Froz

Contē

Prologue	4
Chapter 1	7
Chapter 2	20
Chapter 3	32
Chapter 4	43
Chapter 5	52
Chapter 6	59
Chapter 7	67
Chapter 8	76
Chapter 9	90
Chapter 10	99
Chapter 11	111
Chapter 12	120
Chapter 13	132
Chapter 14	142
Chapter 15	153
Chapter 16	164
Chapter 17	173
Chapter 18	185
Chapter 19	193

S. M. Clair

Chapter 20 205
Chapter 21 222
Chapter 22 234
Chapter 23 249
Chapter 24 260
Chapter 25 268
Chapter 26 276
Chapter 27 283
Chapter 28 291
Chapter 29 297
Chapter 30 305
Chapter 31 312
Chapter 32 319
Chapter 33 325
Epilogue 335

Frozen

For the love of my life, for your unwavering belief in me and all the support making this book possible.

For my children Igor, Isabella, and Isaac, for all the wonder you have brought into my life.

S. M. Clair

Frozen

Prologue

It was her.
It had to be.

He pulled his feet to a quick and sudden stop to avoid colliding with two girls. Rosy cheeks donned their faces, as if they had been moving at a steady but brisk pace. They proceeded to dodge him, and their feet barely stumbled.

Only one caught his attention. She shouted a hurried apology and gave him a smile as their eyes locked.

His head filled with light and something in him clicked into place. His body warmed and his head emptied, until her smile was the only thing left.

Before he had a chance to reply or to even think, her eyes had turned away from him. She had run on like a feather dancing on wind. Graceful and swift.

Was she real, he thought, fixed in place. It had all happened so fast. *How could it have been real?*

****

Days had passed since that first sighting. He hadn't gazed upon her since. He knew little of her or the person that had accompanied her. He tried to remember every detail, but the more he tried, the more it felt like he was clutching at straws. Her eyes and smile were the only detail he could recall with clarity, but this was of little help.

He had gone straight to the Elders about what had happened and how he had felt. He was adamant that she was the one he had been looking for, that had been enough for them. She may be their only option.

The hunt for her had begun immediately and had been fruitless. There was little to go on, but he knew he had to try. There was too much at stake.

****

A week later, before any real progress had even been made, he found her.

Frozen

There was a slight chill on the air that day. Autumn had already begun and the leaves in the tress above him were rich in sunset colours. He looked up from his phone and saw her immediately.

She was making her way into school, wrapped up warm like it was the middle of February. Again, light filled him, and an invisible cord pulled him in.

It was her.

It had to be.

Chapter 1

Tara Kingley's life had always been this way, all seventeen years of it. She was constantly the butt of the jokes and today wasn't any different. *How could anyone find it funny to glue a pin on my chair?* She thought over in her head.

Not only was her butt cheek throbbing, but she could also sense the sniggers that were working their way around the room. She had a hole in her trousers and her white briefs were showing through, in front of the entire class. What a typical Friday morning, she hadn't even made it through her first lesson. She comforted

Frozen

herself with the knowledge that at least this was her final year in high school.

As she looked around the room, she could see the class laughing underneath their breaths. The Majority of which were taking every opportunity to enjoy her embarrassment. While a few only glanced from the corner of their eyes. The feeling was so familiar to her and yet undeniably her cheeks reddened, betraying her as usual. She needed to get out.

"Sir, could I please leave the lesson?" She said this while still blushing to the most wanted and fancied teacher in school. Mr Evans was especially young for a high school teacher. He had worked his way through university and found a teaching position straight away. He had the talent, that was for sure. He also had the looks to go with it.

"What's the problem T?" he said, looking up from his textbook, showing his deep blue eyes, as he did the whole class swooned aloud, well the girls did anyway. The boys just moaned in response. Jealously is what that was, Tara thought as she rolled her eyes. Mr Evans never paid attention to it. Either he didn't notice or was too professional to make a comment.

It was normal for people to call her T, instead of her full name. It was all due to another Tara in her school year. Tara Cooper, she had been the one to start the little nickname, after she decided she wanted no association with T.

"I have a hole in the back of my trousers. I'd like to go and fix them please," she blushed to a deeper crimson red and waited for a comment from her fellow students, but it didn't come.

"Okay, but don't take too long," he said. He moved his rich, dark, curly hair from his face. This caused another swoon and another low groan.

While the class was preoccupied, she picked up her white knitted cardigan off the back of the old, grey, plastic school chair and wrapped it around her small waist, picked up her bag and left hastily.

Tara made her way down the corridor and into the school hall at the far end. The hall was dark at this time of the day. It took time for the sun to pass over the building and shine through all the windows on the west wall.

Tara was moving quickly as Mr Evans had instructed her to. However, she became aware of a sixth form first year – a year below herself – who was lent against the wall with his hood up.

He wore completely dark clothing, and his head was pointed towards the floor. Tara couldn't make out anything about the boy from where she was. She continued across the dingy hall, which was towards the stranger. He didn't move or look up as she got closer, he just stood there like a piece of modern art. It wasn't until Tara was right next to him - and the exit - that he moved to block her path entirely.

"Excuse me," she said anxiously after a slight pause. He did not answer, but raised his head slowly, looked straight into her eyes, and smiled. Her anxiousness dissipated quickly. Past his exterior there

Frozen

was a face full of warmth and friendliness. Not that she could make out much in the shadow of his hood. His eyes caught her attention and held her still. He then moved and opened the door for her, breaking their eye contact.

She walked a several paces down the corridor and curiously looked back towards him, expecting him to still be there. Only, he wasn't there anymore. The door from the hall swung shut with a slight bang. He could move fast, that was for sure. Tara realised that she couldn't recall the colour of his eyes. *Weird,* she thought to herself.

****

When she got to the textiles department in building E, she could see through the door that Mrs Tyrell was preparing for her next lesson. She was intently writing materials on the white board.

Tables were clustered together to form four larger tables. Along the edge of the square room was a work bench that ran the entire length of three walls - only breaking for the door and the fire exit. There were windows above the work benches, covering two sides of the room, letting the space fill with the low October light.

Tara's textiles lesson had been taught by Miss Donahay and she had left the school last term. She had never met Mrs Tyrell before.

She pushed the door open gently, preparing to introduce herself.

"How can I help you?" Mrs Tyrell asked before she had chance to say anything. Tara had to paused for a second before answering.

"Hello, my name is Tara Kingley. I have come from Mr Evan's Class. I was wondering if I could sew the hole in my trousers back together?" Tara reached to take her cardigan off her waist and put it on the desk, along with her bag.

Mrs Tyrell clipped the lid back on her pen, turned around and peered over the top of her glasses to look at the hole – more of a rip - in Tara's trousers.

Tara noted how she did it. Mrs Tyrell could be no older than thirty with long, red ringlets bouncing around as she moved. Her eyes were a brilliant green colour like jade and the way that she peered over her glasses, was something she would have expected in someone older, not this youthful woman in front of her.

Tara chided herself for making an opinion on someone she didn't know. First impressions can be deceiving, and she knew that.

"That hole will not be fixable, at least not without a patch. Which, I would be happy to do for you, but I think that I have a better idea," Mrs Tyrell gave her warm smile and gestured to the corner of the room.

Mrs Tyrell took her into the store cupboard, located to the right of the board. She disappeared from

Frozen

Tara's view and a light flickered on. Tara followed, until she stood in the doorway.

Mrs Tyrell had done wonders at sorting through everything. Mrs Donahay had had a system that was chaotic to say the least. Now everything looked so easy to find. Everything from thread down to materials - folded into a colour spectrum – were easily visible. She had even separated the patterned materials into their own spectrum of colour. Neatly hung on the clothing rail were the works of previous students. The materials so lavish that there was nothing in here that Tara would consider wearing - except to a ball or a fancy-dress event. Although Tara had to admit, they did appeal to her. Instinctively, she reached out her hands to touch all the different silks, satins, and even denim of the outfits in front of her.

"I suspect that you like it in here," Mrs Tyrell declared. She had been watching Tara's shifting expressions for a barely a minute or two.

"Mrs Donahay had her own messy system, that only she could understand. This just makes so much sense." Tara explained waving her arms at the cupboard. That was when Tara noticed the items of clothing that Mrs Tyrell held in her hands.

"Ah, yes, these are for you." Mrs Tyrell handed her a pair of exquisite, black, skinny jeans. But they weren't just black they were jet black, so dark they needed their own classification on the black to white scale. As she held out the jeans, she also noticed that there was a shirt. It was a long sleeved, white chiffon shirt with a lace around the collar and the cuffs.

"Thank you for the jeans… But why the top?" Tara asked confused.

"O dear, I thought that you knew. You have a paint mark on the back of your current shirt, and I would hazard a guess there is some on your cardigan too." Mrs Tyrell pointed over to a free stand mirror in the corner of the cupboard.

Tara went to it and looked. Sure enough, just as Mrs Tyrell had said there was a grey paint mark on the back of her white shirt. The same colour grey as her chair had been. *Clever,* she thought.

"Well at least it is only an old T-shirt." Tara said calmly, while trying to swallow her annoyance. She wished people would stop all their stupid pranks. How old are they? Five?

"It is also a good thing that you are wearing a plain white top under it too." Mrs Tyrell said looking from the straps of her white camisole towards the chiffon shirt in her hand.

"I will let you change." Mrs Tyrell said, as she headed for the door and closed it behind her. Well, she nearly did.

"O and please do the shirt and jeans some justice and take off those horrid worn-out trainers. You have a natural beauty to you. There are shoes on the rack over there. Take which ever you wish." Then she closed the door to let Tara change.

Frozen

Tara had not worn clothes like this in so long. She forgot what it felt like to wear something that made you feel attractive. The material felt new and crisp under her fingers. She stood looking in the mirror at her wavy dark brunette hair, her chocolate-coloured eyes that sat in her pale slim face and then down to her figure.

She was a petite girl but would never describe herself as a natural beauty like Mrs Tyrell had stated. Plain Jane is how she felt. Yet, she had to admit to herself that the clothes helped bring a glow to her skin, a waist to her hourglass figure, and elevated her appearance.

Tara took a second to take it all in. Why had she been hiding behind hoodies for so long? So that she didn't stand out? To hide? *Both,* she thought to herself. She didn't have a choice now, unless she wanted to walk around with a patch on her backside and a paint-stained shirt.

Somehow Mrs Tyrell had got the sizes perfect. As Tara stood into the shoes that she had picked - nothing that was overly girly, just a pair of black flats with a very small black and white bow on top of the toes - she collected her ruined clothes and put them into a plastic bag she found on the shelf and returned to Mrs Tyrell.

"Thank you so much for lending me the clothes. They are amazing. I think I will bin these," Tara said as she motioned to the carrier bag in her hand.

"You are most welcome, they look very good on you, if I do say so myself." Mrs Tyrell smiled at Tara.

"Although, I think you should put your hair up. It would suit the outfit more. Do you need a hair tie?"

"No thank you, I have one in my bag," she said as she started to rifle though her bag to her red make-up pouch. She pulled out a tie and put her hair into a neat ponytail at the back of her head and left it at that.

"Perfect," Mrs Tyrell said admiring her own handy work.

"I will have them washed and brought back to you in a few days," Tara explained.

"No need to worry yourself. You can keep them all. They are only cluttering up the cupboard." Mrs Tyrell watched as Tara's expression lit up with wonder at her generosity.

"Thank you, is there anything that I can do for you in return?" Tara looked to the teacher and saw nothing but kindness on her face. However, Tara was adamant, she wasn't taking them for nothing.

"There is something. Do you know much about textiles?" Mrs Tyrell asked her.

"Yes, a bit. I took textiles for my GCSE's, and my mother and I make a lot of furnishings together at home."

"In that case, I have a taster class going on Monday morning for the year 9's and I could do with some minor help that morning to set it all up. I have already got one more pair of hands. Another pair would make it considerably easier." Mrs Tyrell asked.

"That's fine with me," Tara said as she put her black bag onto her shoulder and picked up her book,

Frozen

which she placed in-between her arm and her body. Leaving her one arm free to get the door. "What time would you like me to get here for?" Tara enquired.

"How about we say eight o'clock? That gives the three of us an hour to get everything out and prepared."

"I will see you Monday then," Tara concluded as she headed out of the door and back to class.

****

When Tara got back to Mr Evans's class, her chair - and the pin - had been removed and a different chair was in its place. She had thanked Mr Evans again, for allowing her to leave and had taken her place on her paint-free chair. She could not help noticing that everyone was staring at her. She was wearing something different… or it wasn't that.

Jake Brown grabbed her attention as the bell rang for the end of lesson.

Jake was a tall boy with short, choppy, blonde hair. He thought very highly of himself and of his body. He had been working out since he was young, but that had more to do with the fact his father was into competitive running.

Tara was sure Jake's dad forced him to participate in sports. She felt sorry for him… well, slightly. It couldn't be nice to have a pushy parent that made your choices for you. However, this didn't give him the excuse to be a nasty person.

"Sorry about the paint and the pin T. It was a stupid prank and I think we should be past it really. It won't happen again," he gave her smug filled smile.

Tara had already known that it was Jake doing all the pranks or at least organising them. He was going out with Tara Cooper and T knew all too well that they stemmed from her.

Tara Cooper suited Jake well. They were both as nasty as the other, getting kicks out of the pain and embarrassment of others. Unlike Jake, Tara wasn't naturally tall, although the 5 inches of heel on her foot made her taller. She had blonde hair like Jake but again it wasn't natural. Tara Cooper could be described as fake, over the top and selfish.

"It's okay. Thank you for apologising." Tara wouldn't forgive him just yet. She had a feeling that this may have something to do with making her comfortable enough to pull another prank. She was not going to fall for it.

"Cool, well I suppose I will see you in maths later?" He asked casually.

"Indeed, you will." Tara held onto her book tightly and walked the rest of the way out of the room.

On her way to History, she went via the back of the cafeteria, where there was a bin large enough to take the bag full of old clothing. As she put it in, she made a vow to herself - *I will not hide anymore, I deserve more.*

Tara was not a confident person, but neither was she completely shy. She had done the popular kid thing

Frozen

and had decided it wasn't for her. She preferred a slower social life and time to read.

However, Tara Cooper had given her reason to hide and to sink into the shadows. She was beginning to see that she shouldn't allow someone else to decide who she was or how she should act. *I will not hide,* she repeated to herself.

Tara turned around from the bin and the student that she had seen in the hall earlier - when she had left Mr Evans's class - was stood a few feet away.

Tara headed towards her lesson, as she did the student said something, but she couldn't make it out.

"Sorry, I didn't hear you." Tara looked towards him as he lifted down his dark hood. Underneath was not what she was expecting, based on the small glimpse she'd had earlier.

Tara had anticipated a brooding face, dark eyes and even piercings. However, that was not what she saw. He was as beautiful as his smile earlier had been. His mid brown hair was not as dull as it would sound. Light danced across it, captivating Tara. His eyes looked on in concern she thought. It was hard to tell when looking into eyes that seemed to captivate her entire being. She tried to place the colour but couldn't. *Hazel,* she concluded.

"Are you Tara Kingley?" The stranger said, as he stepped closer to her.

"Yes, and you are?" She retorted. At this small distance between them, she could smell his aftershave and she found it divine.

"My name in Nick. I am new here and I just came from Mrs Tyrell's class. She told me that we are both working on the set up on Monday. I thought I would introduce myself." Nick seemed very polite, genuinely nice, and pleased to meet her.

"It's nice to meet you and yes, I am helping Mrs Tyrell." Tara stated, offering her hand in greeting. He didn't take it, leaving her to lower her hand, feeling a bit silly and confused.

"It was nice meeting you." Nick smiled, turned, and walked away. Tara thought it was unusual for him to go out of his way to see her and keep the conversation so short.

Tara started heading towards her next lesson. She realised that Nick may need a lift to school that early in the morning. She spun quickly to ask if he did, but he wasn't there anymore. Tara stood there for a moment, wondering how he had moved so fast for the second time that day. She shook herself off and continued to her history class.

Frozen

Chapter 2

It had been a particularly boring weekend for Tara. Her friends were away, and her mother had been busy. Tara had entertained herself by diving into worlds that were pressed into paper via printing ink. The words in the books creating a world within her mind.

She was still half asleep on Monday morning, arriving earlier than usual - at Mrs Tyrell's request. It was partially her own fault for staying up late reading. Her mother had made her an extra cup of ginger tea, to help wake and warm her up. It was the middle of October, after all.

Hopefully, the caffeine would start to kick in, as she made her way to the textiles department. Tara was what people referred to as a 'night owl', meaning she hated mornings.

Tara retrieved her things from the passenger seat and climbed out of the car with her arms full. The travel mug, school bag, library books, and keys made a precarious stack in her arms. As she stood up, she clumsily staggered and dropped a book. *Thank God it hadn't rained,* Tara thought. She could not deal with books being damaged. She bent over and picked it up, while cursing to herself for dropping it in the first place. Luckily, the book was unscathed.

Tara lived in a land of books. It was a wonderful way to escape from this mundane world and in many cases into a better one. It had helped her to understand people and to see the beauty in the simple things. Reading was her passion and it had come from her mother. Tara's mother was the one to introduce her to the wonderful life of a reader. Tara – like her mother - particularly loved fairy tales and anything that touched into the realm of fantasy.

She had been a queen, a slave, a woman, and a man. She had been old and young. Fallen in love and entirely alone. She had been a traveller, a magician, a warrior, and a musician. She was a reader, a very keen reader and therefore, she was anything she wanted to be.

She was stood there juggling her things and trying to open the heavy door into the building, as an arm stretched out in front of her and opened it for her.

"Thanks," she said, turning to her rescuer.

Frozen

Nick was stood smiling back at her. Tara hoped that she hadn't looked too silly while trying to open the door with one hand. Tara stepped through the opening, and she caught her reflection in the window, only to see a massive nest of hair covering her head. The wind had been savage this morning.

"You're welcome," Nick replied while holding his hand out towards her. "I can carry those books for you if you like?" He had asked, but his hands were already holding the spines, trying to gently take them from her. As he did his hand grazed hers. It was a very gentle touch, that normally she wouldn't have even noticed, but a surge of heat ran up her arm, stopping just before it hit her shoulder. She leant into the warmth of it. A couple of seconds later, she realised that Nick was still trying to take the books from her, shaking her back to reality.

"Erm... Thank you, again." She couldn't help but laugh at the situation. It almost felt like a scene from one of the novels he just took from her.

"What is so funny?" Nick asked her with a smile.

"I was just thinking how most people don't really open doors or help carry things for one another anymore. It is more the sort of thing that stays in a book. Generally, because of the mixed feelings on the matter I suppose. Some girls like it, some hate it and others well, they don't really have an opinion on the matter. So, I can..." she suddenly came to a stop, realising that she was mumbling about doors.

"Why did you stop?" Nick said, looking at her quizzically.

"I was rambling. I don't really have much social interaction lately, outside of a couple of my friends. My train of thought took over. Sorry." Tara could feel the heat rising to her cheeks. She began patting down her dress so it would sit neatly. She had decided to wear something that was a little more her, keeping yesterday's promise to herself. Feeling silly she stopped fidgeting and resumed walking towards Mrs Tyrell's room.

Nick strode after her and once he was beside her, he turned his head, catching her attention. "You should not hide your opinions or who you are."

Tara nearly stopped dead in her tracks. Well, she slowed down anyway. Nick continued slightly ahead of her. It was a bold statement to make, considering that they had only met twice.

When they got to the classroom Nick greeted Mrs Tyrell first with an informal, "Morning." Then Tara greeted her with a formal - "Good morning, Mrs Tyrell."

Tara couldn't help but notice how radiant she seemed to be. Not just first thing in the morning, but all the time. It was like an extra bit of sun had shone on her, making her glow. When she looked at Nick, she saw the same glow and began to wonder if they were related somehow. They didn't look the same though.

Mrs Tyrell was average height with thick, long, red hair that curled into ringlets about halfway down

Frozen

and sat on her shoulders. She also had beautiful jade green eyes.

Nick on the other hand had his mid brown hair, sand coloured skin and his captivating hazel eyes. He was also tall and had broad features.

Mrs Tyrell had pale porcelain coloured skin and a delicate shape. Tara still couldn't help but notice the similarity of the glow that they both seemed to have emanating from them.

"Are you two... related?" It came out without her thinking about it. Tara caught them sharing a questioning look. To avoid appearing like a fool she continued, "to tell you the truth, you both have this sort of glow about you."

They shared another look between them, one that Tara could only take as shock. Her unique ability to say what she was thinking, would get her into trouble one day. Although, it had already got her into many predicaments before now.

"Sort of," Nick answered her.

"I am his stepmother. We are not blood related, but I do take care of him." Mrs Tyrell said waiting for Tara's response.

The answer still didn't really explain why they shared the same glow unless it was just an aura, they both gave out.

"Okay, that explains why a guy is helping out in the textiles department." Tara said sounding far more sexist than she intended. She had thought about this last night.

Guys stereotypically didn't have anything to do with the textiles in her school. *I suppose it was not 'manly' enough or too many people judge,* she had thought. It was refreshing that someone had gone against the grain. This made more sense though.

Nick chuckled a little. A beautiful sound that made her feel like laughing herself. Tara went to the back of the room, attempting to take herself away from ability of embarrassing herself anymore.

She started to take out the sewing machines and then by Mrs Tyrell's instruction, started to thread them with different colours of thread. There hadn't been anything as fun as getting to try things out when she was in year 9. It was nice to see that the school was taking the learning and interest of the students more seriously, especially with their GCSE options to think about.

While Tara was threading all eight machines, Nick was getting the scrap fabrics and other equipment out of the store cupboard and laying them out evenly between the groups of tables.

Mrs Tyrell had been getting the clothes – the same ones Tara had spotted the day before - off the racks and was dressing three mannequins in different outfits. She was currently wrestling with the smallest of the three.

One was dressed in a very ornate kimono, one was a male suit - that she supposed was concentrating on the lining technique – and one was a child sized mannequin - dressed in what could only be described as a princess dress. It was pink and covered in frills,

Frozen

sequins, lace and so much material. Tara could hazard a guess as to why Mrs Tyrell had put it out. The dress was extreme, but it showed a lot of skills that the class could use, such as beading work, layering, creating volume, and working with lace.

"You look lost in thought," Nick said, as he passed her with the scrap bin.

"Indeed, I am. I was just thinking about what Mrs Tyrell is putting on the mannequins. I didn't have anything that showcased what you can accomplish if you put your mind to it, when I did textiles. I think it will be great for the other students to get this opportunity and to learn from Mrs Tyrell. You have a great mother."

"I am very lucky. I lost my birth mother when I was a baby and my father a long time ago. Mrs Tyrell was there for me when I needed her the most and has been there ever since." Nick stared at his mother with an expression filled with love and understanding. There was something more and if Tara was right, it was appreciation.

"I lost my father when I was twelve. It tore me apart. My father loved me and my mother so much, he died a hero to many, but he was my hero before he was anyone else's. I never met my birth mother," Nick shared.

"I have a strong mother too. She has managed to get us through everything, including the loss of my father. She always taught me that I was capable of accomplishing all my dreams." Tara explained.

"Well, your mother is right, you can," Nick said to her.

****

When they had finished organising everything, Mrs Tyrell thanked them just as the first bell rang. Tara and Nick left Mrs Tyrell to teach her class and went their own ways.

Tara had a free period for her first lesson and planned on heading to the library to read two or three more chapters of her book - *Throne of glass* by Sarah J. Maas. She had been so engrossed in it, she missed having a small amount of time to read it before she got out of bed this morning. It was a tale of a woman fighting for her freedom. Though she had to make a choice between want she really wanted and what was right repeatedly.

Tara hoped that she would never be in that position, but instead her goals and doing the right thing would always be on the same path. She admired the woman's courage though, something that Tara needed more of.

Her free period flew past so quickly, that Tara had to finish in the middle of the chapter, something that she hated doing. Although, when finishing a chapter, there was always the temptation of starting the next one.

Her next lesson was Art with Miss Bullock. They had been working on mixed media portraits and she had

Frozen

been thoroughly enjoying it. Then break, where she normally went to see her two friends in the library for a quick catch up. But both of them had been away that week in the Maldives with their parents.

Tara and her mother had been invited, but her mother had a deadline for her new book this week. Therefore, Tara had been left to go to school on her own, with none of the support she got from her small group of friends.

She wanted to send them a message and tell them about the new guy, but what was she going to say. There was really nothing to tell. He was really good looking, polite, and Mrs Tyrell's son. That could wait until they got home.

The rest of her day was boring and moved very slowly. Her next and final lesson of the day was Maths. A subject that she was good at. Not great, but she was achieving more than just a pass.

As she entered Mr O'Brien's class, there was group of pupils sat together laughing. Unsurprisingly, in the middle of the group were Tara Cooper and Jake. Jake turned his head in her direction as she walked over to her seat near the far wall. He turned to the rest of the group, and they all fell quiet - generally a good sign to Tara that they were up to something. Tara checked her chair and the table thoroughly this time before she put anything down. However, nothing - as far as she could tell – looked suspicious.

Tara looked back over to the group and received a smile from Jake and a severe look from Tara Cooper.

She was sat with her friends - Gen, Kayleigh, and Chloe. They were all just the same... Fake, troublemakers and - to say the least - mean. They were doing everything they could to fit in with the 'cool' kids, but in the process losing themselves.

Tara was cautious all lesson. She kept glancing over her shoulder while listening to Mr O'Brien's slow and direct lecturing about different equations. He had to be the oldest teacher in the entire school, and no one could understand why he hadn't retired yet. He had family at home, he could spend time with, and he was comfortable enough to afford it. Tara had put it down to the fact he must enjoying teaching maths.

When the bell rang and nothing out of the ordinary had happen, Tara felt relieved and headed to her car.

By now she was tired. The two large cups of ginger tea from that morning had not been enough to get her all the way through the day. She would go home and have a nap.

As she got to her car, she noticed that someone had drawn the word 'loner' down the side. She swore under her breath. Tara turned to see the group from Maths, sat laughing with each other. *So much for no more pranks,* Tara thought.

She unlocked her car to head home and realised that there was a storm coming. She had no idea how she had not noticed it before now, especially with the wind that morning. Tara decided to leave cleaning the drawing off until she got home.

Frozen

Tara threw her bags into the back seat of her new, white Audi TT. It had been a gift from her mother for her seventeenth birthday, as well as driving lessons. Her father had left her and her mother a substantial amount of money and her mother's six novels had also helped boost their income.

She climbed into the car and went to press the ignition, when there was a knock on the window next to her. The sound of it made her jump. After realising that it was Nick, she rolled down her window.

"Just wait a moment?" Nick's face looked grave and panicked. Tara couldn't work out if he had asked her to wait or instructed her to.

"What…"

CRASH!

Tara saw a light flash behind her. She climbed out of the car to find an old streetlamp had fallen to the ground, sending large lumps of concrete across the entire car park.

All the electrical lines were sparking on the floor or sticking up through the small stump of concrete that remained. The rest of the lights on the car park had short circuited and were now dark.

The solid floor of the carpark had taken the impact, creating a slight dip in the ground where the lamp had hit, as well as creating spider web cracks that radiated out from the largest chunk of the post.

Realisation slowly dawned on her. If she had pulled out before Nick had knocked on the window… she would have been under it. She looked at Nick and then back to the sparking wires. Nick looked at her and then turned to leave, intending to say nothing.

"Wait!" Tara called out to him. He just kept walking. *If he had not been there,* she kept thinking.

She felt faint.

Darkness clouded her eyes as she fought to focus.

Then it took her.

Frozen

Chapter 3

Tara woke up to harsh, bright lights shining down on her. She could tell that she was layed on her back in a bed most likely. She strained to open her eyes. She blinked until her eyes began to adjust. Tara heard a muffled voice beside her. Her mother was calling her name.

Her small and delicate face came into view, blocking the light above and creating a halo around her. She had fair hair, blue eyes and looked the opposite of Tara, who had taken after her father's darker features.

"Tara darling, you are at the hospital. Try not to move too quickly." Her mother sounded worried and that was never a good thing. She had been extremely protective of Tara since losing her husband, her soul mate.

The room slowly came into focus. She could see that see wasn't in a private room but in a cubicle, the terrible floral-patterned curtain was pulled across. She didn't have any drips or wires connected to her other than the heartbeat monitor that was connected by a peg on her finger, creating the beeping noise she could hear. Tara assumed she wasn't that bad. Although, the fact her mother had interlaced her fingers in Tara's left hand, meant she wasn't convinced Tara was okay yet.

Tara led there for a short while, trying to process what had happened. She remembered getting in the car, Nick knocking on the window.

Suddenly, the rest of her memories came flooding back to her. Nick had somehow known that the lamp post was going to fall at that exact moment. He had seemed filled with concern. How had he known?

"Mum, how did I get here?" Tara asked.

"A strapping young lad brought you - I can't recall his name. Nathan maybe or Neil," her mother explained. Tara knew her mother would be going through a list of names in her head, trying – and failing - to find the one that fit. Tara doubted her mother had even noticed much about him, especially while her daughter lay unconscious. Tara would bet her mother hadn't even noticed the doctor's name.

"Nick?" Tara put her mother out of her misery.

Frozen

"That's the one," a smile of recognition spreading across her face. She fussed over Tara's hair and covers. "A very polite and kind young man. He brought you here in your car and then called me from your phone. You fainted and banged your head on a curb. The doctor says you might have a concussion."

"Mother, please stop I am fine. A little headache but I will be okay. Can we just go home?" Tara hated being in the hospital.

"The doctor needs to check you over first, sweetheart. I'm not taking you home until he gives me the all clear." Her mother looked at her determinedly.

"Fine, can you go and get him then please?"

****

A few hours later, the doctor had checked her over and he told her mother to keep an eye on her. A short while later they had headed home. Tara went straight to bed – to rest, but mainly to escape her loving - but currently overbearing - mother.

She woke up early the next morning. The sun had barely started to peak over the top of the horizon. It shone a beautiful, deep orange across her room. She led in bed just watching the colours and pondering on the day before.

Her room was large, but she was used to the space. Her favourite part was naturally her own ample collection of books, which could be found on the bookcases, on the shelves, and in the cubby holes below the window seat. The walls were dark blue and were paired with light turquoise and gold. It had been all been pinks and purples not so long ago, but Tara had decided that it was time for her to have a change when she turned seventeen. Her father had decorated her room with her when she was eight years old. It took time for her to feel comfortable with changing it. Afterall, she wasn't painting over the memories, just the walls.

Her double bed did little to fill the room. Some of the space was filled with her dressing table, double wardrobe, and chest of draws. Every remaining wall space was lined with her bookcases, but the floor remained clear. That was how Tara wanted it – an open space that would let the light flood in though the large bay window. It was very much in keeping with the rest of the house - light and airy.

When the sun was finally up and over the horizon, she got out of bed and went to the bathroom across the hall. It was considered the family bathroom, but her mother had her own ensuite. With only two of them in the house, the main bathroom was left just for her.

"If you think you are going to school today, you are very much mistaken," her mother declared, once Tara had got back from her shower. She was sat at the end of Tara's bed and looked insistent. Tara assumed this might happen and wasn't going to argue - she knew it would be fruitless to believe that she could best her mother. Besides, she still had a headache and her car still needed collecting from the hospital.

Frozen

"Anything you want or need darling?" her mother asked, already aware that she had won the non-existent argument.

"To go to school!" Tara said to her mother defiantly, "But clearly, that is not going to happen."

"No, it is not," her mother replied.

"I am fine. I think that I will go and read something in the study." Whenever Tara needed to escape, she went into the library - her father's old study. With all the books her father had collected, and all the ones that Tara and her mother had added to the collection, there was thousands of books to read. That meant thousands of books for Tara to escape into.

"Okay honey," her mother said and headed for the door. "I'm going to finish up my book today. I will get you a copy as usual, after the editors have had it."

"Actually mum," Tara quickly called before her mother disappeared around the door. "I need my car picking up from the hospital." Her mother had driven Tara home from the hospital in her car, leaving the Audi TT behind, as Tara wasn't allowed to drive for twenty-four hours.

"No need to worry about that Tara. Your friend Nick has offered to pick it up first thing this morning and drop it off." Her mother smiled at her, as if trying to suggest something.

"What? Why would he do that?" Tara had no idea where this boy had come from and why he kept appearing in her life.

"He rang me last night when we had got home and said that he felt responsible for what had happened and asked if there was anything that he could do. In the end, he suggested that he pick your car up this morning. He collected the key about an hour ago. I don't see how this is a problem, he seems like a nice guy." Her mother's smile seemed to grow and grow. She was quick to trust people.

"I don't know him. I met him two days ago and now we trust him with my car? Just seems foolish." Tara had no idea why she was getting so worked up. He had saved her life, taken her to the hospital and was now retrieving her car. Was there anything that suggested he could not be trusted?

"Well, it is all done now, he will be here soon. You may want to get dressed unless you plan to receive him in your towel?" Her mother had clearly got it into her head that there was more going on here. Her head was filled with fairy-tale endings, not surprising in light of the fact that she wrote about them. Tara had been the same - was still the same - but sometimes reality got in her way more than it did her mother's.

Her mother left her room and Tara ran over to her bed. She placed her head firmly in her pillow and screamed. Why did she even have to see him? Curse her mother and her romantic notions.

She wanted answers about what had happened yesterday, but she undoubtedly wouldn't get any today. The chances were, that her mother would be stuck to

Frozen

her like glue, trying to observe their every movement for something that was not there.

Tara had only just met him, for pity's sake. Nevertheless, Tara had to admit to herself that he was devilishly handsome. This didn't change the fact there was something that just didn't add up about him.

Tara got dressed into some comfy trousers and a T-shirt - she wasn't going out of her way for Nick. Once ready, she headed to the study to choose a book - she had finished her other one while waiting for the doctor yesterday - and sat in her father's leather armchair. Most of the time the chair smelt like leather, but sometimes she swore she could still smell her father's favourite aftershave. She curled up with the book she had chosen - *Starcrossed* by *Josephine Angelini* – and a blanket she kept draped on the back. The novel was a modern take on Greek mythology and gods. Of course, it also had its romance story. After all, she was a dreamer.

Tara had got a few chapters in when the study door began to open. "Mother, I am reading and I'm fine."

"I will be sure to let her know." Tara closed her book so fast that it made a snap and she had lost her page. She scrambled to get up and out of the blanket.

"No please, stay sat down. I just wanted to give you your keys. Mrs Kingley said that you would be up here." Nick gave her a gentle smile. Tara was going to kill her mother for this.

"Okay thanks," she said taking them from him. As she did a spark ran from his arm into hers. "What was that?"

"Sorry must be static electricity." He said withdrawing his arm.

"I know what static electricity feels like. What is going on? How did you know? How did you…" Tara paused as she realised that the door was open, and it could be assumed that her mother was outside listening. She closed the door making sure it was completely closed - quietly thanking her father for soundproof doors. Then whispered her question, "how did you know?"

"Tara, I don't know what you are talking about. I didn't know what was happening. All I did was take you to the hospital and retrieve your car. Sorry I didn't do more and that you got hurt." Nick's smile had all but faded.

"Stop lying to me. Don't you think I deserve the truth, an explanation?" Tara's patience was wearing thin.

"Yes, you do but I…" Nick seemed to withdraw into himself. "I have to go."

Tara grabbed his arm - she wasn't letting him go until she got an explanation. As her hand grabbed his arm, something extraordinary happened. Light seemed to emanate from beneath her hand on his arm and travel up through him. She couldn't let go. The light consumed them completely. There was no warmth to it and as she began to shield her eyes with her other hand, the light already receding.

Frozen

"No no no no no…" Nick sounded distraught. Tara blinkingly looked for his face. She did not feel any fear or worry. In fact, she felt the opposite. She felt warm, safe, she felt alive. As she looked to the place where her hand was on his arm, the light seemed to absorb back into him. The last traces momentarily leaving a handprint on his skin, as she reluctantly removed it. When the light had completely gone, she looked up to Nick.

"Please do not panic. I will explain everything," he pleaded. She took a step back, all the feelings that she had felt before melted away, as if they had never existed.

"Why would I panic?" She questioned. The light behind his head put him in shadow.

Tara froze. How could there be a light behind him? They were in the study. Tara began to look around him. They were stood on the edge of what looked like a garden. It was filled with beautiful colours and unfamiliar plants. Behind Tara was a large pond that glistened in the sun, which was starting to set behind Nick. Insects flew from one flower to the next, recent rain made the plants sparkle. The sun reflected off every surface making it brighter.

"Tara, I am so sorry. I don't know how it happen. How did even you do that?" Nick's panicked voice made Tara turn and look at him.

She stood rooted to the spot, staring into a face that felt so familiar. She didn't know what to say. Back in the study there was so many questions she had to ask him. So many things that had to be explained, but now there was only one.

"How are we even here?" she voiced.

"I... I don't want to do this." Nick started to walk away from her. She went to grab him but withdrew her hand. What if it happened again?

"Nick, please don't walk away. You can't expect me to act as if this hasn't happened, not that I understand exactly what is happening. Where are we?" Tara looked around. It didn't look like anywhere she had been before.

"We are in Japan," Nick answered but kept walking. It almost seemed like he was running from her.

Tara looked around. Japan made sense, the rich colours of the garden, the type of plants and the red wooden architecture.

"How did we get here?"

Nick didn't answer but sat on the stone bench underneath a cherry blossom tree. He looked at the floor, his head in his hands. Tara moved to sit next to him but kept a space between them. She felt a little lightheaded and was glad to be seated.

A breeze blew and above her, the blossoms tumbled elegantly down from the tree. It was magical, like snow falling and floating slowly to the ground. She looked to Nick who had been watching her as the blossoms fell around her.

This still made no sense to Tara, but she could tell one thing - she had discovered something Nick didn't want her to know.

Frozen

"I'm sorry," Tara apologised feeling a little queasy. She didn't know what she was sorry for but somehow it felt like she had to be. "I am sorry for the pain this seems to have caused you. Please, take me home and we will forget about it."

"That's not what I want." That was all he said as he took her hand and this time there was the minuscule hint of the light she had seen before. As the light faded, her surroundings became familiar, she was back in the study as if nothing had happened, but it had, and Tara would never forget it.

Nick walked over to the desk and turned to face her, "please do not say anything to anyone. I will give you your answers, just not here, not now." And he left, leaving Tara feeling puzzled, sorry, confused, and completely lost.

Once he had left the room, she sat on her father's chair and looked around the room. On top of the dark stained oak desk in the centre of the room, was one single cherry blossom flower. Something so real that she couldn't deny what had just happened.

Chapter 4

The next day was Wednesday and Tara's mother reluctantly allowed her to go back to school. Her mother had been cautious the day before, but to Tara she was being overprotective. In the morning, before she set off for school, her mother still told her to be careful and if she didn't feel well to call her immediately.

Tara arrived at school by twenty past eight, nearly forty minutes earlier than necessary. She wanted to visit the library and deal with her English work that was due next week. She hadn't been able to concentrate on anything yesterday, particularly after everything that had happened with Nick.

Frozen

Tara parked her car in a different spot than she normally did. She would never want to park where she used to ever again - of that she was sure - but also because she couldn't. Two vans were parked haphazardly in that particular corner. Builders and electricians were fixing the damage. She also noticed, as she closed the car door with her hip, that the graffiti had gone. Either that was her mother or Nick, she didn't want to know which one.

She still had questions that needed answers, but for now they would have to wait, her English work was not going to write itself. *Unfortunately.*

The library was only small in Tara's eyes, but it provided the students with what they needed. A desk, for the librarian, was the first thing that you saw when you walked in. The librarian Mrs Norman was a wonderful lady that was always there to help them. To the left after walking through the doors, was hooks and benches for bags and coats. Once past them, it opened into the main room. Shelves lined the back walls, filled with non-fiction. In front, stood bookcases placed back-to-back, housing the fiction books. There were eight circular tables that filled the space in front of them. To the right of Mrs Norman's desk, was a separate smaller room that contained six computers.

Tara spent her first free period in the library, using the computers to write everything up and for research. She accomplished a lot within the hour and half that she was in there and she felt more up to date with her assignment. The harsh shrill of the bell sent

Tara to her second period, Maths. She returned to the library for her lunch, but for a completely different reason.

Layla and Savannah - her best friends - were back from their holiday and Tara couldn't wait to see them. They'd all been going to school together since they were nine years old. Since then, they had been the three musketeers and it was impossible to separate them. They came from remarkably similar backgrounds and lived not far from one another.

Layla was closest to Tara's temperament. She loved sports, language, travel, and books. It was not uncommon for Layla and Tara to read the same book and talk for hours on the phone deliberating over the characters, places, plots, and of course the romance - if there was any. Layla had always been like a sister to her. They had alternated between staying at each other's houses over the weekends. Their mothers had become good friends and often all four of them would go for trips to museums and art galleries all around the country.

Tara would be forever grateful for their presence when her father had died. Layla had been that little bit of light when Tara had needed it. Layla was short, but with a strong build and with all the exercise she did, it wasn't surprising. All those outdoor sports had led to a tanned complexion, which made her light hair, look even lighter.

Savannah on the other hand was very confident, young, black woman. She was tall with a clear

Frozen

complexion, straightened hair, and maple-coloured eyes. She was loud, bold, and unique – it was as if the words were entirely built for her. Savannah's idea of an enjoyable day out was shopping, followed up with decent food. Savannah had struggled with boyfriends for a few years now. She was on a determined hunt to find "The One". However, Tara was convinced that her true love was food. How she could remain a size eight, but consume the amount that she did, Tara had no idea. It was her superpower.

"So, T, what happened to you?" Layla asked.

"What do you mean?" Tara retorted, her thoughts automatically landing on Nick.

"Well, your mum, told my mum, that a guy took you to the hospital," Layla explained.

"Oh, that... I fainted and he happened to be in the car park while I was there." Tara wasn't sure she should divulge all the unexplainable things that had happened to her friends. They would only say she had been reading too much, again. Besides, with the way that Nick had looked at her with regret, she didn't know what she should and shouldn't say.

"Okay, keep your secrets." Savannah retorted.

"There is nothing going on with me and Nick." Tara stated. At least that was the truth. Tara didn't want to lie to her friends, but she would avoid telling details.

"Oh, Nick huh?" Savannah said, as she got her make up bag out. She topped up her lip gloss while sitting on the edge of the table, her feet placed on the chair. Savannah, unfortunately, didn't think she was beautiful, in spite of the fact that everyone else thought she was. Tara only hoped that one day, someone would make her feel as beautiful as she truly was.

"On a first name basis? So, he can't be a complete stranger?" Layla added. It wasn't a statement. It was a question and Tara knew it.

"No, he is new to the school and is a year younger than us. His adoptive mother is the new textiles teacher, Mrs Tyrell. We both helped set up a class the other day, for the year nines." Tara looked down at the book that she was halfway through. She knew if she looked up, they would know she had omitted something.

"Really, wow! Small world," Savannah exclaimed.

"Definitely," Layla agreed. "Is he hot?"

"*Oooo*... yeah, good question Layla," Savannah encouraged.

"Ummm... yeah, I guess," There was no guessing about it, she knew he was.

"You guess?" Savannah questioned. "He either isn't, or he is."

"I bet he's *dreamy*," Layla teased. "I bet he saved her, picked her up in his strong arms, and she fainted from all the excitement." Layla teased.

"I have no idea if he picked me up," Tara could barely contain her blush. "I passed out."

"I must get a look at this guy. Any ideas where I might spot him?" Savannah was clearly thinking that if

Frozen

Tara wasn't going to claim him, he could be her next chance at love.

Japan, Tara thought but instead said, "No, I really don't."

"What did you say his name is again?" Layla asked.

"Nick," Tara exasperated loudly.

"Yes?" A voice came from behind her. There he was, stood smiling at her as if it was the most normal thing in the world. Realising he must have heard, she wondered exactly what he had picked up from their conversation. Thank God for Savannah, who immediately saved her the embarrassment of randomly shouting his name.

"Hey, nice to meet you, Nick. I'm Savannah, this is Layla, we're Tara's friends," Savannah quickly injected, while Tara turned around and tried to compose herself.

"Hey," Layla extended her hand for a shake.

"Nice to meet you both," Nick replied, lifting his hand to Layla's and then to Savannah's. Which Tara thought odd, he hadn't done that with her? *More questions*, she thought to herself.

"Thank you for taking care of our friend the other day. Tara was just telling us about what happened," Layla expressed with genuine gratitude. Although, this left a gap for Savannah to tease some more and of course she had to take the opportunity.

"Yeah, thanks for helping her," Savannah grinned. "Did you have to do much?"

"She banged her head on a curb," Nick explained. "I lifted her into the car and then took her to the hospital. I did nothing really. I wish I could have done more."

"You must work out. Not an easy feat to lift an unconscious woman into the car," Savannah continued, winking at Tara.

"Was there anything that you needed, Tara?" Nick asked her, clearly avoiding Savannah's question.

Tara turned around to look at him. She had gained her composure but failed to find any words and embarrassingly just stared at him.

"Well, we were about to go get some food. Come on Savannah," Layla instructed her.

"Yeah, see you later T," Savannah overemphasised a wink in her direction, put her oversized bag over her shoulder, and followed Layla out of the library. Tara knew that Savannah was giving her a chance before she tried for him.

Nick took a seat next to her at the round table, taking the seat that Savannah had her feet on, only a few moments before.

Tara managed to shyly look at Nick and noticed he was wearing similar dark clothing to the other day, but with his hood down today. Even with the rain outside and the room being darkened by all the bookcases, his hair still caught every ray of light it could. The lustre captured Tara's eyes - it took all the effort she could assemble not to stare.

"Hey," she finally managed to expel.

Frozen

"Hey," Nick reciprocated. He proceeded to take his textbooks out of his bag and place them on the table. This wasn't going to be a quick conversation Tara thought to herself. When he had finally got all his things out onto the table, he began to talk to her.

"How are you feeling?" Nick enquired.

"Fine," Tara replied. Although inside she was barely keeping it together and was close to blurting out all the questions that she had for him.

"That's good," Nick said. Maybe Tara was wrong, this could be short.

"How are you?" Tara queried. Nick lifted his eyebrows at this, it was as if he was half expecting her to burst out with questions too.

"I..." Nick struggled to begin. "I am well." He finally concluded.

"That's good." Tara said getting back to her work, Nick following suit. The air felt thick with awkwardness, like the room had been engulfed in it. Tara struggled to breathe normally. He was so close, but he'd made it obvious that he didn't want to talk. They sat in complete, awkward silence, until it was time to pack up their things.

"I'm sorry about yesterday," Tara said, finally managing to find some scrap of confidence.

"You have nothing to be sorry for. None of it was your fault, it was entirely mine. If anyone should be apologising, it should be me," Nick announced.

"I feel like I have," Tara admitted. "You looked truly distraught the other day."

"You have completely misread me. I am not upset with you or anything that you have done. I am upset with myself, my recklessness. I should have stayed away," he explained. "For your safety, I should have stayed away."

"How am I meant to even react to that?" Tara replied, agitated.

"Shhh!" Mrs Norman warned. Stereotypically, she liked to have a quiet library.

"You have just dropped the biggest bombshell of my life and now you think it is the perfect time for you to walk away?" Tara questioned in a whisper.

"Tara, I don't want to hurt you..."

"But..." Tara continued for him.

"It is dangerous to know what I know. I'm not going to deliver danger at your door. It wouldn't be fair on you or the people you love," Nick continued in a hushed voice.

"And leaving me completely in the dark is?" Tara asked rhetorically. "You know what Nick, just leave me alone. If this conversation has established anything, it's that you don't want to get to know me or know what's best for me. So, let me save you the hassle..." Tara hurriedly picked up her tan-leather jacket from over the back of the chair, "Goodbye Nick."

She promptly left the library.

Frozen

Chapter 5

Tara got halfway to her next lesson when Nick grabbed her arm softly and spun her around.

"You are right. I am sorry." Nick apologised.

"For what exactly? For revealing... whatever yesterday was? For telling me nothing? For being in my life? Which one?" Tara angrily questioned him.

"All of them, except the last. I am not sorry for being in your life. I am sorry for what comes with it," Nick concluded. "Can we please start again? I'm not very good at all this. Can we at least get to know one another before I explain things?"

Tara stared at him. His eyes were pleading. She didn't know what to say. Did she want this guy in her life? Did she want to know him and find the truth? The answer came all too easy. She could deny it all she liked but the truth was, she was drawn to Nick and all the wonder that came with him. She had to at least try to find out what had happened yesterday, or her life would be filled with questions, followed by a series of unknown answers.

"Okay," Tara responded plainly.

"Thank you." Both delight and dread flashed across his face. "Tomorrow at lunch? At the library?"

"Fine," Tara replied curtly, still unsure if she should be walking away from this guy or towards him. Tara was angry at herself for not being able to just end it before anything began. However - try as she might – she was pulled to him, and she just couldn't explain why.

"I look forward to it," Nick smiled, spun on his heels in the opposite direction and put his hood up. He was angry with himself, she concluded. Tara was beginning to recognise his reactions, maybe because they were reflections of her own. Tara continued onto class feeling half upset and half irritated. She would need to consider all this when she got home.

****

When Tara finally got home, she went straight to her room and got dressed for a run. She'd already called Layla on her way back from school and they had agreed to meet at their usual spot. Tara had originally planned to think about everything Nick had said and done, but

Frozen

she had decided against it. Tara could be impulsive if her head wasn't clear. Time, she concluded, was what she really needed.

Layla was waiting at the end of her street, near the road sign that read - 'Watling close'. She was in the middle of stretching her muscles preparing for their run. They would do two or three miles, making it back before it was pitch black. Layla noticed Tara and fell into pace beside her, setting off at a reasonable speed, without needing to greet one another.

"Want to talk about it?" Layla enquired, about half a mile in.

"Have you ever felt like you knew the decision that you should make, but every time it came down to it, your instinct overrides you? Like from somewhere deep inside?" Tara asked, not sure if she could explain.

"Like when you know you shouldn't have the chocolate, but a little voice just tells you to indulge yourself?" Layla guessed.

"That's actually really accurate, minus the chocolate." Tara wasn't shocked. Layla had this incredible knack to understand people. Tara wished she had the insight that Layla seemed to constantly have. "I feel caught between two decisions - either listening to my rational thoughts or follow this unmanageable instinct?"

"It's your subconscious, higher self... people call it many things. Ultimately, it's the part of you that doesn't need to think it just knows. Is this about Nick?" Layla assumed correctly.

"Yeah," Tara felt silly.

"Look Tara, I don't know what is going on. It's obvious to me that you are hiding things," Layla stated. Tara slowed down. She had been caught. "However, I am sure that you have your reasons. I have never known you to hide things from me. Just know, I am here if or when you are ready to talk."

Layla had continued the same pace as before, even when she saw Tara falter. Tara caught back up with her reply,

"Thanks, Layla. You really are the best person I know."

"Aww, you are too sweet." Layla expressed. "As for the other thing… just follow your instinct. There is a reason that we have that little voice. If you listen to it, it will take you many places."

"I swear you are an old, wise woman stuck in a young person's body," Tara imagined Layla sat in a remote location, meditating as the sunset.

"Don't I know it sometimes," Layla laughed.

"Thank you, Layla." Tara felt reassured that she hadn't been making a bad decision. They made it back as the sun was leaving its last drops of light. All Tara had to do now was try and sleep. Which was harder than it sounded for an over thinker.

****

"Tara this isn't working. We argue about everything," Nick explained, as he walked away.

Frozen

"Nick, I don't understand. You said you would explain everything," Tara enquired.

"Yeah, well that was before I got to know you," Nick replied angrily.

"So, you expect me to live the rest of my life knowing that there is more out there. I don't know what you are or who you are? Where you came from or why you even bothered to save me?" Tara expelled breathlessly.

The rain was pouring down both of their faces. It was the worst downpour, so far that winter. It felt like ice every time a drop landed on her face. The wind echoed in her ears, burning the tips. Nick stood barely three feet away from her, barely visible under the deluge of water cascading down in front of them.

"Look Tara it has nothing to do with you," Nick said firmly.

"I think I deserve to know what happened. Why we ended up in Japan for god's sake!" Tara rebuked as Nick continued to move away from her. Every time she tried to get closer, he seemed to disappear and head further away from her, like a wisp of smoke, she couldn't get a hold of.

"I will not give you the answers you want," Nick said from somewhere in front of her. "Why do you think you deserve answers? Go back to your controlled life. You will not see me again."

"NICK!" Tara yelled but nothing came back. He dissolved into the rain.

Tara stood cold and all alone. She wouldn't see Nick again and although she didn't even know him, it didn't feel right. Tara stumbled forward trying to find him in the wall of water.

Her feet had turned to ice under the onslaught of freezing water and wind.

"I am not alone. I am not alone," Tara repeated to herself. "I am not alone." The air became thick with darkness as if it moved to consume her, as if alive. She headed for the light that was behind her. The light shrunk before her eyes. The closer she got the smaller it became and the more the darkness enclosed on her.

Then she saw it - the hands that moved in the blackness. Jet black with claws like razors. They enveloped her, enclosed her. They grabbed at her, over and over, dragging her further from the light, engulfing her very soul in darkness.

****

Tara woke up drenched in sweat. Her limbs stuck to the covers as she tried to get out of bed. She headed straight to the sink in her bathroom and ran the cold water on full flow. Cupping her hands, she lifted the frigid water to her face, cooling herself and spraying water everywhere in the process.

It had been a long time since she had had a nightmare. They were always the same thing, her father's death. This was different. Never, had she had such a dream that felt so real. It made her shudder to even think of it.

Tara resolved herself to a shower. The cooling of the water had begun to calm down her racing heart. Whilst her heart found its steady rhythm, her mind had not. It raced round and round.

Frozen

Tara hated not being able to understand people's actions. Nick left her alone, had made the decision to not include her. No reason or explanation. Tara was glad it was all a dream.

She knew now. She knew what her subconscious was telling her. She needed answers. Life with the unknown would be more than she could bear. However, that meant she had to confront Nick and so far, all her attempts at getting the information that she wanted had resorted in him walking away.

After she had taken a long shower, she climbed back into bed for a few more hours sleep. She needed rest before she worked out how to deal with Nick. Unfortunately, it was a minimal amount of sleep, which was filled with those dark, clawed hands.

Chapter 6

Tara woke the next morning feeling sluggish, she hadn't slept well after her nightmare.

"You look terrible this morning my dear," her mother stated at breakfast. "Is everything okay?"

"I had a nightmare last night, that's all," Tara explained.

"About your dad again?" Tara's mother guessed. The recurring nightmare about her father, had taken its toll on her for years after his death, but it had been a few months since she had dreamt of that day.

Tara had witnessed her father's death when she was twelve years old. They had been in the town getting themselves an ice cream, after a hot day at school.

Frozen

Suddenly and without warning, her father had darted into the middle of the road and pushed a small child. He must have seen the truck coming down the road, seen the young boy fetching his dropped teddy, and reacted instinctively. The truck had swerved away from the child, who walked away with scrapes and bruises. However, it had hit her father. The boy was frantic, but safely in his mother's arms moments later.

Tara had screamed for her dad, took steps to go find him, but she was stopped by an elderly woman, *don't look*. She hadn't.

She was glad she hadn't, but that didn't stop the memory of the screams including her own, the red stains seeping out from under the truck, or the taste of ice cream that lingered on her tongue. Tara still couldn't eat chocolate ice cream without being taken back to that moment. She dreamt that day over and over, hoping every time for different ending, an ending that never came.

"No mum. It wasn't about dad. It was about something else." Tara corrected her. Her mother stared at her, clearly waiting for Tara to explain more.

"Could I have one of those fruit teas, please mum?" Tara enquired, giving her a moment to piece together what she was going to tell her mother. She definitely wasn't going to mention Nick, because that would bring up more questions than she wanted to answer. Not to mention her mother would jump to conclusions, as always. Her mother had already grabbed a tea bag and mug.

"It wasn't anything serious mum. I was just surrounded by darkness, which seemed to be alive, and I couldn't get free. It was like the shadows were these living entities," Tara explained. Her mother went still, then continued to fill the kettle.

"What do you mean by you couldn't get free?" Her mother asked with her back to Tara.

"It felt like it had limbs, like it was holding me in the darkness." Tara told her.

"I'm sure it's nothing to worry about, but if you have the dream again though, please tell me." Her mother instructed. Tara was confused as to why her mother was interested in this random part of a dream. Tara had omitted the biggest part. Nick.

"Sure," Tara quickly agreed, hoping her mother wouldn't press for more information. She was sure the nightmare wouldn't come back.

****

The beginning of Tara's day was like any other. Her first and second lesson went by without issues. On her way to third lesson, Tara noted that Jake had been particularly quiet recently. Was this the calm before the storm? Could he be planning something big? Maybe, she should be concerned, but Tara strangely didn't feel on edge at all.

Frozen

She concluded that Jake was the least of her current problems. Nick however was. In fact, Tara could safely say that he was her biggest problem.

When lunch finally appeared from the fog of the normal day, Tara could barely contain herself. She'd basically ran to the library to meet with Nick. When she got there her excitement sunk. He wasn't there.

"Looking for me?" Nick enquired from behind her.

Oh god! Did he see me practically run up here? Tara wondered to herself.

"Hi. I was just looking for somewhere to sit," Tara tried to dodge the question.

"How about over there?" Nick pointed to a table next to some giggling year ten's, whom were no doubt talking about Nick. Before Tara could suggest somewhere quieter, where she could talk to Nick out of their ear shot, he was already heading over.

"Yeah, sure," Tara said, with an undertone of sarcasm. Nick didn't appear to notice it.

When they got to the table, Nick took his books out of his bag and arranged them onto the table. Did he intend on just doing his homework? This was going to be harder than she thought.

After five minutes had painfully ticked by Tara accepted there was no way she could concentrate on doing the Maths that she had placed in front of her. It wasn't the easiest subject for her and with the girls behind her whispering to one another about Nick, it was even harder.

"Look at those arms!" One mousey hair girl groaned.

"Never mind the arms, look at that chest!" Another, clearly eager girl stated.

"It's not the arms or his chest... it's definitely those eyes," said a small red-haired girl. Now that Tara had to agree on. Even as he sat there reading his history book, he looked gorgeous. Nick's eyes flickering from word to word behind his eyelashes, the greener flecks in his eyes almost sparkling with the fluorescence of the lights. The side profile view that Tara had, still allowed her to see the curves of his full lips and...

As if sensing her glares, more than any of the other females in the room, he lifted his head to see her gawking face. The red-haired girl was right. It was one hundred per cent the eyes.

"You, okay?" He asked, as if none the wiser.

"Ummm... yeah?" Tara replied awkwardly.

"You don't sound so sure," he returned, his eyes lingering on hers.

"I'm sure. Although, I do have questions for you," Tara brought up, hoping that it might get the conversation heading in the direction she wanted.

"I have some for you too," Nick smoothly matched.

"For me?" Tara was confused. Why on earth would he have questions for her? He was the one that had turned her life completely upside down, not the other way around.

Frozen

"Yes. I want to know more about you," Nick said enthusiastically. "I want to know what your favourite book is first."

"My favourite book?" Tara was at a complete loss. Why on earth would that matter? Although - thinking back to her dream - maybe she shouldn't push him. Hopefully, when he had some of the answers he wanted, he might answer hers. "I don't have one."

"You don't like reading," Nick looked puzzled.

"Oh no, I love reading," Tara exclaimed. This settled Nick's puzzlement. "I just don't have a favourite. How could you simply state that one book is better than another. Are the works of Shakespeare any better than Jane Austen's? They are so different from each other. How could one possibly compare? It is not the book but the way it makes you feel. Each book will touch us differently in our hearts, but nothing makes a book less special because it drew a different emotion. Books are fluid. They mould to each person, shaping and teaching them in separate ways, I simply..." Tara trailed off.

"Why did you stop?" Nick quizzed.

"I..." Tara started but was unsure whether to continue.

"You?" Nick pressed.

"First doors and now books. I need to learn when to stop talking." Tara explained, with her face in her hands.

"You are clearly a passionate person," Nick perceived. "Your view on books is enlightening. I believe you to be right about books being fluid. If your mind is in a state of sorrow or in a state of happiness you can read the same words in hugely different ways. A friend of mine once said, "I couldn't read one book for the rest of my life. It would take away meaning from what I saw within the pages." I now understand him better for your explanation and I thank you for that."

Tara just stared at him. Most people didn't pay any attention to her ramblings. She wasn't even convinced that she did.

Nick came across so much older than he was. She'd always thought of Layla as having an old head on her young shoulders. But Nick was so much more sophisticated.

"What about you?" Tara enquired.

"After that speech I would think it a shame to only name one," Nick grinned.

"Any favourites then?" Tara asked, emphasising the 's'.

"I love Fantasy and Sci-fi," Nick expressed. "Although, I am partial to the romantic classics. I am a sucker for a happy ending."

"I couldn't agree more," Tara seconded.

"Do you have any favourite music?" Nick continued with his interview.

"I like classical music mainly," Tara answered. "Anything that can help you relax."

"So, you aren't a fan of pop music?" He questioned. Tara shook her head. "No R&B? Punk? Rock?"

Frozen

"Nope, never been a fan. I think it's all noise or things to listen to on the go. Music to me is like a symphony of someone's thoughts and emotions. I like to really listen to music, to feel the hairs stand up on the back of my neck." Tara conveyed.

"I could not agree more. A composer, a musician, or even the instrument choice, can put thoughts and expressions within the music. It absorbs it and can be heard or - as you said - felt by the listener." Nick was clearly enthusiastic about music. He spoke about it as if he was on the other side of the fence to Tara. Almost like she was the listener. Did that mean he played?

"You play an instrument?" Tara voiced. Nick looked at her intensely. It appeared like he was uncomfortable about releasing information about himself. With Tara or just in general she couldn't tell.

"The piano mainly," Nick offered. "I do play the violin, but not like the piano."

"I would like to hear you play one day," Tara expressed. The thought that there would be that kind of friendship in the future, was presumptuous. That - however - did not stop her. Tara definitively had a say first and then think later brain. Her intentions were not to push him too far too fast, but here she was doing it anyway.

"I would like that," Nick expressed, not just with words, but his eyes that softened as he smiled. Layla had been right. It was better just to follow your subconscious and see where it took you.

And that was exactly what she did.

Chapter 7

By the end of her lunch with Nick, Tara knew little more than she had before. He had got more out of her than she had from him.

However, she was still committed to trying not to push him too hard. If she did, it could mean him walking away again. She would rather wait to get her answers, than never get them at all.

Nick agreed to meet with her again. Tara wasn't sure if he would say anything about what had happened, but nevertheless, Tara agreed to meet with him Friday at same time and same place.

Tara went to Layla's that night after school. She wanted to talk about everything that was going on with Nick, but needed to avoid the things she felt she shouldn't tell Layla about, yet.

"It is obvious that you like him, Tara. I just don't understand what can be keeping you from telling him? He is obviously interested in you, so where is the problem?" Layla asked. Tara knew that if it was Savannah, she would have meant the question in a judging way, but not Layla. Tara knew that Layla only meant to help, but Tara had a secret that wasn't hers and couldn't give her friend the straight answer that she deserved.

"I can't tell you," Tara sighed. "It's not my secret to tell. If I could, I would. Let's just say that we have very different worlds and I want to see his world, but he doesn't seem to want me in it. Even if he says he does."

"That does sound complicated," Layla agreed.

"I really like him," Tara admitted. Not just to Layla but to herself for the first time. She wasn't sure when or how it had happened, but something in her had bloomed.

"I know you do. Follow your heart, but don't let it get broken," wise, old, wonderful Layla hugged her.

"Thank you, Layla. You truly are the best." Tara hugged her back.

The rest of the night was spent doing their usual. They poured over books, watched *Pride and Prejudice*, and fell in love with Darcy, for the hundredth time.

Frozen

Layla had done exactly what Tara had hoped she would do, distract her.

****

The next day brought anxiety from the moment she woke. Tara couldn't seem to shift it. She tried to meditate before school, she tried a cup of tea before she left the house, she tried distraction with lessons, she even tried splashing herself with cold water, but nothing did the trick.

When she got to the library at lunch, she could feel her heart bouncing around in her chest. She thought that if it pounded any harder it would come straight through her chest and land on Mrs Norman's desk as she entered.

She offered a greeting to Mrs Norman, who looked up, gave her a smile and Tara smiled in return.

Nick was already sat at a table, although it was in a quieter place this time. He had ensured there was a table between them and the book stacks. Tara knew they would fill up with giddy, ogling girls in the next ten minutes.

Nick was so engrossed in writing in his book, that he didn't notice that Tara had come in until she was sat down. All the while Tara was repeating to herself -*I will stay calm… I will stay calm.*

It was all in vain because when she sat down and looked over to him, their eyes locked and she could swear for a good five minutes neither of them looked away, moved a muscle, or said anything. The room felt quiet even for a library. Tara's stomach fluttered in response.

It was Nick who finally broke the stare with a quick look to his books, "Hey, how are you today?" He said it so calmly, Tara wished she could be so collected.

"I…," Tara cleared her throat and looked away. "I am well, thank you, and yourself?"

"All the better now you are here," Nick replied, still so collected.

"What are you working on?" Tara asked, before he could hear her heart beating in her chest like a brass band.

"I was just doing on my English essay, it is due next week though, so I can put this down." Nick said, already starting to pack it into his bag.

"Are you going to tell me anything today?" Tara bravely piped up.

Nick stopped what he was doing for a second and then continued. He didn't answer until he had put everything away and was looking at her with a devilish smile. "That depends on if you answer my questions about you."

"I don't know why you want to know so much about me. There is nothing to tell you. I am boring. I am a plain Jane," Tara concluded.

"You…" Nick said grabbing hold of her hand. "… Are NOT a Plain Jane! I have never met anyone like you before."

Tara felt very self-conscious. Heat rushed to her cheeks, betraying her. No one, other than her mother

Frozen

and father had ever thought that she was more than average. She pulled her hand back not knowing what to say or do. She was extremely uncomfortable.

"Yet, you won't tell me anything," she stated. Tara started to pick up her things, getting herself ready to leave. "Why?"

"I can't tell you," Nick sighed. "Please, don't go. I am sorry if I was too forward."

Tara continued to grab her things. She was embarrassed and didn't know where to look or what else to say to him.

"Tara?" Nick stood and looked at her. Now everyone in the room was looking too.

He had said her name loud enough for all to hear and the only person that said anything was Mrs Norman, who simply, but traditionally told them, "Be quiet!"

"I can't do this Nick. I can't keep telling you everything and you telling me nothing. I'm sorry." Tara explained in a whisper and then left the library and headed straight for the girl's toilets. He wouldn't be able to follow her there.

She locked herself in a cubicle and started to cry. *Can this guy be for real? He hasn't told me anything but expects me believe he likes me? Wants me to answer his questions but won't in return.*

Tara sobbed some more and then straightened herself out. *So much for staying calm.* Tara scolded herself with her head in her hands.

There was a little rap on the door, followed by Layla asking if she was in there. Tara wiped her eyes and opened the cubicle.

"What happened?" Layla enquired.

"I was an idiot. He won't answer my questions, tells me he likes me, and then I walked out." Tara explained.

"I thought you liked him?" Layla asked confused.

"I do, I do. I just didn't know what to do when he said it. I freaked out. How can I like someone who doesn't respect me enough to tell me the truth?" Tara began to sob again.

"The heart wants, what the heart wants. You know that as well as me," her friend consoled her.

"How am I ever going to face him again after I ran away?" Tara managed in between breaths.

Layla moved forward, gave her a hug like it was the best solution to her problems and thankfully it was. After a few minutes, her sobs ebbed. She tidied herself up and they went to their last lesson together.

Thank God, it's the weekend and I don't have to deal with anymore of this until Monday, Tara thought to herself.

She would discover how wrong this was.

****

It was a beautiful Sunday morning. After doing her usual morning routine with her mother, Tara had decided that she would treat Layla and Savannah to a

Frozen

lovely meal in town, followed by a lovely walk in the park. A major catch-up was needed, after they had been away.

Layla knew it was all just a distraction and so did Savannah. While the latter was aware of this, the former had to tell the latter to keep her mouth shut about it. Savannah of course did not listen.

"Tara why don't you just go and talk to him, demand that he gives you the answers to whatever cryptic thing that you are keeping from us and tell him that he doesn't get to know you until he has." Savannah suggested to her while they were on their walk. Savannah sounded so matter of fact. Tara wished that she had her gumption.

"Savannah, I can't say things like that. You know that I will bottle up halfway through or worse walk away, like I did the other day. I am not as strong as you are." Tara explained herself.

"You think way too highly of me and way too little of yourself. You are an extraordinarily strong woman, and you know what it is that you want. So... grab the bull by the horns and go take it." Savannah was right and Tara knew it, though it was easier said than done.

"You are right Savannah," Tara told her.

"You just need to tell him in a way that he doesn't have the chance to say anything," Layla encouraged. She knew Tara extremely well. If Tara allowed him to say anything, she would get distracted and loose the little courage she did have.

"Well, why not now?" Savannah asked, pointing to a figure coming down the path towards them.

The path was covered by trees arching over the top and the figure stood black against the green back drop behind him. Even from here, Tara could tell who it was from the way he walked.

Savannah stood in front of Tara and took her by the shoulders and quietly said, "Do you want to know this guy?"

"I don't…" Tara began.

"Yes, or no?" Savannah pushed for an answer.

"Yes."

"Then go tell him how you feel and what you want and then just walk away. Don't give him a chance to ignore you. It will be up to him to make the next move." Savannah turned Tara around and gave her an encouraging pat on the back.

"We will go to the café and meet you there in fifteen minutes or so," Layla planned.

Tara was stood there, watching this figure come towards her at what now felt like a frantic pace.

Nick looked up from the floor and spotted her. He stopped dead in his tracks and stared at her.

"Tara…"

"Don't say anything." Tara insisted and surprisingly, he obliged. Tara took a deep breath and willed her heart to calm down before she continued.

"I can't do this Nick. I need answers to all the questions I have. I like you, but I can't be friends with someone that doesn't respect me enough to tell me the

Frozen

truth," she told him, hoping that it would make a difference. "When you are willing to tell me the truth, you know where to find me. If you aren't then this is where I will say goodbye." Tara waited a second to see if he would say anything. She finally looked up at him properly. His eyes were serious. She didn't know what to make of them.

She turned abruptly and went in search of her friends feeling a little stronger, a little braver and a little more confident.

Chapter 8

As she left the library during her free period on the following day, Nick was stood by the stairwell. He lent against the wall with his arms crossed, staring at the tiled floor like the first time she had seen him.

Tara froze.

What could she do or to say? She opted to just keep walking, hoping that Nick wouldn't even notice her as she walked past.

Nick moved from the wall and with his face still tilted to the floor said, "I will give you the answers that you deserve. Meet me after school by your car."

That was all he said and then he looked up into her eyes. She felt the warmth of it travel through her.

Frozen

Bright and pure white light filled her vision and then he disappeared right in front of her eyes.

Tara looked around to make sure no one had seen, but apparently, he knew what he was doing.

Finally, she thought to herself. At least what she'd said the day before had gotten a result. She made a note to thank Savannah next time she saw her.

This was the result she wanted, but she had to admit that she was nervous to be finally getting the truth and wondered if Nick would be completely honest.

****

Tara was unable to concentrate on anything for the rest of the day. Her head had been floating in the clouds and she was constantly losing her train of thought. Always landing back on all the questions that she had for Nick. Tara had to dig deep to find the will power to finish her coursework but was proud that she had managed it despite her burning thoughts.

The end of the day drew nearer and nearer. She'd even managed to leave her last lesson earlier than usual to head for her car. She was anxious and her heart skipped a few beats like a needle jumping on a spinning record. This could change her whole life.

After everything she'd seen, it appeared that magic and all the things that filled myths and fairy tales, existed. Yet, she found she needed proof. That it wasn't something she could blindly accept.

The tales must have come from somewhere, she had thought to herself. The only truthful way for her to find out was to confront Nick and talk to him. He was her door into this unknown world, and she would open it curiously, like she had opened the cover of every book, discovering what mysteries might unfurled from inside.

Tara ran to her car to get out of the rain that still poured a week after the storm. She put all her things into the back seat, keeping out her purse and climbed into the front of her car. The Audi didn't feel big enough to hold her emotions. It was as if the metal cage was holding her in and kept her from bursting.

Tara spotted Nick striding across the car park, not from the direction of school, but instead from the surrounding football fields. He moved quickly and before Tara knew it, he was so close. Her heart pounded so much faster, and she bounced her leg up and down to expel some of her nervous energy.

When he got closer, Tara unlocked the doors, allowing him to climb in the passenger side. He did it more gracefully than she could ever have managed herself and he closed the door with just a gentle *click*.

They sat there for what seemed like ten minutes but was more like thirty seconds. Tara didn't know what to say and Nick didn't say anything. The silence grew awkward.

"We should…" They eventually said in unison.

"You go first," Tara said before Nick could get a chance and then gently added, "please."

Frozen

"I was going to say, that we should get moving. We need to get to the other side of town." Nick said, as she started up the engine. Tara reached for her seatbelt and heard the passengers belt click into place, just after hers did.

They sat in near complete silence for the majority of the journey. Nick's directions were the only thing intermittently breaking the quietness. Although, the atmosphere was rife with unspoken words.

She didn't know where he was taking her and yet... she wasn't concerned in the least. She had been quick to trust him, and she couldn't explain why, even to herself.

Sooner than it felt, they were pulling up outside a small, white-washed house. There seemed to be nothing special or remarkable about it. It just looked like every other house on the street and all the streets surrounding.

It was a semi-detached house with a small protruding porch and white trimmed windows to match the rest of the house. Ivy climbed up the left side, giving it more of a cottage feel and it was helped along by the wooden flower boxes that hung beneath each ground floor window like a rich and vibrant display of nature.

Tara noticed straight away that the small, square front garden was well kept. It took her a few moments longer to notice all the plants were healthier and bigger in some way. Every individual leaf or flower, looked like something you would only see in a gardening magazine. Tara had a little bit of a green thumb, but whoever was taking care of this garden, must have a hand assembled completely of green thumbs.

"This is Mrs Tyrell's current home. I stay here every now and then. We won't be disturbed for a while. She has after school lessons to take care of," Nick said, as he unbuckled his seat belt and reached for the car's door handle. Tara did the same.

"She has a beautiful garden," Tara remarked, trying not to get caught up with the fact he only called it 'Mrs Tyrell's current home.' If she was his adoptive mother then surely, he would live here too.

Tara kept her curiosity to herself. She had decided not to quiz him, and this seemed an exceedingly small detail compared to the other questions running around in her overactive brain.

"Yes, Catherine gives it a lot of attention," Nick said looking around as they headed down a twisting path towards the front door. "Sorry, I meant Mrs Tyrell," he corrected himself.

"It seems strange knowing the first name of a teacher, but then I assume that you're used to it." Tara thought aloud.

"I do not really know her as a teacher, she is more of a mother to me," Nick told her, as he retrieved a bunch of keys from the front pocket of his dark-washed, denim jeans.

Nick led her inside. The house was just as colourful internally as it was externally. The walls were painted several assorted colours in different patterns, making them art even on their own. Every space was

Frozen

filled with so many wonderful things from all around the world. A small and delicate masquerade mask made with white, shimmering fabric and embroidered with pearls and beads. It looked well used but still stunningly beautiful. In a cabinet there were small trinkets of brass and silver. A didgeridoo lent against the cabinet with lizards sweeping up the length of it. A sky-blue tea pot which Tara assumed was from Japan, based on the ornate cherry-blossom pattern that sprawled across the sides.

It wasn't just things from around the world either – countless antiques were spread out amongst them. There was an entire history persevered inside these four walls. Tara couldn't help feeling like she was walking into a miniature museum.

"There are so many things here. I don't know what to look at first," she excitedly explained to Nick.

"Mrs Tyrell has collected a great many things over the years. As well as received a considerable number of thoughtful gifts," Nick said, looking at all the beautiful objects around him as if for the first time himself. Tara supposed that he was used to it and took most of it for granted.

Tara's eyes fell on more and more objects as she slowly crept through the hall.

A small elephant, the size of a small dog and carved from wood, was sat on floor next to a door that Tara assumed led to the living room.

There were stunning carpets leading from the hallway and into the individual rooms. They were delicately made and covered in intricate patterns. Small tapestry's, photographs, and paintings covered the walls. No matter where Tara looked, there was something that caught her eye.

Nick led her to the front room. The space was dominated by two cream, comfortable-looking sofas, but Tara didn't sit down. She was trying to take in everything around her like a sponge. There was so much to see.

As she looked, she noticed something familiar in some of the photos and pictures that covered multiple surfaces. Nothing seemed remarkable at first, various places and even different times.

Then Tara noticed something unusual. She could see centuries of history in the pictures and paintings. Parties from the fifties. Nurses during WWI. A beautiful painting of a lady in a Georgian dress holding a small dog. Although, every picture depicted something different, one thing remained the same - Mrs Tyrell.

She occupied most of them, but with different haircuts, a variety of dresses, and varying, diverse groups of companions. Nevertheless, in the centre of them all - was definitely Mrs Tyrell.

Tara could see one on the far wall and it looked like it had been taken in the Victorian era. Mrs Tyrell was wearing a simple dark dress and hat and stood unsmiling on the steps of a town house, which was common stance for a photograph of that period.

Frozen

Another portrayed a man in a traditional tailcoat of a circus ringmaster, standing next to a handsome and majestic lion perched upon a large platform. He was brave that was obvious, and it was one of the only pictures that Mrs Tyrell was not in.

Her eyes started to flick to another and another. Finally, her eyes landed on Nick. "How?" It was all she said, but that was all Nick needed.

"I will tell you what you want to know, but I need your word that it does not leave this room," Nick eyes were pleading with her. "What I will tell you could negatively affect many people, if it became widely known."

"I swear," *besides whom could I tell,* she thought to herself. *Well, besides Layla and Savannah,* but she would have to keep this secret from them.

"I am sure that by now you have worked out that both I and Mrs Tyrell are not like your…friends and family," Nick paused as if trying to find the right words before continuing. "We are not…" He continued hesitantly. "…Wholly human. We are what you might describe as demi human or half human."

The information washed over her bit by bit. The information felt strange to process. The thought that it might be another practical joke did run through her mind. Jake had really upped his game.

However, what Nick had said seemed to fit somehow. It was like she should already know this based on what she had seen. After all, the guy could literally vanish in front of her eyes.

"I, we…" He corrected himself. "… are shapeshifters," Nick's eyes met hers. She could see them searching for a response – looking for fear. Tara let all her emotion wash over her, but the only thing that she really felt was curiosity.

Nick stood rooted to the spot, fidgeting with the ties on his hoodie, and trying to be patient with the time she took to process.

Tara's mind ran over every little thing that had happened in the last week and how this fit into what she had learnt. She began to realise, that although it was an answer it didn't explain anything.

"Okay, so say that you are a… Shapeshifter," saying the words out loud felt uncomfortable. *Was this real?* "You can transform into other things?"

"Technically, yes," Nick answered vaguely. Tara's thoughts were a thundering train, but she couldn't get past the conflict of what she had witnessed and what his answer was.

"But that does not account for you teleporting me halfway around the world, or how you knew about that lamppost or even the fact that Mrs Tyrell seems to appear in all the paintings and photos. That would make her over a hundred years old just based of the oldest photo. Which is completely impossible and has nothing to do with shifting…" Tara stopped. She had blurted out everything again.

"She is older. She is three hundred and sixteen." Nick said, as he sat down on the sofa with a sigh.

Frozen

How was that even possible? She didn't know anything about shapeshifters. All the books she had read were more focused on werewolves, fae, vampires and even mythological creatures. If he had said one of those, she would at least of have had some clues to go on.

"How old are you?" Tara asked robotically. It was the next logical question in her mind.

"I am a hundred and forty-two." Nick replied blankly and stared at her.

"You don't age?" Tara asked.

"I do not age. I will never age." Nick showed a glimpse of pain in his eyes. It must be strange to have no ending to a story, a burden of an endless life.

"So why does Mrs Tyrell look about thirty and you look like you are about eighteen?" Tara had no idea where these questions were coming from. It was like she instinctively knew the next question she had before she had settled on it mentally.

"We stop ageing when we ascend into a shapeshifter. We are not born one. We transition, though you must have a close blood tie to the Shapeshifters, to become one." Nick explained things so easily that she felt she was being told a very rehearsed story.

"Then how did you know about the lamp post?" Tara asked.

"I didn't... not exactly. Many of our kind - if not most of our kind - have other abilities. Mrs Tyrell has the ability to see parts of the future. Of course, it is dependent on other people's decisions. As soon as she told me about what was likely to happen and where, I made the decision that I wasn't going to let that happen." Nick said so calmly, like it was an average day in his world.

"I am assuming that yours is teleportation," she paused until Nick had nodded his reply.

"Okay, why save me?" It had been the biggest question of all. Why was this stranger so insistent on helping her, he saved her life and was revealing things to her that he shouldn't?

"I...," he started but didn't seem to know how to answer her. "There is something else that you need to know first. An awfully long time ago, we lost our ability to shift into other creatures. We do not technically have the right to call ourselves Shapeshifters at all. I became a Shifter after our kind lost that ability. I have never shifted into something else. I do, however, have this unbelievable instinct to fly or run or climb. It grows deep inside, willing me to change, but I cannot. I believe that the sensation is worst for those that knew what it was like to shift. Mrs Tyrell, I know longs for it." Nick paused again. Tara understood that he was giving her the chance to take things in and to process them. It also gave her the possibility to ask any related questions which she might have.

"Then how did you become a Shapeshifter?" She asked.

"I was only eighteen when I crawled up the stairs of the place that all Shapeshifters can call home. My father was with me that morning. The sun had only

Frozen

just crept over the horizon and the steps were washed in a morning yellow glow. We had been traveling for months to get there." Tara could see Nick piecing it all back together from a long-ago memory. "My Grandfather was a Shapeshifter. He past those genes through the bloodline to both my father and me.

"My father never became a Shifter. I believe that he did not want this kind of life. He had never looked for our kind, even when his father went missing. My father however, had got an ability of his own. It was not supernatural like mine or Mrs Tyrell, but it was a superpower to me. He had the ability to love, completely and fiercely. I remember even now, the homely smell on him as he held me when I was a small child, and he had a smile that would light up the room.

"When I became eighteen, I thought that life would become easier. Independence would start to become a reality. I had had an incredibly good education and wanted to give that to others. Unfortunately, that was never meant to be.

"I do not remember it all, but I do know that in the middle of the night in mid-May, I could see a light coming from the hallway. It moved strangely though. I never knew and still do not know what it was, although I have tried to find out. It was what happened next changed everything I knew.

"My father and I collected some of our things, but only what we could comfortably carry. He took me to our stables. We had only two older horses that weren't meant for long strenuous rides. We got them saddled up and left. I followed him without question. He was a man that did not do things for no apparent reason. We changed horses as soon as we could and travelled for days afterwards. I asked him repeatedly what was going on. He gave me no specific answer. All he said to me was cryptic. "We need to tell them. I have found them hope." It didn't explain anything and gave me more questions.

"It took us months and months to track them down and we almost made it to the Shapeshifters location, although I did not know that at the time. My father had gotten ill in the first few weeks of travel. He refused to rest, and the illness claimed him just hours before we made it to our destination. If I'd had my powers, then I may have been able to save him," Nick paused as he overcame his renewed grief.

"Just a day before we made it, he gave me a scroll. He told me not to open it, but to hand it to the Shapeshifter Elders. He gave me a brief explanation and told me where to head and that these Shifters would find me. I did as I was told. I found myself in front of a collection of Shapeshifter Elders asking me questions within hours of my father's death. I had to leave him where he lay under his instruction. Eventually, they helped me retrieve him and bury him.

"But firstly, I gave them the scroll, they read it and then again aloud to me. The scroll that my father had somehow got his hands on, was a prophecy. It spoke of being able to find someone that would be able to unlock the power from our enemies, to take back our

Frozen

power. It said that I would find her. That the person who delivered the scroll would find a girl, he would know her when he found her and she would be their salvation, the key to unlocking the binding around our power."

Tara had sat down on the other sofa halfway through his story. She knew that must have been hard for him to talk about his father because it was hard for her to talk about hers. She could sense the love he had for him, still had for him. The loss must have been too much to bear even after more than a hundred years.

"Did you find this girl?" Tara asked.

"Tara... I think that you are that girl. You are the one that will free us." Nick eyes bored a hole through her. Like he was trying to read her very soul as he told her.

Tara couldn't process anything else. Everything seemed to twist and turn and then melt away.

How? She thought, but somehow, she knew. It fit inside her perfectly, unlike anything she had known before. The truth. Not the whole truth but her truth.

She was the Key.

Chapter 9

Nick dropped Tara back home in time for dinner with her mother. He'd been silent since he'd shocked her with the truth. Tara was strangely grateful for the quiet.

Once Nick drove off, Tara went straight to her mother, who had already served her dinner at the dining table. She wouldn't be able to recall what she ate for that meal or what kind of small talk she'd with her mother. Her mind wasn't in the present moment. It was stuck on the hours before, with the words Nick had uttered to her coursing through her thoughts.

Tara had left without questions, for the first time since meeting him. The unexpected answers were enough for her to process. She was sure there was more for Nick to explain, but for now at least, she was done asking questions.

The same sentence seemed to vibrate around in her head like a mantra. *I am the Key*. What did that mean for her? Would she even be able to help the Shapeshifters?

Tara found herself in the study barely moments after finishing her meal. She retrieved a book from one of the many shelves and with a dark blue blanket that she had taken from the end of her bed, she proceeded to sit in her dad's leather armchair. She inhaled his familiar, faint, lingering scent and began to read. She needed to escape from her thoughts and books had always been her way. Tucked between two card pages and revealed to her through printed ink was another world and another life.

It didn't take long for Tara to conclude the short story she had quickly chosen. She began sifting through all the books on the shelves.

Realisation dawned upon her, and she was surprised it had not occurred to her sooner. If Nick was right, there was an entire world out there filled with creatures that were written within these books – described on their pages. How many of them were real or somehow depicted in a slightly different way? One thing didn't add up – where were the books on shapeshifters.

She had read too many books to count. She had grown up loving books, just like her parents before her.

Yet, she had never stopped to think that the stories could be real or at least a warped version of events and facts. As a child she may have wished to get her letter to *Hogwarts* or wish *Narnia* was at the back of her closet. It hadn't taken her long to realise that the worlds and events she read, were bound in paper and separate from reality.

Was everything that she'd read - her entire collection of books - really bound between two covers? Could they be stories told to humans, be to deviate them from the world that unknowingly existed around them? Still, she couldn't recollect a single one that ever enclosed any hint of shapeshifters.

Tara worked her way around the bookcases, one after another. When she got to the end, she was sure. Not a single book about shapeshifters. She had heard of them of them though. How it was possible in a room filled with this many books, that her mother, her father or even Tara herself, had never found a book, or read a book about them specifically?

Tara's hunger for answers returned at a frightening speed. She went back to her room, retrieved her iPad from her school bag and Google searched 'shapeshifters'.

Tara didn't know where to look first. There was so many stories and information - folk lore, legends, paintings and... books. Why didn't she own even one?

There were two things that got close, but not close enough. Werewolves which changed in most cases based on the full moon and only into a wolf. These

Frozen

neither had other powers, nor could they change into more than one thing. The others that she had read about were Fae and they tended to have the other powers like foresight, but rarely were they able to turn into other creatures and if they could it was – typically - only into a singular form.

Her head span with questions again. No that wasn't it… it wasn't questions… no something more distinctive… it was people talking. Did her mother have people over? She went to see who it was, but when she shouted down to her mother, she explained she had no-one coming over today.

She went to her room. Her window was open. *Had people gone past?* She shut it and sat back on her bed. The noise started up again, her head began to throb. She could hear people talking loudly like she was stood in the middle of a crowd.

Where was it coming from?

Tara sat on the edge of her bed and pressed a pillow over her head, but it didn't muffle the sound. It could not muffle the sound, Tara realised.

Everything slowed down all at once. She removed the pillow and grabbed her phone to call Nick. This was strange and he was the one person who knew strange. She had no idea what she'd said to him, but seconds later he made her jump when he appeared from nowhere as she placed the pillow back over her head hoping to stop the noise and find some form of relief.

"Tara, what's happening?" Nick knelt on the floor in front of her. He was simultaneously calm and anxious. Tara led down as the pain in her head became too much. Nick encouraged her to sit up, whilst kneeling in front of her.

He looked up at her. The glow she had seen the other day in the textiles department had appeared again. It was like a human-shaped bubble of light softly clinging to him.

"I can hear people, but it is all one giant mess of noise. It hurts," she explained - concentrating on the immediate problem rather than the bizarre glow. Tara took the pillow off her head - aware that it was making no difference – and held it to her stomach. Nick's eyes lit up with understanding.

"Tara, look at me," he waited for her eyes to focus. His eyes seemed to of changed somehow, the green had gotten lighter, and the brown was more of an amber. To Tara, they looked like they were glistening somehow.

"Tara, you need to try and listen," she strained to hear him.

"You need to imagine a wall. A wall that has no end, no bottom, no top, and build it up in your mind. A wall with the purpose to stand between yourself and the noise. A wall that only you can move, open or change. It needs to be strong. It needs to stop the voices entering your mind."

Nick sat on the floor and watched her. She closed her eyes to concentrate and adhered to Nick's instructions. Brick by brick it went up in her mind's eye. The more the wall grew and the stronger she made it the

Frozen

faster the noise, and all the voices began to fade. No, fade was the wrong word. The more they were held back, waiting for Tara to hear them.

When the noise had gone completely, her head began to feel light, as if it had been relieved of a heavy burden. She opened her eyes and noticed that Nick was still knelt on the floor in front of her, his eyes watching. She was ensnared by his glowing eyes. They drew her in closer.

Only when she broke eye contact with Nick, did she become conscious of their proximity. Somehow, amid everything, he had taken hold of her hand.

As his eyes looked upon where her gaze had landed, he withdrew his hand in shock. He'd not noticed where he'd put his hand.

"What on earth just happened?" Tara asked him as he got up and moved to the other side of the room towards the window. She was a little dizzy but otherwise felt fine and decided to sit up.

"I was afraid that this might happen," Nick looked out of the window, almost searching for the words.

"That what might happen?" She pressed him.

"That after contact from me and the truth, you may become one of us," Nick replied without facing her. She slowly went to him at the window, conscious of her light headedness. What did he mean? She couldn't be one of them. "By the looks of all this you are probably telepathic."

"Nick, you have to explain this to me," she said grabbing him by the arm and turning him. It was the wrong thing to do.

She'd touched him again.

Was this ever going to stop happening? Every time we touched - we ended up somewhere else.

They were no longer stood in her warm bedroom but on a windy cliff somewhere. *It couldn't have been somewhere tropical?* Tara thought to herself, wrapping her zip-up hoody further around herself.

The cliff was long, and the tide was out on the rocky beach below. Though from where Tara was stood, it still looked like they were in Britain.

"I am sorry. I don't understand why that keeps happening. We're going to have to try not touching one another," he said to her.

"But..." Tara tried to push past the embarrassment. "...you held my hand before." Her cheeks began to redden, and she could feel it, which just made Tara's shade of red more of a deep beetroot.

Tara reached for the courage to look up at Nick. He was confused. He stood there for a moment and pondered something. Tara's own thought turned over.

Why hadn't she run away from all of this? It was all too much. Something this big should knock her right down and send her running for the hills. It should all be scaring her, but it hadn't. She didn't want to run, but Nick seemed to want to run away from her.

Frozen

"It's every time that you want to run, isn't it?" That was all she could say. He seemed to understand then.

"Somehow, you seem to surge my ability into my unsaid actions, my thoughts," Nick walked across the cliff. *Running away again,* Tara observed.

Tara just stood there and watched him go, until she couldn't hold it in anymore. "Why must you try and run from me. I know that I am not like other people. I know that I am different, and I am sorry if I have freaked you out, but I am sick of people running from me!"

She'd never said it aloud before. She'd never admitted the thing that she was most afraid of. Everyone left because of who she was.

"I am not running from you," Nick corrected, coming to a stop. "I am trying to stay away. If you are the Key, then I do not want our powers back. You deserve to have a normal life and I don't want to drag you into this. You are not at fault, but I am."

"It seems that you haven't noticed or been paying attention. I'm not a normal girl. I don't fit in. I'm different. What's one more difference?" Tara thought over all the things that she could be. She'd never really thought of her future. It never felt right. Now she knew it was because she'd not been able to see the path that was right for her. Somehow, this felt like all the puzzle pieces falling into place. She was the Key - this was her future. Her future was with Nick and the other Shifters.

"You still deserve the chance to have it," Nick turned around and looked at her, really looked at her.

"What if I don't want that life? What if, this here with you and being the Key, is my path? What if this is what I want? Do I not deserve to choose for myself?" Tara stopped. She'd spewed too many questions again.

"Yes, you do. If this is what you choose. If this is what you want. I will show you, our ways."

"This is what I want. I want to know your world," Tara explained truthfully. Nick walked back to her with the sun glistening on the water behind him, casting his face in shadows.

"Then no more running." He stated, while he reached for her hand and although there was a little light dancing around their hands, this time they didn't jump to another place - even as their fingers entwined together without hesitation for the first time.

Frozen

Chapter 10

For the next handful of school days nothing really happened. Tara just wanted to go escape somewhere with Nick, so he could explain anything else that she may need to know. However, Nick had politely refused.

His exact words were, "You must still fit in and be part of the world around you. You will regret missing school if you leave now." She'd had no argument to that.

Although she'd changed, nothing else had done so. The world seemed to continue as it always had, and Tara started to grow frustrated with all the normality. The only thing that had changed was Nick. He told her trivial things about some of his own history. Nothing significant, nothing to do with what he was, but still it was something.

Tara had learnt things like the music he loved - classical. He had always dreamed of traveling and now he could go anywhere he wanted to. She'd also learnt that he was born in Italy, which was where he'd stayed, until his father had them leave on the trip that took him to the Shifters.

Nick's mother had died when he was young of a disease - that Tara couldn't recall the name of - when he was four years old. He could remember her long beautiful golden hair and the way she sung to him as a child. He thought that it might be where he got his love of music from.

Other than that, Tara had not learnt much at all, but surprisingly she wasn't at all bothered about the slower pace of learning. She felt like she had time for explanations and if there was a particular thing she wanted to know, she only had to ask Nick. She was the Key and she supposed that no matter how slow the shift into their world, she would eventually be part of it.

She was sat in the library finishing up some work that she had left to do. Nick was sat across the table from her. He was wearing his usual dark jeans, dark t-shirt, and hoody. Tara didn't know how he did it, but even in the plainest things he looked gorgeous. His hazel eyes were travelling from word to word, his muscles in his arms flexing slightly as he turned over each page or reached for something.

Frozen

"You're staring." Nick said without lifting his eyes from his book.

"Sorry," she blushed. She didn't think she'd been that obvious. Nick looked up.

"There is something I would like to show you over the weekend. If it's okay with you?" Nick said graciously ignoring her blush.

"What is it?" Tara's curiosity peaked.

"I thought I would take you to meet everyone. You would also see the place we all call home. It might be your home one day, and I think you should get to view it," Nick explained. She got the impression that it was important to him.

"Of course, when do you want to go?" Tara asked.

"I was thinking tomorrow afternoon we would go to the Manor and then in the morning I thought I would take you for a little trip." Nick replied.

"You never said anything about it being a manor. How many of you live there?" Tara had always had a passion of all things old.

"Well, there was ordinarily about a hundred rooms altogether, but some rooms have been split into two to accommodate more Shifters, or to allow for apartments. So just under two hundred now, at a guess. Although, there is only about a hundred of us that might call it our permanent home. Many have lives of their own and visit rarely," Nick shrugged it off like it was nothing, but Tara supposed he was used to it. He'd lived there for approximately a hundred and twenty years.

"I can't wait to see where you call home and meet your extended family," Tara concluded.

"I can't wait either," Nick smiled.

****

The rest of the week dragged in anticipation for Saturday. When Tara woke up that morning, the light from the sun was so warm on her cheeks that she had got up at seven instead of eight. In the end it worked out for the better. She'd had no idea what to wear. The entire hour and then some, was spent scrutinising everything in her wardrobe.

She was sure she could have worn anything, but somehow it didn't feel right to her. She was visiting a manor house for goodness' sake! She refused to wear jeans and a t-shirt.

When Nick arrived wearing the usual dark jeans but had a shirt on - rather than his usual t-shirt – she knew that her choice of a white short sleeved shirt dress with a belt around her waist, a navy-blue jacket and pumps had not been a bad one. An even balance of smart and casual.

"Tara, Nick's here," her mother bellowed up to her. Tara was already at the top of the stairs when she heard her. She'd already seen Nick pull up to the house and get out of the car. Her bedroom faced the road, which was perfect for constantly checking the drive, and her mother knew this.

Frozen

Tara had told her mother that Nick was taking her to visit a stately home and she didn't know which. Her mother hadn't really cared where she was going, as long as she went with Nick. You could always trust her mother to have her head stuck in a fairy tale, imagining things before they even happened.

Tara nearly ran down the stairs. She grabbed her bag from the hook on the wall next to the front door, gave her mother a peck on the cheek and departed before her mother could say or do anything embarrassing.

They'd just got to the bottom of the drive and were climbing into Tara's car, and she had thought she'd made it when her mother shouted from the door. "Take care, both of you. Be safe." Her mother smiled.

"So, embarrassing," Tara said aloud.

"I think it's wonderful, she cares a lot about you. You can see that straight away." Tara felt guilty, recalling that Nick hadn't had his mother and father around for a long time now. It made her feel like she should treasure every moment she got. Her mother wasn't perfect but there was something about a parent's unconditional love that made you feel safe. At least she had been lucky enough to have it.

"So, where am I heading?" Tara enquired, as she headed towards the end of her street, but had no clue if she needed to head east or west after that.

"We shall go to Mrs Tyrell's first. Drop the car off there and I will take you to where we are going. You would not be able to drive there and back today, not even with this car." Nick explained while gesturing towards the engine.

"Okay," Tara didn't know what else to say. She wasn't a car person - she just knew that she liked hers.

"You look beautiful," Nick expressed. Tara glanced at him for a second to find him gazing right back at her, but she quickly turned her focus back to the road. She needed to concentrate on driving.

"You don't look too bad yourself," Tara managed to say. Nick chuckled.

****

It took them no time at all to get to Mrs Tyrell's. Neither of them had said anything else on the way over. Tara hadn't known what to say and by the time she'd thought of something, it just felt too awkward.

She pulled into the driveway and cut the engine – silence immediately filled the car. She looked up to Nick, who was staring out the window. Tara couldn't stand the awkward silence, so she just climbed out of the car while holding her dress down. She didn't want the errant wind to send it flying up.

By the time she had closed the door there was a faint flash and Nick was standing at the front door of Mrs Tyrell's home. He had teleported and she noted that she was beginning to get used to the unexpected. Especially when Nick was around.

Frozen

"I thought that I could take you somewhere first, before we got to the manor," Nick finally found his words.

"Okay, where are you planning on taking me?" Tara asked enthusiastically while walking around the car and up the beautiful garden. Tara stopped a short distance away from him.

"I don't know. My plan was to take you somewhere that you would like to go. Somewhere you may have wanted to visit but couldn't." Nick explained.

"Right now, I can't think of anywhere, that I haven't been that I would like to go and see," Tara replied. Nick began to chuckle, a sound that was filled with happiness.

"I was thinking more worldwide, rather than just the local area." Nick retorted. "I kind of have unlimited air miles," he continued, with a gorgeous smile.

"You can go anywhere?" Tara asked, trying not to stare at his mouth and those perfect, full lips.

"Nearly, but it is best to be dressed for it." Nick replied.

"So, what you are saying is - no visiting Alaska or Mount Everest while I'm in a dress," she said, tugging on the lightweight fabric of her dress. She was wearing thick tights and the jacket over the top, trying to keep the chill of October at bay. However, it definitely wouldn't be enough against artic temperatures.

"Exactly! So where would you like to go?" Nick asked her again.

Tara stood there, racing over the list of places she has wanted to go. Although her mother had the money to take them anywhere, her mother did as little travelling as possible. Tara knew that it was fear of an accident and Tara couldn't blame her. Her father after all had been taken from them prematurely by a truck. If her mother could use teleportation for transport, she knew it wouldn't be that big of an issue.

"I really don't know. Where would you go?" Tara asked Nick.

"I would like to take you everywhere you want to go, but we don't have the time right now. So, how about we go grab something to eat in Paris? We could get some food, grab a blanket, and sit underneath the Eiffel Tower?" Nick replied, as he removed his house keys from his back pocket.

"That sounds great. I have always wanted to see Paris," Tara commented. "There's so much history and culture to see."

"Shall we?" Nick said, as he gestured into the house.

Once inside, Nick dug out a thick blanket from a cupboard upstairs and took what looked like money from a side table in the dining room. The notes looked strange to Tara, until she noticed that they were Euros. Of course, Sterling Pounds was not going to help them when they got there. Nick seemed to think of everything and of course he would. He had been doing this for a long time, probably since before the Euro. It was easy to forget that he was a lot older than her.

Frozen

"What are you thinking about?" Nick enquired. "You look absorbed in thought."

"I was thinking that due to the way that you travel, the euro must have made things easier," Tara partially explained to him.

"I have never really thought about it, but you are right. It means that I don't have to keep as many currencies around." Nick smiled. "Are you ready?"

"Yes," Tara confirmed, and Nick offered his hand. It seemed like such a dangerous way of touching – given what happened before – and she hesitated just before she did. She took a deep breath and then placed her hand in his.

At first, all she could feel was Nick's skin touching hers, then it was followed by a gentle squeeze of her hand. An electrical spark began spreading across her skin. She looked up to Nick - who seemed quite happy - and then back to their entwined hands. A light began to build in between them, until it swallowed them whole. It was so bright, that Tara had to blink to adjust to it. Next time she would close her eyes. Once her sight had cleared of little, black dots, she looked upon an entirely different scene behind Nick.

"Where are we?" Tara asked, peering around. It just looked like an ordinary alley way. They could literally have been anywhere.

"Come with me," he said, pulling on her hand gently. "This way."

Nick led her down a couple of busier streets, never letting go of her hand. If she was being honest with herself, she didn't want him to let go, not now that they had the confidence to do so without repercussions.

As they walked a little further, she could see an iron giant looming above her, the Eiffel tower. The sun shone off its surface and through the gaps in the iron. Surrounded by well-kept grassy gardens and encased by French buildings further away. There were sounds of people going about their day, on foot or by bike and the sound of children playing on the grass. It was a remarkable sight.

"Wow!" Tara exclaimed.

"People get confused if I appear out of nowhere. I like to get as close as possible, but where there is no one that can witness me." That made sense to her.

"Let's go get something to eat and then we can sit down under the tower, and you can look at it some more." Nick said, still leading her by the hand.

****

They sat close enough to see the details of the tower, but not so close that Tara would have to look up by craning her neck all the way back.

Once they had finished eating their warm and buttery croissants, Nick told Tara facts about Paris and the Eiffel tower. Tara supposed that if you had lived for as long as Nick had, it would be inevitable to have a wide range of knowledge. It did make her question how much he knew about the world. Instead of asking him,

Frozen

she was quite happy to sit where she was, under the tower with the warmth of the sun on her face, listening to Nick's silken words.

"It was completed on March 31st, 1889, and at the time was the world's tallest structure and held this title for forty-one years. It's three hundred and twenty-four meters up to the very top," Nick said pointing up. "It would actually take you over sixteen hundred steps in order to reach it, but the lift is much quicker."

"You shall have to take me up there one day." Tara smiled back. He nodded his agreement.

"It was named after Gustave Eiffel who engineered and designed the tower, as well as the Statue of Liberty. He kept a small apartment in the tower itself," Nick recalled. "The structure comprises of eighteen thousand parts and held together with over two and a half million rivets, all made of iron. Due to this it got its nickname, The Iron Lady. She sparkles with twenty thousand lights when turned on, another thing that I will have to show you."

"Well thank you, for the education," Tara appreciated his attention to detail.

It had been a lovely way to start their day together. Tara was getting very comfortable around him. She thought it was due to the way he made her feel at ease, not only with him and the surroundings, but also with herself. After no time at all, the morning seemed to slip away.

Nick had taken her back to the alley in which they had emerged from earlier. It was a dark alley, covered on all sides by the tall buildings that ran down a slightly curving street. There only appeared to be one-way in. The smell of the bakery that was on the opposite side filled the air with the warmth and aroma of baking breads. It was a good thing they had eaten something earlier or she would have insisted they go and acquire a French snack. The rest of the buildings, Tara couldn't determine from the backs of them.

"Are you ready to meet everyone?" Nick queried with her.

"I think so," Tara replied anxiously.

"Don't worry about anything. I am sure they are all going to love you. You are extremely easy to be around." Nick complimented her, leaving a tingling feeling in her cheeks.

"You are blushing again," Nick pointed out. "You are not used to compliments, are you?" Nick's question was easily replied with a simple shake of her head. Tara was glad of this because she had lost her words in the embarrassment of her blush.

"If you would do me the honour?" he asked, extending his hand for hers again. Tara took a few steps to reach him, but her shoe got caught on an uneven cobble stone and sent her tumbling into Nick, just as she was consumed by light.

Frozen

Chapter 11

When the world started to reappear around Tara again, the first thing she saw was a singular colour - green. She could feel Nick's arm wrapped around her back pressing her body against his. Her hands were located on either side of Nick's body, and she could feel the texture of grass between her fingers. She glanced down at Nick, and he smiled back up at her.

"Are you okay?" Nick asked calmly.

"Yes, I'm fine," Tara replied nervously. "Are you?" She reciprocated, their proximity becoming her foremost thought. Tara rolled off him and onto the grass next to him.

"I am," he replied. He stood up and offered her aid, with the gesture of his hand.

"Well, that was certainly a theatrical entrance," a stranger's voice giggled in a very child-like manner. Tara turned in its direction but could only see a variety of trees and plants.

"Up here!" The mouse like voice explained.

In a tree that towered over Tara and Nick, about ten feet up, on a thick branch, perched a young girl of maybe eleven or twelve. She had rosy cheeks and long, dark hair, which was tied neatly in a bun. She wore a beautifully decorated dress that dangled over her legs as she swung them back and forth with vigour.

The girl began to undertake the climb down the tree, one branch at a time and with a grace and swiftness that suggested she had done this hundred times before. Tara noted her own small jealousy of the child, who plainly had more balance than she did.

Tara glanced towards Nick. He shrugged his shoulders then turned his attentions back to the tree. The elegant girl landed softly on a mossy patch that circled the base of the tree.

"I would like to introduce myself to you, Tara," the girl announced, as she extended her delicate hand forward. "I am Jenifer."

"It's very nice to meet you," Tara replied taking the little girl's hand in hers.

"Jenifer is a Shapeshifter," Nick explained. "She is also a member of the Council or as we refer to them - Elders."

Frozen

Tara paused mystified. *This child - with an overtly girly dress and reddened cheeks - was a Council member? An Elder? She doesn't even look like she's entered high school.* Tara thought to herself.

"Jenifer became a Shifter when she was only twelve years old. She is the youngest to ever join our kind. Nobody is sure as to the reasons why," Nick elaborated. "She is now eight hundred and seventy-two years of age but frozen in her twelve-year-old body."

"Thanks, Nick, for adding an additional year on to my age. You know how to make a girl feel young," Jenifer retorted. "If I could go back and choose a different body the day we froze, I would. I chose to wear this form that day. Why - is a question I plague myself with. But here I am twelve forever."

"My apologises, Jenifer," Nick said, performing a slight bow.

"Does being so young in appearance, but being older in your mind, not get disorienting?" Tara thought aloud.

"It is what I am used to, and it is my body. Before our powers were taken from us, it was not an issue. I just took on my mother's appearance when it was necessary to look older or I even used another shape. However, after losing our gifts I am unable to make my body reflect my mature mind," Jenifer leaned in closer to Tara. "It is a good thing that I am not interested in chasing down boys."

Tara chuckled out loud. She instantly likely Jenifer and her sly quips.

"I am going to take Tara up to the house. Show her around the old place. If you would please excuse us, Jenifer?" Nick politely requested.

"Of course, Nick. Just don't keep her all to yourself. I think that Tara and I, will get along splendidly," Jenifer smiled sweetly, reciprocating Tara's earlier musings.

"It was nice meeting you," Tara smiled back, as she rotated her body to follow Nick.

He offered his bent arm, and she happily took it. She slotted her hand slowly around his upper arm above the crook of his elbow. She could feel the movement his muscles through the sleeve of his shirt. She felt tense for at least the first few minutes, her heartbeat was echoing through her like a yodel against the faces of a mountain. She was half expecting to kick start his powers for him, but fortunately nothing happened.

"How come we aren't at the house?" Tara had assumed he'd be able to just appear in the manor, as he wouldn't have to hide his powers there at least.

"I wanted you to see the whole house from the best angle first. I thought we would walk up to the front through the gardens. Besides, you wouldn't want me to land on anyone," Nick joked, referring to their earlier mishap.

"How did Jenifer know where to meet us then?" Tara puzzled.

"That is my usual spot for landing outside of my room, if you want to call it that. I suppose appearing might be a better word for it." Nick explained. "But her

Frozen

knowing when I would appear, was no doubt information gathered from Cather... Mrs Tyrell."

"Oh! That makes sense," Tara exclaimed wondering if she would ever get used to all this.

"I know that it's a lot to take in and it will take you time to adjust to everything.

"There are so many diverse types of people and powers that come and go, even I can't keep up sometimes," Nick tried comforting her. She wasn't sure how he had managed to touch on the one thing she had been thinking about, but she was glad of the reassurance he was attempting to give her.

"That isn't as comforting as I know you meant it to be." Tara rolled her eyes. "But thank you."

"I'm sorry. You will get used to the chaos eventually though," Nick said as matter of fact. His reassurance for her did have the desired effect of slightly calming her. He stopped and said, "We are nearly at the house. Are you sure you are ready for this?"

"As ready as I'm ever going to be," Tara tried to reply confidently. Nick took her around - what she came to realise - was the final cluster of evergreen trees.

There it was... the manor house. It stood encased in the surrounding environment. Ivy was climbing over the east side of the building, causing a slow blend from the nature of the gardens to the manufactured bricks that the house consisted of. Rays of light shone down from directly above, as the sun was hitting its highest point in the sky.

Tara could see huge French bay windows. Beams of light cascaded onto the hundreds of window panels, which were reflecting the dazzling glow. Exquisite sandstone brick work and mouldings made the house look soft and inviting. In fact, everything about it drew Tara in.

The gardens flowed organically up to and around the incredibly large building that bordered on a palace. A variety of plants lined gravel and stone pathways that all seemed to ebb towards the house like veins to a heart.

As with Mrs Tyrell's Garden, from where she stood everything seemed greener, larger, richer, and healthier than those she'd ever seen before. She wondered what they would look like up closer.

"Would you like to see inside?" Nick offered. His words snapping Tara out of her trance.

"Yes, I would love to."

It took them ten minutes to walk the rest of the distance and be officially in the garden. They'd had to circle around the pond that stood before the building. Then they weaved their way along gravel pathways and up sandstone stairs. They flowed and weaved towards the house, like a feather caught in an errant wind.

The closer they both got, the more that Tara could see. All the intricate details around the edge of the buildings became clearer. The stonework gave a sense of strength and magnificence. It must have been carved by expert hands and looked completely unweathered. The frequently cleaned stone, bathed in the warmth of the

Frozen

sun and looked ablaze. Tara could have sat and sketched the building all day and she would never have been able to show its true grandness or its captivating beauty.

"The building has changed and adapted over years. Grown from no more than a small house to this," Nick said, gesturing towards the Manor. "It has been the works of many of our talented builders. They have the great ability to move and change the building to fit what it is needed."

"That would explain why no other Manor has looked this perfect." Tara gawked at the house some more.

Nick led her towards a large wooden door that was carved with a pattern of foliage. He dropped Tara's arm, walked forward, and pushed both doors inwards, letting the light from the outside to the inside. Then he retook her hand and led her inside.

Tara had thought the outside was exquisite, but the inside was even more so. The walls were clad halfway up with a whitewashed wood. The rest of the wall covered in a duck egg wallpaper, that was covered in delicate, pale pink, floral pattern. The floor was a magnificent cream marble that made an enjoyable noise with each step Tara took. The ceiling was embossed in an intricate flowery design.

Along several of the walls stood display cabinets filled with artefacts of every era, with tiny white cards in front of each one. Each card was inscribed in an elegant hand, with a small description, a date, and a place.

It's far more organised than Mrs Tyrell's own display, Tara noted.

Paintings were every few meters on the walls and covered a substantial portion of the wallpaper behind. There were water colours, sketches, oil paintings and other medias Tara couldn't name. They portrayed different scenes, people, and places. Like with the objects in the cabinets they also had a small, engraved plaque underneath each with similar information, but with the addition of the artist.

The one thing that dominated the space, was the staircase. It that was opposite the doors but several meters back, leaving a large entryway. They lead up to the next level of the building in a sweeping curve of elegance and sophistication. Each stair was lightly carpeted in the middle of each marble step. Tara was glad of this. She would be likely to fall flat on her face if she ever had to climb or even descend these steps. Light poured in from the window above the front door and straight onto the marble, creating a glistening lake of a thousand stars.

Tara exhaled sharply as Nick touched her hand. She had been holding her breath and was completely absorbed. Nick must have been watching her reactions.

"Tell me what you are thinking," he finally enquired.

"I… I don't know where to begin. It's truly amazing and all I have seen is the stairs. You really live here?" Tara explained, managing to get some words out.

Frozen

"Yes, I do, but my room is situated on the other side of the building. It's a little more practical, than lavish over there. I just wanted to show you this." Nick pointed towards one of the cabinets and then gently directed her by the arm towards it.

Inside on the third shelf, which meant she had to lean down to see what Nick was pointing at. Right there at the front and centre of the shelf was a scroll. On it were faded letters and drawings in a language Tara could not read but could identify as Italian or French. On the card placed in front of it were only two words, not a date or a place, just 'The Prophecy'.

"Is this THE prophecy about me?" she inquired.

"It is the one that I told you about, but I'm not completely sure if it attains to you yet." Nick's hope radiated through his deep eyes. Tara wondered why he wasn't sure it was her.

"Would you like to see the rest of the house?" Nick offered, before she had chance to ask him more about what the scroll said.

"Sure, lead the way." Tara agreed, she would try to bring it up again later.

Chapter 12

Tara was exhausted by the time they were halfway around the house. She was glad she'd decided to wear sensible pumps and not heels. Her feet would have been killing her before she'd even had the chance to truly see anything.

Nick had taken her to every corner, nook and cranny of the building. It wasn't a short distance that they'd covered.

After showing her the Prophecy at the entrance, he took her down many large corridors - big enough to be rooms themselves.

Almost all the walls were shroud in beautiful paintings. Differing in size, shape, and style from the

Frozen

ones she had seen earlier. The floors flowed through different styles and colours as she walked. Wooden to tiled, carpeted to marble. The hallways weren't bare by any means. If all the furniture was removed, it would have felt cold in Tara's eyes.

However, there were sofas, chairs, and tables that lined the edges. Spaces had been left in between each item, allowing art viewers to get closer or to read information that was provided underneath the paintings. The tables were littered with objects. They nearly all displayed a vase filled with the brightest of flowers - the aroma filling their path with the scents from the garden. Tara had expected it to smell musty - like those buildings she had previously visited - but she found that she enjoyed the fresh floral scent immensely.

Tara could see that the house was well lived in, that it was obviously a home. There were objects like clothing and technology left about here or there. The sound of bustling people moving about and talking to one another, could be heard through the walls. As of yet, they hadn't come across anyone face to face since they had met Jenifer.

Nick knew everything there was to know about the building and everything in it, just like he had with Paris. Naturally therefore, he had given her a tour that you would have expected at a museum – like an audio tour. All that she had been missing was a map and pamphlet with "please visit again soon" written on the back.

Nick took her around the living spaces, the terrace that overlooked the lake – located around the back of the house - the music rooms, ballroom and even the kitchens.

She'd particularly liked the music room. Stands were covered with sheets of music ready to be played. Most of the surfaces were littered with them like confetti. Around the room, laid instruments ready to be picked up by a band that may have only gone for a quick break. It pulled her in immediately. There were many instruments that she had never personally seen before - like a hand pan or harp.

However, there were two places that she had loved more than any others. Tara's second favourite room had to be the gallery. When Nick had taken her inside it was as if she had walked into history.

It was different from other galleries she had visited before. This was not filled with a particular style or a set era, but filled with paintings from every era, in every place and in every style. There were even some artists that she recognised - Paul Klee, Monet and even Picasso.

It didn't stop there because not only was every inch of the wall covered with some kind of painting, sketch or tapestry, but in the centre of all these stood sculptures, ceramics and other installations. Tara stared in awe.

Nick didn't look at the art very much. His attention and focus had been on Tara and her reactions. He looked nervous and watched her intently. Tara was

Frozen

aware of his stares, but was far too engrossed in soaking in her surroundings.

They'd finished walking around the enormous room and Tara declared that she loved it. He had replied that there were two more places he wanted to take her.

This was the place that captivated her far more than any other of the other truly splendid rooms. She loved it above everything else in this beautiful manor.

Naturally, it had to be - the library.

They approached it from the main corridor. Two seven-foot, arched, oak doors loomed over them. Tara had stood waiting for Nick to tell her something about the ornate carvings in the wood, but this time he stayed silent.

He stood in front of her with his back to her. He pushed open the doors with some apparent effort. *They must be heavy,* Tara thought watching the doors swing open. A familiar smell hit her then and she looked deep into the room, already knowing what she would find.

Books. Thousands and thousands of books.

Tara didn't know where to look. As she glanced at Nick, she could see the smile spreading across his face. Her jaw had literally dropped open.

She became aware that she'd been holding her breath since the moment she'd caught a hint of what was inside - she drew in a deep breath. The fragrance of ancient, earthy books hit her once again. She had grown up in a home filled with books but even so, it didn't come close to the extent of this library. It dwarfed her little collection.

The ceiling above never seemed to come into focus. There were four levels that ran from the basement to the very top. It could be viewed by a central space that was left clear of obstructions from the floor to the ceiling. Someone had cleverly changed the roof to glass, allowing the space to be flooded with light. Each level had a walkway along the stacks and stacks of books. Rolling ladders occupied each level to make access easier. Tara mused that it would require a ladder at least forty feet long to reach the top shelf.

There must be millions of books here, Tara thought to herself. Nick led her further into the enormous open centre, so she could view the library that surrounded her.

Tara noticed that they had barely let go of one another's hands since they had entered the gardens. She didn't feel uncomfortable like she thought she would. Most shockingly to her, was how little time she had known him and yet still, she felt content around him. This had to be the first time she trusted someone, at least this much outside of her mother, Savannah, and Layla. It felt like her heart was on a delayed express train, that desperately needed to get to its destination after being stuck on a platform for far too long.

"Do you like it?" Nick finally asked her.

"You're asking me if I like it? I mean really? I have my own library at home, I love books, I read all the time that I can spare, and you are asking me if I like it? Just look at it. There has to be millions of books here, I could never have imagined this many books in one

Frozen

place. I don't like it... I love it." Tara spilled in a flurry without pause, finishing with a much-needed inhale.

"I'm glad that you like it. It must be one of my favourite rooms," Nick beamed at her.

"I should hope so too. Books after all hold so much meaning and knowledge of life," a familiar voice echoed through the library. Mrs Tyrell came out from behind a bookcase on the second level, clutching an open, aged, green leather book in her hands. She began to walk down the spiralling staircase closest to her. She wasn't looking at them or where she was going at all, but at the book, she was too absorbed to look away even for a few moments.

When she reached the last step, she shut the book together with a snap and looked up. She moved her glasses on to the top of her head and smiled at them both.

"I was just doing research. Have you finished your tour?" Mrs Tyrell questioned her adopted son.

"Not yet," Nick answered.

"Then I will leave you both to it. I will be here for a while," Mrs Tyrell informed them.

"We will come and find you when we are done," Nick told her and turned to Tara. "I have one thing left that I want to show you."

"We are coming back here though, right?" Tara asked, impatient to explore the library. Nick's only reply was a smile.

Tara and Nick bade Mrs Tyrell fair well and they set off to this mysterious place. They headed down, what seemed like endless corridors, until they arrived at just an ordinary, wooden door. Nick opened it and showed her in.

"This is my room," Nick informed her.

Tara looked around. The room was filled with light which streamed through from the bay window directly opposite her. Tara judged the room to be a little larger than her own. It had a fireplace that wasn't currently lit, with an old red couch sat right before it. A small side table sat just to its side, with a stack of books and a ceramic lamp placed upon it. There were a few dressers around the edge of the room, but that pretty much concluded it's contents.

"No bed?" Tara asked.

"That's through here," Nick took her to a door on the right side of him. He opened the door but remained outside, gesturing for Tara to look. Tara hesitantly walked into the room.

It was dominated by the biggest four poster bed she had ever seen. It was draped with the richest blue silks that invited her to discover how soft they were, but she resisted. The wooden floorboards were partially covered with a large carpet, echoing the colours in the drapes decorative pattern. Two fairly basic – at least in comparison to the bed - bedside tables sat either side, with nothing except lamps visible on each. The walls were clad in a lightly varnished wood. A singular wardrobe – the same colour as the panelling - sat in the corner. The rest of the room was bare.

Frozen

"What's through that door?" Tara enquired, spotting another door that looked just like the one she'd just walked through.

"My bathroom," Nick responded.

"That makes sense," Tara agreed. "This space is all yours?" She was completely taken back by how big the space was. It might as well have been a flat. The rooms were not grand in size but enough for one person or even two.

"Yes. Not many people get this amount of space. Generally, the ones that do are the permanent residents or the Elders," Nick explained. "There is one more room. If you would like to see it?"

Tara walked towards him nodding, wondering what could possibly be in this extra room.

Nick revealed another door on the opposite side to his sitting room – if it could be called that. When Tara got inside, she understood why there was another room.

The room was approximately the same size as the front room but contained a lot more furniture. It appeared to have been split into a few different areas. One corner was filled with books, that she thought must be Nick's own collection. The other side was filled with art equipment. There was an art easel, which had a blank canvas sat upon it, waiting for an artist to depict what window it would open for the viewer. It stood looking out a small window and had a clear view over part of the manor's gardens and the grounds beyond them.

Paintings covered the walls and littered a section of the floor. They were all in a similar style, telling Tara they were all painted by one person - Nick. He was evidently incredibly talented.

The final area in the room was filled with Nick's biggest passion, Music. A white piano took centre space, and the other beautiful instruments were hung on the wall, sheets of music covered most surfaces like a musician's tablecloth. A smaller section of the wall had deep shelving, it was filled with CD's and records. To the side of these was a record player and stereo. Tara hoped that he had discovered *Spotify,* or he might run out of space.

"It's amazing. A bit like a miniature version of all the best rooms in the manor, collected in this one room. Without all the walking though!" Tara exclaimed.

"I'm sorry. I have made you walk so far today," Nick needlessly apologised. They both took a seat on the piano bench.

"I am so glad that I have. This place is so beautiful, and I don't think I could have rested, until I had seen almost all of it. It's filled with so much history, knowledge, art, music, beauty and of course books," Tara said, heartedly impressed.

"I am glad that you like it so much," Nick resolved.

"Would you play something for me?" Tara asked excitedly nodding to the piano.

"Of course." Nick got up from the bench and walked over to a pile of music sheets, which were sat

Frozen

neatly on top of some shelving. After rummaging through them all, he pulled out a worn, discoloured piece of paper that he had been looking for and returned to sit next to her, facing the piano.

After taking a moment to organise himself, music began to fill the room. It started calmly and quietly getting more intense as the music continued. Tara watched his hands run effortlessly across the keys. They created the beautiful sound that entered, not just her ears, but her soul. True music.

When Nick finished, Tara clapped her hands together and said "Bravo!" To which Nick replied with a slight bow of his head. Tara let out a small chuckle and Nick reciprocated.

"That was a gorgeous and very happy piece. Who was it written by?" Tara queried.

"Thank you. It is one of my own pieces," Nick explained. "Catherine enjoys music so much that I wrote it for her. It reminds her of her life and the gatherings before her powers were taken. It reminds her of being free."

"You wrote that?" Tara asked for conformation. Nick nodded his reply. Tara was amazed by his talent and passion for music. "Can I ask what you mean by gatherings?"

"I forget that you don't know everything yet. It feels like you have been here all along. I surprise myself with how at ease I am around you." Nick smiled at her, but Tara could see his nervousness.

"It's the same for me too," Tara blushed. She was trying to make him feel less embarrassed, but caused herself more instead.

"I…" Nick stopped before he had even begun. He edged closer to Tara and the space between them electrified. They looked at one another, both apprehensive of taking the next step. Nick lifted his hand and touched her reddened cheeks gently with the back of his fingers. Tara closed her eyes trying to take in the moment and calm her heart. His warm breath melded with hers. She wanted this.

Nick closed the small gap between them. He pressed his lips against hers gently and Tara returned the pressure, allowing little space between them. Nick encircled her with his arms pulling her even further in. Tara felt secure and yet her heart would not calm down, like it had been made to beat for this exact moment. Their lips danced upon each other's, entwining, and moving with the flow of the kiss until they finally parted.

Tara slowly opened her eyes, moving back only by the slightest amount. She instantly saw Nicks gentle eyes softly gazing into hers. He didn't let go of her. She could still feel the heat of his body. It hit Tara then – that was her first kiss. She felt elated, but this was soon taken over with the worry. Worry that she had been a bad kisser, and this made her blush.

"You are blushing again. Why?" Nick asked as Tara cursed her body for giving her away.

"That was my first kiss," she explained and was surprised she had managed to divulge it.

Frozen

"It was mine too," Nick shocked Tara.

"How is that possible? You are a hundred and forty years old and you have never kissed anyone?" Tara questioned.

"A hundred and forty-two," Nick corrected. "I have never been that interested in chasing girls. There have been one or two that I thought I might, but they just became friends. I had to be sure before I kissed anyone."

This revelation made Tara feel more comfortable, at least she wasn't getting compared to anyone else. It seemed incredibly odd that he'd never kissed anyone but - finding that she couldn't talk anymore on the subject at present - she diverted the conversation.

"So, what is this gathering?" Tara said firmly - giving Nick no room to revert the subject back.

"I have never been to one," Nick told her. "So why don't we go and find Catherine. She will explain more clearly than I can."

"Okay," Tara replied. Nick stood up and embraced her hand in his and steered the way. He didn't let go of her, not once.

Chapter 13

About ten minutes later, Tara and Nick approached Mrs Tyrell at a table in the library. She was reading the same green, leather-bound book, but now Tara could see it was covered in symbols.

Instantly, Mrs Tyrell lifted her head towards them, but her eyes continued to finish the sentence before settling themselves on Nick with a smile. She proceeded to turn her head towards Tara and gave her the same warm smile.

"How was the tour?" She asked, simultaneously removing her glasses, and sitting them upon her currently closed book.

Frozen

"It's pretty big! I haven't seen it all yet, but it's a lovely building with so much history," Tara said with true enthusiasm.

"Indeed, but not just human history. There is what you would call 'mythological' history too. There are more books in this place, than I will ever get around to reading. Even though, I have been here for a truly lengthy amount of time, and I plan to be here for a lot longer yet."

Tara's love of books meant that her interest had peaked in the library, and she found she was truly glad to have come back. If Tara previously had to guess, she would have said Mrs Tyrell was a great reader. Seeing her in this environment and how comfortable Mrs Tyrell was, cemented her prejudice almost immediately.

With an extensive library like this one, she couldn't imagine that anyone in the manor didn't read. Tara had dreamt of fairy tales filled with creatures of myths and legends since she was a little girl. Some part of her knew, that all the books she had read as a little girl, would now be more than just fairy tales. Now they were just looking glasses peering into their worlds. There had been truth in those pages, unbeknownst to her at the time.

"Mrs Tyrell, can I ask you something?" Anxiety washed over her. Tara didn't like to pry into other people's lives – especially painful memories - but her overriding need for information, meant she had to ignore her anxiousness.

"Of course, Tara, but please call me Catherine," she softly replied. Tara was coming to realise how caring and thoughtful Mrs Tyrell truly was.

"Could you please tell me what happened to the Shapeshifters, all those years ago?" The question cautiously rolled off her tongue. She watched Mrs Tyrell's expression as she sank into thought.

"It would be my pleasure," Catherine answered, but she seemed reluctant. Tara hadn't witnessed caution in her expressions before. Tara assumed that she would've seen it coming, but she supposed it didn't make it any easier to drag up such an awful part of her history. She gestured to the two chairs opposite her and Tara took the one to the left, while Nick took the chair to the right.

"It was a long time ago - nearly two hundred years. Only a handful of us remember the gathering clearly." Mrs Tyrell started, wincing. She seemed to bite down the feeling and continued her tale. Tara felt awfully guilty for asking this of her.

"Once, every hundred years or so, we gather in large numbers to pass our inner light back and forth between one another. You might call it love, perhaps. It is not necessarily love of a passionate kind, but of fondness or kindness or of life.

Frozen

"You might think that we are skin changers. We are and we are not. We use the light that we absorb from nature, and this provides us with the ability to bend the light, energy, and our shape. We are changing your perception and our own. It looks and feels real, but we cannot stay as an animal or as someone we are not for too long. After all we are still human, and we crave familiarity. We do not think and act like the animal of choice, we only replicate their shape. We remain always conscious of ourselves, our desires, and our needs. We don't change our mind and bodies like werewolves, for instance. Alas, changing is more painful for them.

"The gathering is more than just a ceremony. Most of us go to see family, friends, and meet new Shifters.

"That particular year, I went to see my grandfather - one of the twelve Elders - and my sister, Amber. She was much younger than me because my mother had remarried. She had never been to a gathering before then.

"I'd lived separately for quite some time and missed them greatly. The gathering was a suitable place to meet up with them. You must remember that time is less finite for us.

"We were having the most wonderful time. We talked for hours. There was always dancing and music that could fill your soul. My grandfather remarked to me that this year, the party was substantial, and Amber was excited to be part of such a large ceremony. She said, "I will never forget this one." Of course, she could never have known, that she was talking for each of us.

"The sun set, and it cast a beautiful glow, an amber glow. I had never seen that depth of colour in the sky and haven't since. As I watched, it intensified across the horizon, beaming through trees. I was sat on a hill side, just above a sweet stall and I could smell the most delicious, sweet honey, a smell I have never forgotten to this day.

"The sun finally dropped from the sky and the gathering started to congregate, to the centre of the field. We were all anxious to get started. Small floating lights began illuminating above us, appearing like a star filled sky, casting its light on to us. Adding to the billions of lights already suspended with the moon.

"Once we all got to the middle space. We clutched each other's hands, creating a connected circle. My little sister was on left side of me and my grandfather on the other. The ceremony started and we began passing our light - our love - to one another.

"The middle of the circle becomes this heightened centre as light bounces back and forth across it. I closed my eyes to experience the warming sensation, but I could still hear the wonder in the small noises my sister was making beside me. I remember thinking about my joy for her wonder in that moment.

Frozen

"As we all amplified our light to become its own liquid ball of gold, like a sun made entirely from love.

"The light from the centre should have sent tendrils into each of our bodies. Filling us with heightened light. We should have felt ourselves become something more – something higher. We should have felt the connection to those around us, to the surrounding nature, and to our own powers. However, that was when our entire world spun on its axis.

"I had opened my eyes slowly, adjusting to the light in front of me. I turned my head to look at Amber expecting a smile spreading infectiously across her face. But all I saw was horror, pain, and shock. She looked down at her chest. I followed her eye line and what I saw haunts me even now.

"Where her cotton, yellow, polka-dot dress was tied in a bow on her chest was a gaping hole. Blood ran out of it, drenching her. It gushed down her front and before I could catch her, she fell. I broke the circle, the light wavering and fading as I did. I couldn't breathe or think. I just stared into Amber eyes. They had gone cold and glazed instantly.

"I remember looking around the circle seeing an increasing number of shifter bodies hitting the floor. The same red hole, yawning in their chests.

"Screams echoed off the hillsides around us. Chaos spread like wildfire, catching everyone in its grasps of pain and fear. People began to shift to run, to hide, to escape, but it was a fool's errand. As the final bit of light disappeared in the centre, I saw something.

"I saw a human figure. It wasn't of flesh and bone, but as if a shadow moved in place of one. It extended its hands forward. The light – our light - appeared forced into the centre of its hands, until it became a ball.

"It resembled a glass ball filled with a honey liquid. The fluid captured inside was trying to find its own way free, swirling freely beneath the surface. The figure pulled it against his chest and bent around it in a strange movement. Darkness descended and with it the figure disappeared.

"That night we lost sixty of our kind. We lost our ability to shift. We lost our ability to trust. Worst of all we became soaked with fear." Catherine looked from Nick to Tara, a tear rolling over her bottom eye lid and down onto her cheek. For what seemed like ten minutes, both Nick and Tara stood waiting. The loss must have been crushing.

"To have witnessed such horror must have been beyond heart breaking," Tara stated.

"There was and has been no pain like it," Catherine confirmed.

"I have some questions though," Tara asked after a pause. She wanted to leave adequate time for Catherine to stop her if it was too much to handle. But Catherine nodded her response promptly.

Frozen

"Who was it and why did they do it?" Tara asked softly. Almost believing that the pitch of her voice would make the query easier.

"There are a few things that we know about that night. Firstly, that it was the Shadows that attacked.

"Secondly, that they took the sphere of light that contains our ability. It wasn't all of it, but enough to weaken us. Enough to cease our shifting ability.

"Thirdly and most shockingly, it was definitely an inside job. It was one of our kind that had to of released the whereabouts of the gathering.

"The answer to who and why – I can not give you. We were and are all perplexed by the individual's actions and motives.

"Thus far we know that the Shadows did it for power. You see we are yin and yang. Without light there are no shadows and with no shadows there can't be the contrast of light.

"The Shadows have taken the source in order to exist in any world - even worlds with the darkest of nights – in corporeal form.

"We additionally know that they haven't released the light from the original container, giving us a slight upper hand. Releasing it without finding an adequate container would be catastrophic for them."

Sensing Tara's next question Catherine continued, "See the light is too powerful for them. They need a small amount each. Something that they can carry for themselves. Until they solve how to syphon the light out, we still have the possibility to win this war."

"What about those of you that weren't at the gathering. Surely, the Shadows didn't get their powers?"

"No, unfortunately, even they were affected. When the gathering takes place, the people there will have some connection to those who did not participate. It is something that every Shifter links up to. No matter how far away they are, we are all connected - through love, friendship, memories of one another, or family. There is no absence from our connected energies. Hence, when non-shifters with blood ties become close to us, you also become linked, and your dormant genes become active.

"It is the one time that we are weak and most vulnerable, and someone exploited that."

"Then, why gather in such a way?" Tara quizzed.

"You must understand this, in two different ways. The gathering is kept secret. Its location is known only to the Elders and those in charge of security. At least until the last moment, when the speaker - as we call him - announces it to the people the day before.

"The speaker is an enormously powerful individual and respected by all. His name is Ivan, and he is capable of pushing thoughts into people's heads. Ivan tells everyone the location this way. Meaning it is not spoken to anyone aloud. There are procedures and they must be adhered to for the safety of our kind.

Frozen

"There are reasons why we gather this way. One is to be near one another for celebration and fun. Like a very large Christmas gathering, I suppose. The second reason is the main reason. The light that we can pass to one another gives us our abilities. If we only connected to those that live close to us, we would only have a faction of what we can achieve. We collectively enhance and distribute our powers at a gathering.

"Do not misunderstand me though. We do not do this for individual power, but the collective. The stronger the bond, the stronger we are as a whole and therefore, the more we can protect one another. We gather every century because that strength diminishes over time, and you could say it needs recharging before it runs out."

Tara could tell from Catherine's speech, that she was passionate about the gathering. That she had grown up with it. But she could see in Catherine's eyes the agony that these memories gave her.

"Thank you, for explaining that to me and I'm sorry for your tremendous loss," Tara sympathised. Nick stood up abruptly next to her.

Nick glanced her way conveying that it was time to leave. Tara understood that Catherine would need time to herself. Time had healed the wound but discussing it in such detail had made the scar burn.

S. M. Clair

Tara had been supplied with a lot to think on and more things to discuss. However, for now it could wait.

Frozen

Chapter 14

Upon re-entering Nick's room, Tara discovered a small table that wasn't there before. Glasses, plates, and cutlery were arranged into two place settings. A meal was laid out for them. It looked and smelled delicious. Nick led her to her seat and helped her slip the chair closer to the table. He walked around to his side and took up his own seat.

"When did you do this?" Tara asked him.

"I didn't personally. I organised it with the butler and chef. I thought you might like to eat here with me before you go home," Nick suggested.

"That would be really nice," Tara responded warmly to his romantic gesture. "Thank you."

"We have beef wellington, served with creamed potatoes and asparagus. Then for dessert we have strawberry cheesecake. Is that okay?" Nick asked her, while he played the devoted host and poured water into her glass from a large jug. Tara watched as condensation dripped from the ice-cold glass.

"That's completely perfect," Tara exclaimed. "Beef wellington was one of my father's favourites. I have fond memories of making it with my mother." Tara fought back the tears that threatened to fill her eyes. Talking about her father still made her heart ache.

"I'm sure it will not live up to your family's recipe," Nick said respectfully. "Although, I still hope you enjoy it."

Tara enjoyed every succulent mouthful. It wasn't the home-made version she was used to, but it was mouth-wateringly good. The pastry was flaky and crisp. The meat was juicy and tender. She had to admit to herself that the only reason her mother's recipe was any better was nostalgia.

They were soon onto the sweet, heavenly cheesecake. Tara enjoyed it so much, that Nick offered to box some up for her to take home to her mother.

When the meal was fully and happily ingested, and the cake ready to go, they grabbed their jackets and head out of Nick's apartment. They travelled down

Frozen

endless corridors and Tara soon began to wonder if she would never find her way around without a guide.

Nick offered his hand to her as they left his room and Tara had happily taken it. The feel of his hand in hers was a comfort Tara never knew she was missing out on until that moment. A kind of connection she had never been privy to before. His fingers entangled around hers. Tara's palm fit perfectly inside of his and a radiating warmth emanated between their hands.

Tara was still amazed about how fast things had been progressing. She questioned her sanity, but it just felt right. She'd only known him for a few weeks, but that didn't matter to her, not when it felt completely and utterly right. It was like her whole being had been calling out it him and his to hers.

Halfway down one of the wider corridors they bumped into a girl as they turned a corner. She was taller than Tara. At a guess she would say the girl was about five foot nine, with long blonde hair that was tied back into a sleek ponytail. She had the deepest blue eyes that Tara had ever seen and looked to be about Tara's age. Although, it was technically impossible to age anyone that lived here.

"Sorry Stephanie," Nick apologised.

"Who is this?" Stephanie probed bluntly, her face showing nothing but distain. Tara thought this was strange as she had never met the girl.

"Stephanie, I would like you to meet Tara Kingley. Tara I would like to introduce you to my friend, Stephanie." Nick smiled.

"Oh! It's you. Spend two minutes with this one..." She jabbed her finger towards Nick. "... And everyone thinks that YOU are the Key? I mean look at you…" Stephanie literally looked her up and down. "… I mean have you even picked up a weapon before?" She glowered at Tara.

"No, I …"

"See," she aimed her words at Nick. "What use is she going to be in our war? She'll just hold us back," Stephanie complained. She barged past Nick with her continued attitude and rounded the end of the corridor.

"What was that all about?" Tara enquired, but only when she was sure that Stephanie was far enough out of ear shot. She didn't want to offend her further.

"I will explain in the car," Nick offered.

"Okay," Tara agreed.

It became apparent to Tara, that with this many people in one building, you were bound to bump into someone on your way around. To prove her point, they bumped into two more people. Tara began to wonder where everyone had been while she had her tour earlier.

"Greetings, you must be the ever-anticipated Tara," a tall man said to her. He had short, choppy, brown hair and appeared to be about twenty-five. His smile was small, but still he instantly felt approachable.

Frozen

On his arm was a petite woman with similar coloured hair, but hers was longer than his and reached her shoulders.

"This is Cain and Mary. They are two of the twelve Elders," Nick explained to Tara.

"It is a pleasure to meet you," Tara replied formally, while mentally making note that she had met three in totality. At least so far.

"You mean to say, that you introduced her to other Elders before you introduced her to us. Shame on you, Nick," Mary said with a grin. Tara could hear an accent in the way she spoke and supposed it to be North European, but she couldn't be more specific than that.

"No, Jenifer came to meet us when we first arrived," Nick explained to her.

"In that case I will forgive you," Mary chuckled.

"You are very generous," Nick smiled and bent into a slight bow.

"Now, now, Nick. You will let it go to her head. I do not need any more theatrics than I already have," Cain insisted.

"What are you trying to say?" Mary roused.

"That you can be overtly flamboyant and dramatic, and it gives me a headache!" Cain produced a big grin in Tara's direction, and she began to realise that both Nick and Cain were teasing Mary.

"You tease me," Mary concluded with Tara.

"Would we do such a thing... Nick?" Cain smirked.

"No, of course not. That would be disrespectful to her grace!" Nick joked in return. This caused Mary to wave her hand in playful dismissal, leading to a chorus of laughter from them all.

"Well, it was nice to meet you, Tara. I hope that we get the chance, sometime soon for us to get to know you better," Cain stated.

"Yes, I agree," Mary chimed in.

"I would like that," Tara agreed as Mary and Cain walked in one direction, and they headed in the other.

Tara would've assumed the Elder's to be twelve stuffy, entitled leaders. However, the evidence provided by Jenifer, Mary, and Cain proved otherwise. She mused about what the other nine might be like.

It wasn't long, until they had reached the spot they had clumsily teleported onto when they had arrived earlier. The sun was starting to leave a streak of warm hues across the sky. The trees and plants around the manor seemed to be reaching up to the last drops of light before nightfall. Oranges, browns, reds, pinks, and some touches of lavender filled the horizon. It was such a beautiful view, that Tara paused for a moment to admire it.

Frozen

"Why do you teleport from here?" Tara enquired. "Surely you can't hurt anyone while you are leaving."

"I could. It is just an old habit I have, from when I was getting used to it. Plus, it has the bonus of getting to spend some extra time with you." Nick charmed.

Nick took a hold of Tara's hand and lent in towards her. Their lips intertwined in a slight and gentle kiss. Tara slowly noticed the building light behind her closed eyes, and knew he was taking them back to Mrs Tyrell's, but the majority of her attention was on the way his lips guided hers.

When their lips parted, they stood rooted to the spot, indulging in their closeness. Nick drew her even closer. Tara could feel the warmth of his body, smell his deep, rich, earthy scent, and could hear his beating heart. She was pleased to realise that its rhythm was just as wild as her own. His arms locked around her body in a gentle and loving embrace. Tara was hit with the sensation of belonging.

After a few minutes, he relinquished her. Nick firmly took her hand in his once more and guided her through the house out towards the car. It was dark outside - the sun had set on one of the best days of Tara's life.

"What is the deal with Stephanie?" Tara queried moments later. It was a cloud that had been cast over her day, an absurd notion considering everything that Catherine had told her.

"The straightforward answer is that a few decades ago, several people - including Stephanie - thought that she was the Key," Nick winced.

"You didn't?" Tara inquired.

"No, I didn't," Nick sighed. "She didn't match the all the descriptions in the Prophecy. There were a few things that did fit, and she is more than capable of holding her own. The Council put her through vigorous training to shape her into the weapon that they needed. However, she was not the one. She carried on believing that she was the Key all the way up to me finding you. She feels like you took her role away from her. She feels lost and without purpose.' Nick concluded. Tara was inclined to believe there was a gaping hole in the middle of this story.

"What made you so sure that she was not the Key?" Tara tried to press.

"The Prophecy states that I would find the Key and deliver her to the Shapeshifters. I did find Stephanie that is not deniable. I found her in a terrible situation, and I took her to the mansion to receive healing. After several years, she became better, and we became close friends. I believe that she always wanted more, but I didn't. I just knew in my heart that she was not the Key and that I was still searching.

Frozen

"Subsequently, I found you and that feeling of searching just left me." Nick facial expressions portrayed his despondent emotions. Tara knew that he was still hiding something. He was skirting around some information, but she would not press him anymore.

"Stephanie said that I would not be suitable as the Key. She made it sound like I need to be a warrior to defeat the Shadows," Tara had been wondering what Stephanie had meant by it.

"Many hold the belief, that to defeat the Shadows we require a great warrior," Nick clarified.

"What do you think?"

"I believe that there is more than one way to bring down an enemy. What it will take to bring down the Shadows, I do not know. What I do know is that it begins with you."

Tara was conscious that Nick had gone from questioning whether she was the one, to being sure that she was. Tara pondered what might have caused this shift.

As they pulled into the driveway of her home, Nick asked what her plans were for the rest of the weekend.

"I haven't really thought about it," Tara told him honestly. "Normally, Sunday is homework, yoga with my mother and then reading a good book."

"Would you like to go on a walk with me," Nick queried.

"I would love to," Tara replied.

"Okay, I will pick you up in the morning and I will drive us there."

"Can you pick me up for about eleven tomorrow? That way I still have time to do yoga with my mother in the morning. I don't want to let her down after being out all day today," Tara explained. Nick got out of the car and Tara unbuckled her seat belt. Before she had time to open the door, Nick had done it for her.

"You don't have to do that," Tara told him.

"I know that you can do it, but I want to. I come from an era where it was the right thing to do for a woman. Chivalry is someone extending their hand in kindness. It doesn't mean that I think you are incapable. They are actions that are driven by the fact that I care." Nick enlightened her to his way of thinking.

"Then I will not stop you," Tara concluded, blushing at the idea that he cared for her.

"Thank you. I know that it is not a modern notion. Women are more capable than men have given them credit for in the past. I have always believed that. However, it doesn't mean that we cannot rely on one another for small acts of kindness to each other. No matter the gender."

Tara stared at him in awe. "Have you ever thought of doing public speaking?"

"Would be a bit difficult if I still looked eighteen in ten years," Nick laughed.

Frozen

"I wouldn't say eighteen. I think that you look more like twenty," Tara looked at him. "I get what you are saying though. It must be hard for you to create stability in the human world, when everything keeps changing except you."

"It can be, but we have our own Shifter spaces. There are also other places for other... kinds of people ...that we use too," Nick explained, stumbling over what to call himself. "We can carry on talking tomorrow. I think your mother is waiting. The blinds keep twitching. Tomorrow at eleven?"

"I swear that she purposely tries to embarrass me," Tara said, as she headed for the door. "Tomorrow at eleven," Tara agreed. "Night."

"Good night, Tara," Nick returned.

Chapter 15

The next morning, Tara woke up at her usual Sunday time of nine. She got dressed in her gym gear and headed down to the conservatory for yoga with her mother. The conservatory was the best place for it. It continually poured light in through the windows, even on overcast and gloomy days. It gave both Tara and her mother the chance to soak in some Vitamin D.

It was a beautiful day, and the sun was out in strength. The room was heated to a lovely temperature and even the plants that lined the windows, seemed to be reaching out their leaves, like little hands trying to grab the sun.

Frozen

One thing was different today though. Tara was about to get a whole bunch of overprotective parenting. Last night, she'd been very lucky in managing to avoid it. The questions came as soon as she entered the house, but one of her mother's friends turned up just at the right moment. Tara had received a 'get out of jail free card'. There was no chance of that today.

They led their mats out in the middle of the tiled floor and faced the garden. It was filled with herbs, flowers and plenty of fruit and veg. Tara's mother had always believed in organic food and believed the best way to accomplish this, was to grow her own. Tara always helped at the beginning and end of the growing seasons, but she never really had the proverbial green thumb.

"So, are you going to tell me how it went?" Her mother asked, as they exited the cat pose. It hadn't taken long for the questions to start.

"It was good. He took me for a picnic first and then we went to see the house. I also met with some of his friends," Tara told her. She couldn't tell her everything, but she would tell her what she could. Paraphrasing would be her only way to get through this.

"Did you kiss though?" Her mother asked bluntly.

"Mother!" Tara exclaimed.

"What? It's a perfectly normal question."

"You don't have to be so direct about it. I've only known the guy for two weeks," she tried to evade, but to no avail.

"Did you kiss?" She pressed.

"Yes," Tara let out, there was no avoiding it so she might as well get it over and done with.

"I knew it!" Her mother squealed. "You like him then?"

"Yes, I really do," she said candidly. Her mother was lapping it up. Somehow, her mother had never given up on romance, even after her husband had died. Tara had no idea if her mother was ever going to end up finding someone else or if she would continue to idolise the love story she had already lived.

"Do you love him?" Her mother pressed a little more serious this time, as they moved into the Halasana pose.

"I've only just met him," she reiterated. "How am I meant to know if I feel that way yet?"

"Sometimes you just know. Sometimes, two people in love, just are," she explained.

"Not everyone's love story is like yours and Father's," Tara exasperated.

"No. Maybe not. But they do exist. True love is a fickle thing. It can be grown and tended like a delicate flower, or it can be love at first sight." Tara's mother continued.

"Who is to say that he will love me?" Tara bounced back.

"I think that ship has already sailed, my darling. I think it is obvious that he is in love with you. He takes you places, introduces you to his friends and then kisses you." Tara's mother smiled at her.

Frozen

"That doesn't mean love mother."

"Maybe not, but the way he looks at you. The way his eyes light up, especially when you look at him. That. That to me says he is in love with you. Time will tell," she stated, determinedly.

Tara's mother always had her head in the clouds and if Tara was going to take anything with a pinch of salt, it would be this. It didn't, however, stop Tara from blushing because deep down she hoped, and she wished that this feeling in her might last forever.

****

Tara and her mother had done another thirty minutes of Yoga in relative silence. Tara had then gone upstairs to shower and get ready for the walk.

Nick arrived no more than three seconds after Tara had finished putting her hair into a messy bun. She quickly grabbed her bag and ran down the stairs, reaching Nick before her mother said anything embarrassing to him.

"It is a pleasure to see you again, Mrs Kingley." Nick politely addressed her.

"It is nice to see you too, Nick," her mother offered her hand for a handshake. Nick took the offer with a smile.

"I believe that you are taking Tara for a walk today?" Nick nodded in agreement. "Thank you for taking her to see the Manor yesterday. It is nice to see my daughter enjoying activities that I have not seen her doing in a while."

"I am glad that she is too,' Nick agreed with her. He glanced up and smiled when he saw Tara. *This doesn't mean she's right*, Tara thought to herself.

Tara greeted him and said goodbye to her mother. She led Nick out of the house as quickly as possible.

When they got to the driveway, Tara climbed into Nick's car without hesitation. Nick gave a final wave goodbye to her mother, then he climbed into the car. While Nick backed the car out, her mother gave her a thumbs up. *Could she be more embarrassing?* Tara thought.

It took them a little over an hour to get to their destination. While Nick could teleport them, he had suggested that a drive would be better. "Sometimes it is nice to enjoy the journey," Nick expressed.

It was definitely worth the wait, and she had to admit, that she did enjoy the drive. They had talked about many different things along the way, but it was all nothing of consequence - small talk.

They arrived at a stretch of the southern coast and parked in a quaint little village. Stone cottages were topped with thatched roofing. Hanging baskets swung slightly in the salty breeze from the coast. Small stone walls were filled with flowers and shrubs of every colour.

It was a picturesque village and at its centre stood a small, but beautiful church. The clock tower chimed the hour with a beautiful ring. People began to

Frozen

exit the church onto the road, passing through an arched gate way. A Sunday service must've been held inside.

Nick pulled the car over. He went into the boot and retrieved a picnic basket. Tara looked at him quizzically.

"We will have to eat at some point," he explained. Tara hadn't failed to notice that Nick always brushed off romance like it wasn't a big deal. She just wasn't sure if this was for her benefit or for his own. He took her hand and led her forward.

The horizon offered nothing of what lie beyond the rolling hills. They walked through a small woodland area and across green fields dotted with cows. It didn't take long for Tara to spot a slight blue line on the horizon. The ocean advancing towards them.

The views - once they got to the cliff edge - were nothing short of stunning. The cliffs we chalky white and the sand a golden yellow in the sun's rays. The grass hugged and covered every nook and cranny that it could get its fingers into - clutching to the safety from the salty onslaught of the sea. The water was as still as ice, except the last few feet of water. The foam of the crashing water creating a boundary along the sand. Marking where one world ended and the watery depths of another world began.

"What do you think?" Nick enquired.

"It's stunning," Tara expressed. "The water is so clear."

"Today it is. Though, I have watched countless storms from here," Nick told her.

"I can imagine the view would be quite spectacular and yet humbling, to witness so much of nature's strength," Tara noted, and Nick nodded in agreement.

They meandered further around the cliffs at a slow pace. They appeared incredibly tall from this height. Tara imagined they must look like white sheets hung out to dry, if viewed from further out at sea.

They continued their walk, enjoying the views of the coast subtly change. After about twenty minutes of walking, they came across a small cove. The cliffs made a perfect crescent shape, welcoming the water into its centre.

Many people were spread out across the beach below, some with their dogs. Tara could hear several children laughing and playing below them. They ran away from the waves that threatened to dampen their shoes, chuckling as they pursued the receding wave, only to be chased down again.

"Shall we sit and eat something?" Nick enquired.

"I think that would be a wonderful idea," Tara replied.

They headed down to the beach and found a spot that was drenched in sunlight and looked out at the water. Nick got a blanket out of the basket, laying it out for them to sit on.

Tara removed her shoes and socks. She dipped her feet into the cool sand. She felt every coarse, damp

Frozen

grain dance across her skin and tickle in between her toes. She closed her eyes and took in the salty smell, the unseasonal warmth from the October sun on her skin, the sound of the waves hitting the sand calmingly and took a deep breath.

Tara felt so calm. She knew it as more than just the sounds, smells, and sights around her. Nick's presence calmed her.

They sat and ate their food, while they watched the waves ebb back and forth. Clouds floated across the sky, making shapes as the wind twisted them in unusual ways. They talked about Mrs Tyrell and the people at the Manor and how he had met everyone.

Eventually Tara brought up a subject that she had been avoiding, but she couldn't keep herself in the dark any longer.

"Nick, can you tell me why I heard voices the other day?" Tara queried.

"I can. Are you sure you're ready to know?" Nick checked.

"Yes, I am," Tara firmly told both herself and Nick.

"What do you want to know first?" Nick asked.

"I suppose how it is even possible. I'm not a Shapeshifter."

"I... I am not sure that you aren't," Nick said vaguely.

"I think I would know if I was," Tara retorted.

"It's the only explanation. I think that your mother or father carried the gene and after you had been exposed to me and Mrs Tyrell it has begun to trigger your dormant traits," Nick explained further.

"You're telling me that my mother is, or my father was a Shapeshifter?" Tara quizzed.

"Not necessarily. I believe that one of them or possibly both carried the gene onto you," Nick clarified.

"Let me get this right. You think that I am becoming a Shapeshifter, after being near you and that my mother or my father, or both may have given me the gene in the first place?" Nick nodded in response. "They would have told me. That's not something that you hide from your child."

"Unless they did it to protect you and wanted to keep you from becoming a Shifter. I cannot tell you why they haven't told you or if they planned on telling you. That would have to be a discussion that you have with your mother," Nick explained. "What happened the other day was not the kind of thing that happens to just anyone. You are a telepath, Tara."

Nick said it so matter of fact. This is what Tara had been dreading. She wanted to fit into Nick's world, but she didn't want to be different in any more ways than necessary.

"Does the Key have to be a Shapeshifter?" Tara wondered aloud.

"We do not know. No-one knows who or where the Prophecy comes from. We've not been relying on it to fight our battles. We did try and find out who it came from once. My father wrote it, that we know, but who

Frozen

gave him the information we can only guess," Nick enlightened her.

"Okay, so let's say that I am turning in to a... Shapeshifter and that I am a telepath. What happens now?" Tara quizzed.

"That is your choice. I will not let anyone force you into this. We can train you and teach you, or we could continue as we are and see what happens, or…" Nick paused, and Tara looked up into his eyes that seemed to burn with sorrow. "…or we can part ways, and no one will ever bother you again."

Tara stood up and moved away from where Nick stayed sitting on the mat. She looked up at the sea and felt the sand shifting under her toes. Her heart felt like a raging tide, and it was crashing down to earth, with the heavy realisation that nothing would stop the flow of energy that was inside her.

What did she want? Who did she want to be? Tara Kingley loved by few and hated by so many? Tara Kingley the saviour of the Shifters? She didn't know.

She turned and looked at Nick whose eyes blazed like the sun and his hair shone like light hitting water.

"I do not know what or who I want to be…" Tara started. "… but whoever that maybe… I want to discover her with you."

Nick stood up, grabbed her around the waist lifted her close to his body, and clean off the ground. He spun her in ecstasy. He dropped her back to the ground took hold of her cheeks and kissed her as a wave broke across the sand.

Tara had been sure of one thing and one thing only that day. No matter what the future held for her she wanted him to be in it.

She was falling completely in love with Nick.

Chapter 16

The next week of school flew by. Every day had - pretty much - been like the week before. She went to lessons and at lunch she met with Nick or Savannah and Layla in the library.

She told both Layla and Savannah about her weekend with Nick. They had been supportive like Tara knew they would, but she'd felt terrible about omitting so many things.

It was apparent the Shifters kept their existence private and secret. She didn't want to release information that was not hers to share and may also endanger them.

"Nick?" Tara asked him on the Monday morning in the school's old canteen.

"Yes?" Nick replied.

"Why is it that you keep it ALL secret?" Tara emphasized the 'all', hoping he would understand what she was hinting about.

"There are many reasons, but the two big ones are simple really. It is safer for us all to remain hidden. Many people in normal society would be far from accepting. However, it's not only humans," Nick explained in a hush tone. "We stay hidden from the Shadows. They are powerful beings that have already taken advantage of us once."

"Will you always remain hidden?" Tara quizzed.

"I believe so, yes. As technology and human advancements continue, we will be more at risk. It is easier to prove what they have seen with video or photographic evidence to back them up. The fact we don't age is a huge give away. Several hundred years ago, when portraits became more common, it was easy to pass them off as being a distant family member. It is hard with the quality of the photos you get now a days. A birth mark for example does not get passed down" Nick went on.

"It can be unbearable to not tell the people around you at first. Time will heal this. The people that you know will age and pass, but the family you create with the Shifters will last several lifetimes over," Nick comforted her. "Why is it you ask?"

Frozen

"I need to tell Savannah and Layla something about the other weekend. It's obvious that I will have to hide things and I understand why. I'm just struggling to come to terms with not sharing everything with them. Especially, when I always have," Tara sighed.

"It will take time for you to adjust into the Shifter community. You have a long time left with them yet," Nick was trying to comfort her. Tara hadn't really thought about what this change would fully mean to her current life.

Tara stayed quiet and kept her thoughts to herself. She wasn't ready to dump all her worries on to the table. She was worried about losing Savannah and Layla. She was worried about confronting her mother. She was worried about being a Shifter. She was worried about being a telepath. She was worried that she might not be able to save the Shifters. She was worried about everything. Except Nick.

They were getting closer and closer. They spent little time apart and this suited Tara perfectly. She had never felt the way that she did with Nick. She hoped that whatever they were would last. She would deal with everything else as it happened.

****

The week continued just the same, but the more that the week went on, the more that she wanted to know. She posed more questions to Nick, but his answers left her with more, not less queries.

By Friday, she'd decided she needed to find out more about her own history. Which parent had given her the shapeshifter genes? The only person that she was able to ask was her mother. If she didn't have the answers, then it was her father that had kept the secret of his past quiet.

Tara talked to Nick about her intentions to ask her mother and wondered about how much her mother might know. It niggled at her. Nick had suggested that she try and ask her mother indirectly. If she knew something it would become apparent after a few simple questions. It was good advice, and she took it.

At dinner time that evening, she confronted her mother. The room was dark by the time they'd finished eating. Her mother talked at length about her current book coming back from the editors.

The lamp in the corner of the room cast light onto the large, handmade, reclaimed, wood table - it had been a gift from her mother's friend about fifteen years ago. A mix match of antique chairs surrounded it. Her mother always sat in the same seat opposite Tara. Her father had always sat at the head of the table in between them both. Since his death they had never sat in his space. It was tacitly reserved in his memory.

"Mum?" Tara started. Her mother was gathering things together, clearing the table of their meal. They'd had organic home-grown ratatouille.

"Yes darling?" Her mother looked up at her.

Frozen

"Is there any reason that I would have any abnormal genes that I may have inherited from you or dad?" Tara asked nervously.

Her mother stopped dead in her tracks and went sheet white.

So... she knew something, Tara thought.

"Why do you ask?" her mother answered, continuing to scrape the food scraps into the bin.

"I'm different, aren't I mum?" Tara asked looking straight at her. Mrs Kingley looked up to meet her daughter's stare. She put down the plates and returned to her chair.

"I had hoped that I wouldn't have to explain any of this. What do you know?" Tara's mother genuinely looked sick.

"I know that I carry a different gene, one that makes me different for everyone else. That you or dad had the gene and have given it to me," Tara stated.

"I wish your father was here to explain all this," her mother said, putting her head in her hands.

"It was my father that was a... Shifter?" Tara tentatively dropped the unspoken word.

"Yes and no," Tara's mother looked up at her. "It was your father that carried the gene and gave it to you. He told me because he knew that any children that we had may become one."

"His parents carried the gene?" Tara asked.

"Yes, it was his mother and his father. Do you know about the attack on the Shifters?" Tara nodded in reply. "They had Harry after that happened, so they went into hiding. They decided that it would be best to raise their son in the human world, away from all the problems.

"Your father grew up and when he was about twenty-five, his parents told him the truth about their past. Your father had noticed strange things about himself. He didn't want to be a Shifter for many reasons, but also because he had already found me. He suppressed his Shifter side. You can never truly be rid of it through. It lies dormant until you may choose to use it or surround yourself with them.

"He aged just like everyone else, got a job and married me. It wasn't until after a few years of trying for you we finally fell pregnant, and he told me the truth. I didn't want to know everything, and your father said that he would take care of it, when your time possibly came."

Tara and her mother sat there for a minute in the darkened - now silent - room. Tara took that time to take it in and process it. Her father had carried the gene. She was a Shifter and couldn't be anything else.

"Why didn't you tell me?" Tara asked calmly.

"There was no guarantee that you would become one. We did everything so that you would have the chance at a normal life and be far away from all the trouble that comes with being a Shapeshifter. It is a dangerous life and filled with uncertainty," her mother explained.

"Is that why I couldn't find any books on Shifters in the library?" Tara thought allowed.

Frozen

"Yes. Your father made sure no books that even hinted towards them, found their way into the collection and since your father died, I have done the same. If we ever noticed that you had bought or picked up one, we would sneak it out of the house."

"Was that really necessary?" Tara questioned.

"Tara, you must understand that we were - and I am - trying to protect you. You become a Shifter because you are exposed to it. After that, you must suppress it if you don't want to be one. There is so much your father didn't do because he was trying to stay hidden. We kept away anything that might expose..." she trailed off. After a few seconds and then asked, "It's Nick, isn't it? He's a Shifter and has exposed you to their world."

"Yes, Nick is a Shifter, but he saved my life. He never exposed anything, until I pressed him," Tara defended him. "There is more to this than you realise. More than I can even wrap my own head around."

"What does that mean Tara?" Her mother was upset, and Tara couldn't recall ever seeing her mother upset, outside her husband's death.

"Do you know what the Key is?" Tara questioned.

"Yes, it's the person who is..." Tara's mother went whiter than white. "No, no, no... Tara you can't be."

"They think I am. Nick seems to be surer now," Tara explained. 'I don't know if I am or not.'

"My poor daughter..." Mrs Kingley moved around to the other side of the table. She took a seat next to her daughter and took her hands. "You have a choice."

It was a simple thing to say and the right thing to say, but to Tara it felt wrong. There was no choice in her eyes. What her mother was saying was she had a choice between a simple life without Nick or a complicated life with Nick in it. To her that wasn't a choice.

She would be a Shapeshifter.

Tara knew who she was and what she was. Since spending time around Nick, she felt like a piece of her had been found. It was becoming clearer to her now. There was no escaping what she was anymore. Destiny had her meddling hands in the middle of Tara's life - deep into it.

****

Saturday brought a new day and with it her acceptance of who she was. Nick was both sad and elated at the same time. He took her to the Japanese garden he had accidently taken her before. It was situated in the grounds of an ancient meeting place for Japan's Shifters.

Tara had told Nick all about what her mother had said and about her past. There was more that Tara had questions about, but her mother's knowledge only went so far.

Frozen

She had been unable to calm her mother last night. In some ways, Tara understood. Her mother had been protecting her from this life for seventeen years. Her natural worry for her daughter was to be expected and with the added fear of the Shadows, Tara could place little blame on her mother's response.

Her mother had said one thing that was definitive the night before. One thing that would never change and it gave her comfort.

"No matter what choices you make or what you become, you will always be my daughter," her mother had said while embracing her.

She was incredibly lucky to have that kind of support. She would be thankful to her mother and father for their unconditional love until the day she died.

Now Tara's journey had begun. Her choice had been made. She was a Shifter and if Nick was right, she was the Key. What did this mean for her next?

"Nick, if I am the Key, is there more that I should know?" Tara wondered.

"There is a lot that we need to teach you. There is plenty of time. The Prophecy may have said that I would find you at the beginning of this century, but it never said anything about when that Key would be needed," Nick paused on a tiny wooden bridge that arched over a stream of water. He took her in his arms and said, "There is time for all of that. Let's just enjoy today and we can begin teaching you tomorrow."

Tara's rushing heart wasn't easily convinced. Now that she knew what she wanted, she wanted to know more. For now, she would enjoy her time with Nick.

Tomorrow was a new day.

Frozen

Chapter 17

It was busier the second time Tara visited the manor. People travelled here and there, down this corridor and that corridor. It felt more like a home or a headquarters than it did the last time. Nick held her hand tightly as they strolled slowly through the confusing maze.

There were people dressed in ordinary clothing - at least that is what Tara would call it - but there were other people dressed in fully black attire, carrying weapons in holsters around their waists, thighs and anywhere they could attach them. She was sure she'd even caught a glimpse of a sheath on one man that walked past, but before she had chance to take a second look, he had been blocked out of view by a group of Shifters stood conversing.

Nick didn't seem fussed about these highly armed people. It was normal she supposed. Stephanie had said something about training, but she would ask Nick about it later. She had other answers to find.

They were heading for the library, where they had seen Mrs Tyrell last time. They were on a quest to find more information about the history of Shifters and Shadows. Tara was unable to keep her curiosity contained.

Nick understood he had been through the same experience. Many of the Shifters had been born and raised within their community. There was only a few that had been transitioned with no - or very little - knowledge.

Nick knew Tara would have to start training at some point, but for now Nick was adamant that she wouldn't be put headfirst into danger, after only just becoming aware of his world.

The library turned out to be quiet that afternoon, but they did spot Jenifer going out as they went in.

"Hey, kids," the small girl shouted. Tara smirked at this. What fun she must have joking about her age.

"Jenifer," Nick bowed his head slightly. Tara didn't know if she should bow or curtsy or what. This woman was an Elder and deserved respect. Tara settled on a head nod too.

Frozen

Jenifer was wearing a little white dress with green flowers embroidered around the bottom hem. It was a cute dress and didn't make her look older in anyway. She looked just like an innocent little schoolgirl.

"I was just taking some books back and taking a few more out," Jenifer explained.

"Anything interesting?" Tara enquired. The stack of books in Jenifer's arms contained many older looking books. One was a large, green, leather-bound hardback with gold thread trim. One was a dog-eared paperback that sat on the top of the pile. It had been well read and Tara couldn't say what colour it had once been. *Possibly blue,* she thought.

The one that struck her attention most was at the bottom of the pile and was pitch black. The thread that bound the leather was blood red. It looked old and air worn, but it didn't look like anyone had even opened its covers before.

"No, just a bit of light reading and I'm looking into ancient herbs," she said, showing Tara the green book titled - *Ancient herbal potions and their properties.* "I'm hoping to find something that can unlock our powers again. I have been searching for one hundred and eighty years now," Jenifer explained for Tara's benefit.

"We have all been looking for a long time," Nick agreed with her.

"Yes, we have," Jenifer said with a sigh. "What are you two here for?"

"I was going to show Tara some books on our history," Nick clarified.

"If that is the case, why don't you go and see Cain. He is with Mary in the western reading lounge as usual," Jenifer suggested.

"That's a fantastic idea," Nick replied.

"You are most welcome," Jenifer smiled. She adjusted the stack of books in her arms and headed off.

"Mary and Cain are two of the eldest Shifters. It is one of the reasons that they are on the Council. You met them briefly on our last visit. They have been great warriors and a great guidance throughout time. They can tell us far more than any one book can," Nick explained to her.

Tara and Nick headed straight to them. They had walked past walls and walls of bookcases and it took everything Tara had not to stop and look at every single one. The volume of books was more intense than she had ever thought possible. There were more books in one tenth of the library than anyone could ever read if they lived for a thousand years.

Tara assumed that there was some form of magic at play in the library. It didn't seem possible that it could fit into the Manor, it seemed to keep stretching on and on. She wasn't sure how it was possible but made another assumption that one of the Shifters had the ability to create more space within a smaller space. *Another question to ask,* Tara thought to herself.

The lounge or large study was darker than Tara thought it would be. There were only a few sources of light, and all of these were from slightly dimmed antique lamps. One had a gold stand with a horizontal, half barrel-shaped, green, glass shade. A short, gold chain dangled from the side, to turn it on and off.

Tara's eyes slowly came into focus in the dimmed light. Cain was sat with a book in his hands and Mary was led with her head in his lap holding her own book. They were on a tanned leather sofa, which had scuff marks adorning the cushions and the arms of the chairs.

All the wooden furniture in the room was dark mahogany, which contrasted with the soft teal walls. A table with eight chairs sat on the opposite side to Mary and Cain. It was scattered with many more books, papers, and scrolls. This room had only one bookcase half filled with more reading materials. The large coffee table sat in front of them with carved legs, each one was representing a different season. A leaf representing autumn and a snowflake representing winter. Tara couldn't see the other two legs.

"Nick to what do we owe the pleasure?" Cain asked, looking up from his book. It looked small in his large hands.

"Tara has some questions about our history and that of the Shadows," Nick replied, bowing his head like he had with Jenifer.

"Well, that would only be natural," Mary expelled, as she sat up, but kept physical contact with Cain.

"Jenifer suggested that we speak to you," Tara illuminated them as she too bowed her head in respect.

"How prudent of her," Cain smiled.

"You have definitely come to the right people, my dear," Mary pointed to a chair that was on the other side of the coffee table and was not as worn as the sofa.

"Thank you," Tara said, as she sat down. Nick sat in the chair next to her.

"Let us have some light," Cain said, pulling a gold chain next to him with a half-smile and half grimace.

"I see you notice even the small things," Mary looked at her. "My husband lost his powers as well as his shifting abilities."

"I'm so sorry," It was all Tara could think to say. She hadn't realised that they were married, but now it just seemed obvious.

"I have lived without them for so long, but I am still shocked by the loss of them every day," Cain explained.

"Cain was able to illuminate any space by manipulating the Shifters collective light," Nick explained quickly for her.

"I can, with much difficultly, control the light that emits from plants and animals. Though, it usually comes at a cost," Cain went on. "This may be a good place to launch our history from."

"Yes, dear," Mary agreed. "It is not our history that comes first, but the worlds."

"When life began to flourish on this earth, it was filled with little energy," Cain began after a little pause. "As things grew so did their energy. It would be safe to assume that an ant will have less energy than an elephant

Frozen

for example. Life flourished on our world, unlike on any other. You may call it creation or evolution. That choice is yours and is also a debate that I will not get into now.

"Time passed. Plants grew, animals came, and then people, all small and insignificant changes over vast expanses of time at first.

"Your ancestors started out like any other homo sapiens. They were hunter gathers that moved from here to there, tribes' people that questioned the things around them.

"We do not know where or when the first people to notice the energy round them came to be, we can only guess. The best guess we have is before settlements and stationary living became widespread," Cain continued, still holding Mary's hand.

"You see all around you are things that you may not see, but you will most definitely feel. One of our ancestors discovered that they could see what others around them ignored. Eventually, they found a way to show others, make them aware of the beauty that exists around them."

Tara had no knowledge on what Cain was talking about and didn't fully understand. When her brow crunched into a frown, Mary stopped Cain's story.

"May I show you?" Mary asked her.

"Of course," Tara answered. Mary shuffled to the edge of the sofa to sit up straight. Tara copied.

"Can you hold your hands up like this?" Mary held her hands opposite each other, with her index fingers – one on each hand - extended towards each other but leaving a small gap in between. "Try to look at the gap in-between but let your focus fall."

Tara thought this was a weird thing to do, but continued to do as she was asked. She looked at the gap trying - with difficulty - to focus, but not focus at the same time.

"I don't…" Tara began, but never finished. She saw something, a wisp of air that moved between her two fingers but, it wasn't. The swirl continued moving purposefully, edging over her finger, then she saw it on the other. A warm coloured light danced across her fingers, her hand, and her skin. It was like she bathed in it.

"I see it. It's like light dancing over my skin. What is it?" Tara said, barely looking up.

"That is your light. Your energy," Mary explained. "It is not just your own that you will be able to see, but other plants, animals, humans and even Shifters."

"I think I have seen this before, but not so clearly," Tara said turning to Nick and putting her hands down. "I saw it that day we set up class for Mrs Tyrell, didn't I? The light that I saw from you both was your energies?"

"I think you did, yes," Nick nodded at her smiling.

"Overtime, it will become easier for you to see. However, you will have already been aware of it for a long time and just not seen it," Mary continued. "Have you ever felt like someone was looking at you, even though you were facing the other way? Have you ever felt drained around horrible people? Or have you felt energised after a walk in the woods?"

Tara thought over each question. She'd felt everything that Mary described. She nodded in answer to her.

"Everything is made with energy. The trees in the woods, people around you, and your body. There is much to explain about it all, but I will give you the basics and Nick can teach you more," Mary looked to Nick.

"The first thing that you should know is that we can share energies. At least on a human level. Shifters can still share energies, but not to the level our powers require, not since we lost them.

"Secondly, Shadows do not have energy that grows or emits like everything else on this planet. We don't know why or how they came to be, but they drain everything around them.

"Thirdly and finally, that people can take energy from you, making you feel powerless and making themselves feel powerful. They don't necessarily understand what they are doing, but you should avoid people like that at all costs," Mary explained and looked back at Cain, silently telling him to continue.

"It was a long time after this was discovered, that people shared this energy. Energy will grow the more it is shared through good intentions. It makes us feel wanted and loved," Cain smiled.

"On the other hand, there was a negative. The more we shared our energies the more of a target we became. The Shadows found us, but as humans there was nothing we could do to stave them off.

"Until one day when everything changed," Cain explained.

"They became Shapeshifters?" Tara guessed.

Cain nodded in reply and then continued. "It is no longer known what the first person transformed into, but it was enough to save their village from attack.

"It was not long after this, all in the village could transform. Mostly, it appeared that when they reached late teen years or early twenties, most learnt to transform but it was not uncommon for some to be older. Those that left the village before transformation never did. However, all spread the Shifter gene.

"The more that we shifted, the easier that it became to transform ourselves. We were able to turn into many different animals and even change our appearances, eye colour, hair, facial structures, and height.

"This wasn't the only change. We came to notice that a small percentage of people could do more than shift. Some…" He said glancing at Mary, "…could not. As to why, we still can't answer."

"As you can imagine we became hunted not only by the Shadows, but also by people," Cain sighed. "We were dangerous to them. As peaceful and giving as we are, we weren't accepted by other civilisations. People do not like what they cannot explain. Therefore, we hid

Frozen

ourselves while we continued to learn and share our energies, away from humans."

"What about the Shadows?" Tara questioned.

"It took several hundred years and many, many deaths for us to discover that Shadows - although they feed on energy - cannot touch concentrated energy.

"We protected ourselves with energy shields made by multiple people, but a single person would not survive an attack. That was when Mary and I worked on a project to create a weapon that could be wielded by an individual, to defend themselves."

"It was really this genius that came up with the idea. I just helped to create them," Mary proclaimed. "He is too modest to take credit for the difference that he made to our people."

"What was it you made?" Tara asked.

"Essence blades," Mary told her with pride.

"Swords that are made from quite ordinary materials, but are made to receive and contain concentrated energies," Cain told her. "They are given energy that is powerful enough to kill a Shadow, while they are held by a Shifter. This wasn't enough for some Shadows though, so we altered the design to be able to pour more of your own energy into the weapon as a last resort."

"They are very powerful, and you will need training in order to wield them," Nick stated to her. Tara nodded back to him with a smile but was unsure about wielding a weapon.

"This all took hundreds of years, from discovering light to making the essence blades and it wasn't the only thing we discovered.

"It also became evident to us that we were not the only people who knew about energies. There are more species and types of semi-human species that are out there, more dimensions than we can name. While we know that they exist, we do not go near most of them. We are safer away from all these places and creatures. Something worse than the Shadows could be out there. I would recommend that you learn about them, but not to seek them," Cain looked at her sternly.

"I won't," Tara agreed. She needed to get her head around this world. Let alone the fact there were more worlds out there. How did she even begin grasping the concept of more worlds?

"The rest I believe you have been told," Cain concluded. "The gathering was devastating to our people, and we have become complacent since. It is time to fight, and we are ready. If you lead us in battle, you will have my sword," Cain and Mary both lowered their heads to her.

Tara shuffled awkwardly in her seat.

Frozen

Chapter 18

School was more tedious than ever. There was so much more that Tara should be doing with her time. At least that's how she felt. Nick disagreed. The conversation they'd had about it, was a short one. He would not teach or tell her more unless she continued as normal with school. Nick was protecting her future and Tara understood that. However, that didn't make it any less tedious.

They sat together at Monday lunch time they sat together with Savannah. She excessively talked, barely pausing before jumping to the next topic. She continually kept asking Nick if he had a brother or a cousin that she might meet. Tara found this incredibly funny. Savannah wasn't aware of why that would be impossible. Instead, Nick explained that as he was adopted, he didn't know his birth family.

"Well fine," Savannah sighed. "But if you ever discover one... let me know."

"You will be the first to know," Nick played along.

"Anyways, I promised Layla I would go and meet her after she got some piano practise in," Savannah explained, gathered her stuff. "You two love birds can enjoy sometime on your own."

"See you later," Tara replied blushing slightly.

Savannah bounced out of the library looking pleased with herself as always.

It was busy in the library. The rain pelted against the windowpanes and the wind howled through any gap it could get through. Winter was undoubtedly setting in.

"Nick, I have a question," Tara asked, turning her head from Savannah's parting to look at him.

"Hmm... I am sure I can guess the subject," Nick smiled.

"Your ability," she whispered. "How long did it take you to control?"

"There are things that I am still learning now," Nick told her. Tara looked down disappointed and Nick continued. "However, I got the basic use down after a month or two from discovering them."

"Oh," Tara said, looking displeased. "How did you learn that you had them?"

Frozen

"Well, that's a rather amusing story," Nick began. "It was about a year after I delivered the Prophecy. Mrs Tyrell had taken me in by then and we travelled the world together. We stopped in Croatia. Mrs Tyrell wanted to visit the national parks. It's a beautiful country, I will take your there one day," Nick smiled.

"We were at a famous waterfall - Veliki Slap or Big Fall. It's aptly named, being two hundred and fifty feet tall," Nick told her. "We were stood at the bottom looking up and Catherine was discussing about taking a dip in the waters. All I could think about was the view from the top and how amazing it would be. The image in my head became what my eyes could see. The air rushed around me, and I almost slipped over the edge."

"Catherine had of course seen this coming. She was a tiny spec at the bottom of the fall. She simply shrugged and got in the water. I trekked all day to go around it and get back to her. She laughed so hard and said the shocked look on my face had been priceless."

"I can imagine," Tara giggled.

"It took me a while to understand how it worked, but I got there in the end. My ability works on my thoughts. All I do is, think of where I want to go, picture in my mind and I'm there," Nick explained.

"All I have to do is picture what people are thinking?" Tara asked.

"Not exactly," Nick explained. "Every power works differently. I would assume that you would have to imagine a stream of thoughts entering your mind to access your powers. Though, I can't be sure until you try it."

"I want to try it. If we have to go up against the Shadows..." Nick grimaced as she said it. "... then there might be a reason I have this particular gift."

"Okay, but we will start small," Nick told her.

"That's fine with me," Tara agreed. After what happened last time, she was glad to take it slowly. She waited for him to tell her how to start.

"Not here," Nick said understanding. "It's too busy."

"Then let's get out of here," Tara said grabbing her things.

They headed into the local town to grab something to eat and find somewhere quiet. There was a little café tucked down a street. It wasn't frequented as often now there was a commercial fast-food chain on the main street.

The sign outside read 'Slade's' and had an old fashioned red and white stripe canopy - though it looked well cared for. Inside was kited out very much the same. The walls were an off-white colour and covered in framed photos and certificates. The tables had the same red and white strip plastic tablecloths and were surrounded by wooden chairs or benches.

At the very back of the café was a counter and glass display case. It contained an array of cakes in glass domes inside. A middle-aged lady, whom Tara assumed owned the place came out. Her hair was a mousey brown - with the odd streak of grey — cut to the length of her chin and framing her face. The name badge pined upon her red and white checked pinafore read 'Freda'.

"What can I get you?" She smiled at them as she removed her note pad and pen from the front of her apron.

Tara ordered a jacket potato and Nick ordered a toasted sandwich. Freda rang the bell on the counter behind her and shouted, "Mick, order up," and left the order on the side.

A tall man, with his hair mostly silver-white with a kind and loving face, walked up to the window and took the tiny piece of paper. Smiled at Freda and went to prep food.

"Take a seat anywhere you like," she said, as she turned around. They took a table close to the window.

The food would take a short while to arrive and as they waited, Nick began to walk her though what he thought might help her access her gift.

"You see that lady in the corner?" Nick nudged his chin towards his left. The woman was sat alone in a booth on her own with papers laid out around her. She had a pen in her hand and was tapping it against a large note pad.

"You know the wall I asked you to put up to block it all out," Nick asked, waiting for Tara's response in the form of a nod. "I need you to take a brick out. That space is only allowed for this woman. As you take it out, I want you to concentrate on her."

Tara closed her eyes and pictured the huge endless wall she had created in her mind. She was nervous, but excited at the same time. She took a deep breath, removed a brick slowly and thought about the woman leaning over the table, who was now scribbling out something on her note pad.

Nothing.

"It's not working," Tara sighed.

"Okay," Nick thought for a moment. "What happened the first time you heard them?"

"I can't remember much. It was like my head was filled with voices. I couldn't break the connection until you helped me put up the wall up."

"I have an idea," Nick said. "Try to imagine a line that connects you and this lady, through the hole in that wall."

Tara did as Nick had advised her. She thought of the light that Mary had taught her to see between her fingers - the energy. She looked at the woman and saw her energy pulsing and moving around her.

As she struggled to find a connection, she noticed that from the edge of the woman's aura there was a light blue energised ribbon. It connected her to Tara and others in the room. It was like a web strung out around her.

Tara watched it and as she did, a pulse of energy went from her, down this web, and too the lady sat at the table.

It needs more clarification or needs to be more structured.

"I can hear her," Tara noted aloud, with a bit too much enthusiasm. She really didn't want to draw attention to herself right now. The web continued to

Frozen

pulse. She stopped trying to intrude in the woman's thoughts. The web went back to slightly glowing blue and returned to a stationary position. When she tried to do it again, the same thing happened.

This needs more attention. Come back here tomorrow and finish it?

The web wasn't something connecting them to each other. It was what connected Tara to them. It was her road map to each person. If she followed the connection in the web, she could hear them. The woman had packed her things up and was leaving.

"How did it go?" Nick asked.

"I did it," Tara said, a smile spreading on her face. Then her smile dropped. "It isn't nice intruding though."

"Every ability has a purpose. I know that you will only use it when you have to," Nick said confidently. "You do need to learn to use it. You can practice on me."

"I think that would be better for now," Tara agreed. She put the brick back in her wall as Freda brought their food. She would try again later.

****

The rest of the week smoothly sailed past, except from the occasional prompt from Nick to try and work out what he was thinking.

Nick had been thinking of places, numbers, shapes even just single words all week. Tara was now finding it easy to read him and could recall his thoughts on her first try.

Tara still felt uncomfortable, but both her and Nick agreed that it was a skill that could come in useful. They still didn't know who had betrayed them to the Shadows.

Nick suggested she would be best trying to learn on others around her, but she was reluctant to invade their privacy. Tara thought that they could ask Catherine. Nick had done just that. Though Catherine thought it was a bad idea. They didn't know what kind of effect Tara would have on her Catherine's gift.

Tara resigned herself to have a break from it over the half term, which began Friday. The dishonesty of it weighed heavy on her mind.

Frozen

Chapter 19

The final few days, before the half term break, went quickly. Nick had continued to teach Tara, how to use her abilities and how to control them.

Tara was now able to access most people's thoughts, by simply following the net, which cast out from her to everyone around her. She had learnt some very personal things about the people she was around every day.

Tara's Math teacher, Miss Bennett had a thing for one of the other Maths teachers, Mr George. It was also apparent that he had a thing for her. Yet, both were refusing to acknowledge the other. Tara made a mental note to somehow nudge them together and they could stop living with the 'what ifs' for the rest of their lives.

Tara's own mother's brain was like a whirlwind of thoughts. After Tara had done it once, she had felt dizzy and refused to listen in again until she was able to control her power properly. It did, however, explain why her mother was so ditsy and clumsy like Tara. She was too busy thinking about what could or would happen, to concentrate enough on what was happening currently.

She had also learnt that a stranger in the street had just found out they had cervical cancer. A young girl, no older than eighteen. Tara had wanted to stop and hold the girl. To let her know, that she could fight this fight and win. It would take strength, but Tara could see that strength in her.

After learning these personal things about people, Tara understood how much she was violating their private thoughts and vowed she would never share what she had learnt about someone, with anyone. Unless it was to save or protect.

Tara recognised how having these powers, could send her down a slippery slope to the misuse of them. She never wanted to be that person.

The Saturday after school break, Nick picked up Tara and took her to the Manor again. There were more lessons that Tara needed to learn. Not only if she would be the Key, but also as a Shapeshifter.

"What's on the lesson plan for today?" Tara asked him.

Frozen

"I think that we need to work on your ability to see energy," Nick told her. "If we are to get you trained..." Nick grimaced, "... then you will need to see and understand energy. As Mary and Cain have explained everything is made with energy. If you are to fight with an essence blade, then you will need to understand how they work."

"Plus, the fact that the Shadows want your energy," Tara continued for him.

"Our," Nick corrected.

Tara still struggled to accept that she was one of them. She knew deep down that she was and everything she had seen and was learning about herself, made it evidently true. However, it rocked the one foundation she'd been so sure on. If she was anything for the last seventeen years, then she had at the very least been human.

"Our," Tara agreed. She would adjust to it given time.

Nick took Tara into the gardens and paused by an old stone bench, close to the tree line. Tara hadn't seen this part of the garden in close proximity but had seen it from the balcony that overlooked this area.

There were many different plants around them. Lavender was the first one that Tara recognised. She leant over to touch the leaves, releasing that familiar floral smell.

"What do you see Tara?" Nick asked her.

"Many plants that I can't name," Tara replied sarcastically.

"Me either," Nick chuckled back. "Look closer at the lavender there, at it leaves and flowers."

"I see a healthy plant," Tara exclaimed.

"Now look at the space around the plant, just like you did in between your fingers with Mary."

Tara looked at the lavender closer this time. She followed the edges of the plant. Though it was hard to do in the breeze. She shifted her focus to try and see what she had seen before.

She couldn't see it and the more that she strained to look, the harder it seemed. It didn't take long for her to grow frustrated and for her to turn away.

"You can do this Tara," Nick reassured her, taking her hand. "I know that it isn't easy to focus and yet not focus, at the same time. I can promise you though, that the more you practise the easier it will be to see."

Tara turned back to the lavender and crouched down closer to it. She told herself that she would try repeatedly, until she got this right.

Tara focused on the space that existed just beyond the plant and she let her focus drop slightly. A wisp of light was dancing around the edge of the plant, flowing along and around the entire sprig. She shifted her eyes to try and take in the whole plant.

She lost the sight of it and then regained it very quickly. The entire plant seemed to glow. A warm pure light danced around every surface of the lavender.

"I can see it. It's... it's like liquid light," Tara explained.

Frozen

"Yes, it is. This is energy in the purest form that you will see it. Energy that comes from people can be complicated. It can be filled with malice and hatred. Even those with the purest intentions can carry or give negative energy. It is especially important that we learn to let go of bad energy and cleanse away this negativity. I will teach you how to do this," Nick offered.

"I would appreciate that," Tara stated. Her gaze travelled from the lavender to a plant she couldn't name. She could see the same flowing and twisting light that she had seen on its neighbour. Her gaze danced around the garden, and she could see the light everywhere. It ebbed and flowed around every living thing. How could she have lived her entire life, with all this around her and not been able to see it?

"How? How could I not have seen this before?" Tara questioned out loud.

"You probably have, but didn't know what you were seeing," Nick explained to her. "You may have seen something out of the corner of your eye. Or you may have notice that some plants look better and fresher than others. There is no doubt that you would have felt it before. Humans tend to justify and rationalise things that they see. Although, there are humans that can see, what you can see now.

"Now that you have awakened your Shapeshifter genes, it will be much easier for you. They will give you the ability to see things more openly and clearly than you ever have before."

Tara turned to look at Nick. To really look at him. She could see the same light pulsing and moving over his skin. The light being brighter at his core, almost like his heart was pouring energy out to the things around him.

"You are so beautiful," Tara spoke aloud without even meaning to.

"Not as beautiful as you," Nick replied gently, as he moved towards her.

"NICK! NICK!" Someone shouted from the distance.

"Yes?" Nick replied, stopping in his tracks.

"You need to come to the house immediately," a male voice shouted urgently.

Tara didn't recognise the man that came around the corner. He was shorter than Nick, with short blonde hair. He was wearing the same black outfit Tara had seen on some of the Shifters before. Hanging from his belt, he had a sheath containing a sword. The man didn't look any older than twenty-four years old and had a rough stubble across his jaw, but Tara knew better than to trust what she saw, particularly as far as age went.

"Why? What has happened, Charles?" Nick questioned.

"It's Catherine. She has been found unconscious," explained Charles.

"Where is she now?" Nick asked urgently.

"In the infirmary. They took her straight there and asked me to come find..." Charles never got to finish his statement because Nick had taken a hold of

Frozen

Tara's hand and teleported them right into the infirmary. Nick had aimed for the corner of the room to try and avoid a collision and by luck, he had managed it. Tara, however, had not expected the jump and stumbled before she was able to regain her balance.

Mrs Tyrell lay in the second bed closest to the infirmary door. The first was occupied by a girl, who had taken a nasty cut to the side of her face. Tara thought it required stitches. The girl was sat on the edge of her bed, watching Mrs Tyrell.

"How is she?" Nick asked the older looking lady, who stood at the edge of the bed with a clip board in hand and donning a white lab coat.

"There doesn't appear to be anything wrong with her, Nick. I just can't bring her around. There are no physical signs of injury, not even a singular cut or bruise. I have taken some bloods and I am running a toxicology. Until I have the results back, it would be presumptuous for me to assume what has happened to her," the lady - Tara assumed to be the doctor - replied.

"Will she be, okay?" Tara asked.

"I cannot say at this moment in time. Although, I will say that her vitals look good and so far, I have no concerns other than, I cannot revive her," the doctor said warmly.

"Where was she found?" Nick queried.

"It was I that found her," a small voice said, entering the room. Jenifer approached Nick and embraced him. "I found her in the library, collapsed against one of the bookcases. Several books were scattered around her. She must have been carrying them. There doesn't seem to have been any struggle."

"Thank you for sending Charles to come and find me," Nick expressed, taking a seat next to Mrs Tyrell and he tenderly stroked her hair.

"Tara, let me introduce you to Sandra," Jenifer said, gesturing towards the doctor. "Sandra, this is Tara."

"Hello Tara," Sandra greeted.

"It's nice to meet you doctor," Tara replied. "Though I wish it was under better circumstances."

"You and me both," Sandra replied, tucking her golden-brown hair behind her ears. Sandra was in her late 30's. Time had aged her skin and hair gently, doing nothing to truly age her, but only to mature her. Tara did wonder to herself about Sandra's appearance. Was this how she had always looked or if this was an appearance she had chosen to take before the gathering, to fit her role as doctor?

"Nick, I think it best that you take Tara home now," Jenifer said. "We will have to start an investigation soon."

"Of course," Nick numbly replied. He seemed shocked.

"And Nick?" Jenifer called as Nick was walking Tara to the corner of the room. "Maybe you should grab some of Catherine's things, on your way."

Nick nodded in agreement, taking Tara's hands and teleported them back to Mrs Tyrell's without a single word.

Frozen

"Are you okay?" Tara asked worriedly.

"I'm okay. Just hope that Catherine will be too," Nick replied. Tara didn't feel convinced, but knew better than to press Nick for something that he wasn't ready to share.

"Well, shall we get some of her stuff together and then get me home, so that you can get back to her," Tara asked, trying to help anyway she could.

It only took ten minutes for Tara and Nick to gather some things together. They were in the car and on the way back to Tara's only moments after that.

"If there is anything that I can do Nick, you only need to ask," Tara offered.

"Thank you, Tara. I am sorry that our lesson got interrupted," Nick apologised.

"Don't worry about that. You need to look after Catherine. I can practice while you are..."

Crash

The sound rang in Tara's ears. Her seat belt jolted into her chest. Glass rained down on her and Nick, leaving small gashes across their skin. The car spun around. Tara lost all sense of direction. They had been lucky that the car hadn't flipped. The car came to a sudden stop.

"Are you okay?" Nick checked, leaning over, and scanning Tara in search of injury.

"I think so," Tara answered. "Some cuts and bruises, but I'm okay. What happened?"

"I don't know. There was nothing in the road," Nick answered. He unbuckled his seat belt and tried to get out of the car.

A pair of dark hands pulled Nick's door off the hinges and launched it into the air. The door skidded across the floor, leaving a trail of sparks as it went. Tara screamed. Nick too was pulled from the car.

"TARA!" Nick yelled.

Tara climbed out of the car. Nick was being pulled away, by what she assumed was a Shadow.

Its hands were like dark claws. They were digging into Nick's flesh. Their bodies moved like black smoke. Neither solid nor gas. There was no light to them at all. Like they'd drained any light from around them.

"NICK," Tara screamed, running for him.

"Tara, RUN!" Nick shouted, but Tara couldn't leave him.

Another Shadow appeared from the darkness of the street. Working its way towards her. Its body weaving in an unnatural way. It looked like it was wearing a hooded cloak for there were no features that Tara could make out.

"TARA, GET OUT OF HERE," Nick yelled. He had somehow managed to get an arm free. He reached for something behind him.

A blinding light filled the space. A light that was coming from something that Nick had in his hand. It took a moment for Tara's eyes to adjust. Nick was

Frozen

wielding a sword. Moving quickly to repel the Shadow that had hold of him.

Tara's world went black. Something had hold of her and she couldn't see anything. Her back burned from its touch. It was a nightmare. It had to be a nightmare.

A wailing noise filled the air as Tara's world filled with the honey yellow glow of Nick's sword. The Shadow's claws, dragged down Tara's back, leaving three deep gashes that oozed blood instantly. Tara's screams were left to fill the air, after the Shadow's wails died out.

"I told you to run," Nick exasperated. He took hold of Tara's arms, dragging her along.

They had managed to take several paces, but they were surrounded. Darkness encircled them. There was no direct way out.

"Stay close to me," Nick said in a rush. Tara squeezed his hand tighter.

Shadow after Shadow charged at them. Nick cut them down one by one, only for more to appear. One seized hold of Nick's sword, gasping in what sounded like pure pain.

They were defenceless.

A shadow ripped Nick from Tara's hands. She senselessly chased after him.

"NICK!"

She ran to keep up, but he was just out of reach. Their eyes met across the space. Nick's eyes pleaded with her. She stretched her hand out towards him and he did the same.

But then he was gone. Vanished in front of her eyes.

Tara sunk onto the hard ground. The pain in her back was blinding. The blood was flowing down her and onto the road, pooling in front of her.

Her whole body felt heavy. She led on her side and began to cry. Nick was gone. She couldn't save him.

A different kind of darkness claimed her.

Chapter 20

The anticipation of not knowing what is going to happen next, produces one major issue – it won't let you focus on anything else.

Surprises are great fun when it's a birthday or a celebration because you know that in the end, you'll probably like it, hey, you may even love it!

However, when it is the opposite and you are waiting for unwelcome news, you ponder on every outcome, on every conceivable situation you may find yourself in and on all foreseeable, disastrous endings.

The anxiety builds as you think through them. We immediately forget that there can only be one ending. Yes, we are not aware of which one, but the anticipation and anxiety for all of them is not helpful in that moment. The pain only begins when most of them - no matter how much you try to be positive - are not positive outcomes. That is when you know you must do something - anything - to change or bend the path to a better outcome.

Tara was sat on the end of the bed staring at the plain wall in front of her, dreaming up the worst possible outcomes. What if something happened to the Shifters? What if something happened to Nick? What if something happened to her? How would her mother find out if something happened to her? How would she cope? The list went on, getting worse and worse until she just couldn't take it any longer.

Grabbing her jacket off the back of the door, she headed down the hall, with no idea where she was heading. Knowing only that she had to do something. In the end, she did what she always did when she needed a distraction besides into a book - headed for the closest freezer to grab some ice cream.

Tara had been found on the road the night before by Stephanie. She had taken Tara back to the Manor and straight to the infirmary where Sandra had taken care of the cuts and scrapes.

Tara couldn't remember anything until she woke up with a blinding headache and a terrible burning on

Frozen

her back. She had needed twenty-six stitches and the doctor had said that it would scar.

Someone had messaged her mum to explain that she wouldn't be home that night. Tara had counted her lucky stars that someone had, or she would have woken to a series of voicemails and messages.

Tara was moved to a spare room not long after she had woken. She didn't want to be in the infirmary near the still unconscious Catherine. She didn't want to be in Nick's room either. She had let them both down. She must have had about two hours sleep, when she woke, started staring at the wall and then made herself head to the kitchen.

After grabbing a dessert spoon and a tub of B&J's - cookie dough, of course - she went to the closest bar stool on the breakfast table and dug in. All she could think about was sitting with Nick, she should be sharing it with him. It took some time for her to really take in that he wasn't there, and he wasn't going to be. Tara quickly put another spoonful into my mouth, the coldness going straight to her head.

"Drowning in ice cream," a voice made Tara jump. She looked over her shoulder.

"Jenifer, you made me jump."

"Sorry, I forget that you are not used to being around us, we can be quite quiet when we need to," Jenifer went over to the cutlery draw and pulled out a spoon and held it up. "Mind if I join you?"

"Not at all."

Beats the loneliness, Tara thought.

"Could you not get away from all the possible endings?" Jenifer took a big spoonful of ice cream like a big kid who couldn't get enough.

"How did you know?"

"Because it's what I would be doing, if I was in your situation. Nick gone, Mrs Tyrell in the hospital wing and the weight of the Shapeshifter's future on your shoulders. What else could you be thinking about?"

"I suppose you're right. It just seems impossible. A few weeks ago, I was a high school girl with no issues or worries outside of my grades, but now so many people are expecting so much from me. Worst of all, I don't even know if I can do what it is that they're asking of me."

"It is a lot for us to ask from you. We all understand that. If it is too much, we will have to find another way. It shouldn't have been put upon you. You are new to this, and it would be unfair to treat you like our deliverance." Jenifer sat in the chair looking at her spoon. It seemed strange to Tara, that this little girl, was not a little girl at all, but a grown woman. She had a history and many lifetimes on her side.

"I don't know what I am going to do, but I will do whatever it takes to get Nick back. If that means I must stand up against a whole hive of Shadows, then that is what I will do," Tara concluded. Jenifer started to shake her head and even started to chuckle. It seemed to

Frozen

Tara like a weird moment to start laughing. "Why are you laughing?"

"Well, it's quite simple really. After all the meticulous research, planning, and ensuring things went the right way. Of course, it would be 'young love' to get in the way. I suppose I should have seen that coming." Tara stared at Jenifer confused, but the longer she sat looking at Jenifer's face, it turned from the cute, innocent girl that was there before into something sadistic and twisted. Things clicked into place.

"All this time, all those moments you were scared, I thought that this moment would come, and I would be able to twist you into my puppet. You would not have realised it of course, but that's the beauty in it."

"What are you saying?" A lump jammed in Tara's throat, she got off the chair backing away. She knew what was coming, but she just didn't want it to be true. Surely, it could not be true.

"That I have been planning this for years, decades even. The one thing that gets in my way of course, is a young, love-sick, high school girl. You are all pathetic. I thought when you started to get your mind reading skills perfected, you might get through my mind block, but you haven't managed to even do that," Jenifer sat there playing with her spoon as if she had no care in the world. It was unnerving for Tara to watch.

"How?... How can you?... They are your family... I... I just don't understand. How can you do that to them?"

"My family? Really? The have held me back, controlled my powers, and distributed it between themselves as if they are worthy of it. The power is mine now. All I have to do is unlock it from the globe."

"You! It was you all along. It was you that took Nick. It was you that put Mrs Tyrell in the hospital."

"Yes, it was all little, innocent me! Who would suspect a face like mine?" Tara looked into her eyes and for the first time, all she could see was the hatred that flowed behind her dark eyes. A darkness of the purest kind. Tara could feel her heart pounding against her ribs, filling her ears. She looked to the doorway for just a second. It was a mistake.

"You think that I am going to let you leave? Let you run off and tell everyone? You take me for a fool?" Tara was still inching her way out of the room, as Jenifer dropped off her chair, like a dainty, little girl. She stalked towards Tara like the true villain she was. A completely unforeseen villain.

"Where is Nick? I want to see Nick!" Tara watched Jenifer's smile spread to her ears.

"Of course, the love-sick girl wants to see the boy she thinks she's in love with. Trust me Tara, when you are as old as me, you will understand that love is a fleeting feeling, that will not stay with you. No matter how well you try to keep hold of it."

"You're wrong, I love Nick and I will always love Nick." The feeling cascaded her. She was in love with him, and it did not matter how he felt, she had to get him back.

Frozen

"That may be true, but you think that he will love you the same way for all of eternity? What a childish Disney princess scenario you have dreamt up out of nothing?"

"No, I may have dreamt of the fairy tale as a child, but I know now, that love is more than romance. It grows and evolves with you." Tara stopped to think for a second. Jenifer was jealous. She did not know of this kind of love. Tara turned her thoughts back to Nick, "Besides, Nick does not love me."

"Of course, he doesn't! Got to hear it from the source I suppose?" Jenifer looked towards Tara, but she couldn't move. She clearly had Nick. She held one of her hands up in front of her and clicked.

****

"Tara?" She spun around to see where the sound was coming from. She was no longer in the kitchen but in a dark cave. Nick stood illuminated with a bruised face and blood pouring down the side of his head. Her heart skipped a beat, her instinct was to run to him, to hold him, but try as she might her feet wouldn't move.

"Nick...Nick are you okay? I... you're bleeding." She saw nothing, but grief in his expression.

"I am sorry Tara. Did I forget to mention that he is mine to control? You see I have more power than the average Shapeshifter has.

"I made sure that I had more power in me that night, the night that I took away everyone's 'abilities' and well a side effect of it... is that I can do this." Jenifer clicked her fingers again and Nick was no longer in human form, but a mouse on the floor.

It took Tara by surprise, even though she knew they could do that, she hadn't witnessed it before. This was not what Tara had imagined. Nick being forced to change under the will of another. His first transformation should have been a happy event, not this.

"What have you done? Put him back!" Tara screamed at Jenifer, not that it had any effect other than a grim smile from her.

"If you wish."

Click.

Tara turned to check Nick.

"You see Tara, he IS mine to control. Let's see if you like this little trick."

Click.

"Tara," Nick was moving closer to her. "I don't love you. I never have. All I wanted from you is your ability, I never wanted to be with you. I never will."

"No Nick, you're just saying that because she's making you. I will not listen." Tears welled up in her eyes, she did not need his love, but to hear that she didn't have it that bluntly, stung more than she ever thought that it would.

Tara, please listen to me. Do not listen to what I am saying aloud, I am not in control.

Frozen

Jenifer was laughing in the corner. Enjoying the pain, she knew that both Tara and Nick were going through. Not paying attention to Nick cautiously reaching out his hand.

I am sorry Tara. Save yourself. Forget about me. Be safe.

He finished reaching out to her. As he touched her face, he used his gift. It was too late for Tara to move away from him. The last thing she saw was his eyes looking at her, filled with regret. Then the horizon.

It was raining, the wind slashing at her face. The rain was soaking through her thickest jumper. Tara's hair was blowing in the rain, it grew heavy with water. Slashing at her cheeks like miniature whips that she could not escape. It took her a few short seconds, to realise where she was - the cove. It was Nick's way of saying 'goodbye'.

She sank to the sand. Her heart falling further. What was she supposed to do now? She knelt on the sand and let the weight of her mind take her to the floor and into sleep.

****

Tara woke up back at the mansion, staring up at the painted ceiling of angels. It was like looking at a church ceiling. Not wanting to deal with the emotions on their faces, she rolled on to her side and looked at the room around her.

The room seemed to focus and then become unfocused. All the beds around her were empty, all but one. Mrs Tyrell was still unconscious, with an IV in her arm and blankets covering her up to her chest to keep her warm. Tara could see the movement of Catherine's eyes behind her eye lids. It looked like she was trying to process something, a dream maybe. Tara tried to sit up. The smell of the hospital wing's cleanliness hit her, making her dizzy. She had to steady herself on the bed.

"What do you think you are doing?" As Tara looked up, the white figure in front of her started to come into focus.

"Sandra?" Tara's voice was hoarse, her throat drier than sand. Sand... the beach... Nick!

"You need to take it easy you have been out for two days." Sandra walked over to the IV and seemed to check it.

"No, there is no time..."

"There is plenty of time to talk about what happened once I have checked you over. Not only have you had a terrible injury to your back only days ago, but you have also been exposed to the elements for hours." Sandra interrupted her.

"No Sandra, its Jenifer. She is the one that is helping the Shadows." Tara needed her to listen, she had to listen. Everyone was in danger.

"We know." Sandra stood in front of her, using her body to stop Tara from getting out of bed. "When Stephanie found you again, you were mumbling something about Jenifer taking him. Stephanie understood straight away. She came and told us and went in front of the Council members."

Frozen

"Stephanie? She found me? How?"

"She knew that whoever had taken Nick, was using him as bait to get to you. She had been following you. When she went to the kitchen to check on you, you were gone. There was a tub of melted ice cream and two spoons. She knew you hadn't been alone. She searched everywhere for you. Finally, she started to check out Nick's usual haunts and sent others out too. That was when she found you on the beach."

"I don't understand, Stephanie doesn't like me."

"Well, I wouldn't say that." Tara spun around, a little too fast, putting things out of focus and sending a jolt of pain through her back. Tara winced.

She knew it was Stephanie from the voice. Tara could see her lounged in a chair in the far corner of the room, spinning a knife around in her hand. "I was a little jealous of you though, but that was maybe a bit rash of me."

"Stephanie, I... I don't know what to say."

"Don't go getting all mushy on me." Stephanie climbed out of the chair and walked over to exit, still twisting the knife around and around in her hand. 'Look the Council will want to see you soon. You may want to get washed and changed. You look and smell awful.' Stephanie stalked out of the room.

"She is starting to grow on me," Tara looked up to Sandra and she smiled.

"She does that."

****

The corridor that led towards the Council chamber was cold and damp. It felt much colder because her hair was still wet from having a shower. Stephanie had walked with her. Neither had said anything. They didn't need to.

They approached the doors leading into the room filled with Elders, when Tara's nerves peeked. She knew they were going to ask her what had happened with Jenifer and if there was anything that they could use against her. The honest truth was that she didn't. All she knew was Jenifer had Nick and she was using him as leverage to get at her. Which meant that Jenifer wasn't going to kill her, at least not yet anyway. That meant that they had time. Time to counter act Jenifer's moves. She would use Nick as her bargaining chip.

Tara and Stephanie stepped inside the room, and everyone quickly fell silent. The Elders were sat on stone seats on an elevated stone platform, which arced around the room. It allowed all of them to look down at her. All twelve chairs were full. All but one. Jenifer's.

Stephanie placed her hand on Tara's shoulder and nodded to the chair in front of the curved benches. Stephanie then looked at her, smiled and then walked to the seats on the left. Sat down, put her feet on the seats in front of her and started playing with the knife again. A chuckle began to build up inside of Tara, until she turned and saw eleven pairs of Elder's eyes staring at her. She walked forward to the chair and stood in front of it waiting to be told to take her seat.

Frozen

"Tara Elizabeth Ashleigh Kingsley," it was Cain that bellowed down from the chairs. "Welcome. Please take your seat."

Tara sat nervously, placing her hands within her lap. Holding them together so tight, she could feel the erratic beating of her pulse.

"Tara, you have been summoned to the Council today as a witness, you have no need to panic, if you could just tell your story and answer our questions truthfully, please." This time it was Mary who spoke. She looked at Tara with a warm smile. Then inclined her head as if pushing for an answer.

"Erm... of course," Tara felt like she was on stage and all she wanted to do was run, but this may help them. It may help find Nick, to bring him home to them, safely.

"Tara, please tell us from the beginning what happened on the evening three days ago." Everyone stared at her, waiting for her story.

She told them about the events of that night. Starting with leaving the room she'd been given, up to the point of blacking out on the sand. She stumbled a few times, especially when talking about Nick, but she didn't leave anything out. When she got to the end, she sat patiently waiting to be told what to do next.

Ummm... this is a mess.
There is nothing we can do with this.
She's so brave to have come forth, but nothing here is going to help.

What are we going to do?

"Stop! Please just stop!" Tara couldn't hold it in anymore. Elders or not. "Just because I found nothing doesn't mean there isn't any hope. Jenifer needs me. We can use that. We must get him back," she could feel the heat of her tears streaming down her face.

"Okay, I think we have everything that you're going to get from her. She can hear everything that you are thinking. Every negative thought. This is not fair on her." Stephanie was stood in front of Tara now, looking up at the Council. She had guts - more guts than Tara would ever have.

"I am sorry Tara," this time it was a male. An older male that she had not met before. "There is one more question that I have for you. If I may?"

Tara looked towards the older man. "Yes?"

"I am Catherine's grandfather. I believe she may have spoken of me," she nodded in agreement. "My name is Adam."

"It's nice to meet you," she said removing the tears away from her face. She had to be stronger than this for Nick's sake.

"Tara, I know that this must be awfully hard for you. However, I am going to have to ask you the one thing that none of us want to ask." He paused with a concerned look, took a deep breath, and said, "It may come down to using you as bait. We do not want to result to this - it would have to be a last resort. What we need to know is, if you are going to be up to the task?"

Frozen

Everyone in the room seemed to suck in a gasp of air. None of them clearly expected Adam to ask this from her, but they all waited in hope of her answer. She moved out from behind Stephanie, who looked for the first time - concerned for her.

"If it means saving all of you, getting back your powers, getting back Nick, and stopping the Shadows. Then... I will do it. Last resort or not. If it is the best plan we have, then I am in."

She stood tall and proud of herself. Inside she was mush, scared and nervous, but she knew that she would have to have courage, if she wanted to save Nick.

"Thank you, Tara. We will need time as a Council to discuss this. You may leave."

"Thank you, Adam." Tara smiled at him, as he smiled back. She could see why Catherine spoke so highly of her grandfather.

"Stephanie, you will be on protection duty of Tara. Who knows when Jenifer may strike again?" Stephanie nodded. She didn't look pleased.

"Find Samuel and Alistair, they will accompany you on this. Understood?"

"Yes, sir," Stephanie agreed. They both walked out the rest of the way, leaving them to discuss a plan of action. Stephanie turned to close the double doors behind them but left them open slightly.

"Stephanie, what are you doing?" Tara looked at her confused, as she sat on the floor staring intently through the gap.

"Shhh... I'm trying to concentrate." Tara was not going to probe. It seemed that Stephanie was on her side at the moment, and she had no idea how long that was going to last. "God, I can't hear anything! Argh!"

"I have an idea," she figured that Stephanie was trying to listen in.

"Okay, genius what's that?" Stephanie looked at her sarcastically, tipping her head to the side.

"I don't know whether you've noticed or not, but I kind of have a hook up to everything that's going on in there," she stood waiting for a response.

"Well, what are you waiting for then?" Stephanie stood up gracefully, like the warrior she was. Tara suddenly felt self-conscious of her clumsy ways.

Tara concentrated for a few minutes, it took a while to lock on to the people that she wanted to hear. After being able to turn it off. The next thing that she would have to get better at would be homing in on particular people. Currently, it was like one big mess of noise.

Jesus! Is this what I have to work with. Give me strength.

"I'm trying my hardest you know. I am new at this."

"Okay, listen. I know that what I can do is completely different. However, they both run on waves. You need to feel the waves that are entering your sphere. Draw them into yourself and separate them. You will notice that each one has a different feel to it or a different sound. Work out which are the strongest.

Frozen

They will be the ones that are closest to you. Have you done that?"

Tara took a second and within her mind's eye, she could see all the blue pulses that were travelling down the net towards her, but there were too many. They were staggered upon one another. She nodded to Stephanie, not wanting to lose concentration.

"Okay, next step is to remove the largest one. That one will be me," she gave her a second to do this. Then it all started to click into place. She continued by removing the smaller waves that travelled down the net.

Now it was more defined, and she was able to see what part of the web led to who. Allowing her to hear thoughts from one person to another, giving her the ability to single out any thoughts.

We cannot do this to the girl.
But we may not have any choice.
There is always a choice.
She's too valuable to the cause.
We are going to have to find another way.

"So? What did you hear?" Stephanie's patience had run out.

"I don't think they are going to use me as bait," Stephanie threw her knife at the wall.

"God damn it!"

"What is it?"

"It's the only way that we are going to draw Jenifer out," Stephanie took her knife out of the wall.

S. M. Clair

"Looks like it up to you and me, Tara."

Chapter 21

Tara had no idea where Stephanie was taking her. Tara could now navigate the main corridors with ease, but wherever they were heading now, brought no recognition at all.

Once they reached the end of the main corridor - on the east side of the Manor - she went up to the first floor, via a small spiralling, staircase hidden round the corner of the dining hall. Tara supposed these stairs were long out of main use. Perhaps, they had once been used by servers and maids.

When they reached the top of the stairs, they went back down the east wing corridor. To find yet another hidden staircase. Tara was lost passed that. *A maze would be easier to navigate,* Tara thought to herself.

There was an eerie silence that filled the corridors. Stephanie hadn't spoken two words as they meandered the labyrinth. Tara was itching to ask question after question, as she normally would. However, Tara didn't think that Stephanie would take to it as well as Nick did.

Stephanie appeared to be the kind of person that wore armour – mentally and physically. Someone who, safeguarded themselves from the troubles and hurt that surrounded them. Tara hoped that one day Stephanie might let down some barriers, but she was happy that this strong, capable woman was her bodyguard.

Taras's focus came back to the empty, strange silence around them. Her curiosity got the better of her. She let down her barrier and allowed the thoughts to follow within her, while trying to keep up with Stephanie.

> *It can't be Jenifer.*
> *What are we going to do?*
> *How can this have happened?*
> *Did the Elders not know?*
> *We need to leave.*
> *It's not safe here.*

Fear. It wasn't silence that was filling the air, it was fear. Tara may have been new to this way of life, but

Frozen

she understood that they had placed their trust in Jenifer, and she hadn't just broken it, she had crushed it.

Jenifer hadn't just taken their powers. She had taken their faith and trust in the system that governed them. It threatened everything they knew.

Everything had shifted and with the threat of an attack imminent, their fear was rational. They had children to protect.

Tara tried to think of things from their point of view. No matter how hard she tried her thoughts were drawn back to - how could Jenifer abandon her people, take from them, and destroy their way of life?

"We are here," Stephanie said quietly. It snapped Tara back to reality and away from her own thoughts.

"Where is here. Exactly?" Tara asked.

"This is one of the training rooms. Some of us choose to train harder than others. You have no choice, and you need to do it, now," Stephanie told her. "You can learn to fight, to defend yourself or others, or you can play the victim."

"I never want to be that helpless again," Tara stated. "Teach me?"

"If you want to save Nick, this is how we do it. You are going to have to learn quickly. You need enough skill to at least put down or slow down a Shadow," Stephanie pushed open the creaking, grey door as she talked.

Inside the room, she could hear the faint clanging of metal hitting metal. The further that Stephanie led her into the room, the louder the sound got. Until they were in a well light room, filled with all sorts of training weapons and equipment.

In the middle of the space there was two huge men. Tara couldn't recall ever seeing them. The larger of them she found instantly intimidating.

Stephanie lingered back from them, giving them enough space to continue what they were doing. The sound of metal on metal continued, as their swords made contact. Each contact leaving a vibrating twang echoing from wall to wall.

The more Tara watched, the more it seemed less like fighting and more of a delicate and precise dance, that only these two males could understand. They spun around one another, their swords touching only for a brief second, but with a great enough force to push and guide the other.

The larger male – easily six foot six and with a build that was so powerful and commanding - made the other man seem small and squashed beneath the weight of him. Tara would have guessed, that the smaller one was at least six-foot tall.

They finished a brief while later and to Tara's surprise, it was not the larger one that had won. The smaller one had used the larger guy's size against him. He turned so fast, that the larger one had no chance to move from underneath the blade. The smaller one now held a blade upon the other's neck.

"Hey boy's," Stephanie called out to them. Both of their expressions had softened, as they looked towards the familiar sound. Stephanie walked closer to them.

"Hey Steph, you weren't here for training," the larger male stated, through it seemed more of a question.

"I was busy," Stephanie scowled.

"Always with the attitude. Jeez girl, you need to lighten up," it was the smaller one of each of the men, who had mocked her. Tara held back a laugh. She needed Stephanie on her side.

"Well, it's who I am. Live with it!" Stephanie proclaimed and then nudged her head in Tara's direction. "I would like you to meet Tara Kingley. It would seem that she's the Key."

"My name is Alistair," he introduced as he held his hand out. "Ignore her, she's always this grouchy." Alistair was apparently the bigger one of the two. Though his personality was softer than what his physique would imply.

"Samuel," the other said, as a way of introducing himself, "I am very pleased to meet you." He was the smaller one, but Tara's earlier assumption had been right - he was over six-foot. He took her hand with a gentler touch and shook.

"It is nice to meet you both," Tara returned.

"Well now that we have introductions out of the way... maybe you could explain to me Stephanie, why you missed training and why Tara is here?" It was Samuel that had spoken to Stephanie.

While Stephanie, Samuel, and Alistair stood talking amongst themselves about the situation and what had happened at the Council meeting, Tara began to wander around the room.

As she looked at everything, something caught her attention, it looked like nothing more than an ordinary blade on the wall, but as she moved passed it, she could see that the blade looked more like glass than metal and a faint light seemed to glow within it.

"It is quite extraordinary that you came and stopped at this particular blade," it was Samuel. He smiled at her and then continued. "This is an essence blade. It has its own light, it's a being of sorts. The blade thinks and feels for itself. Not like us, but it will accept or refuse a wielder. It is made from a very precious metal. They are essential in our defence and strategic moves against the Shadows. You see…"

"It emanates light, Shadows cannot exist in light. Fill them with it and you can vanquish them, I assume." Tara interrupted. "Sorry, you were telling me."

"Do not apologise, I wish that half the students I have had, would've learnt and observed as quickly." Samuel looked at her in what Tara could only see as intrigue. "I think we should skip the introduction level and get straight to the wielding of weapons. Do you have any previous experience?"

"It depends on what you call experience, I did an eight-week course of fencing about eight years ago. I barely remember any of it." Tara had gone with her father when she was nine. The course finished weeks

Frozen

before he had died. He had said, she needed to learn discipline and control to be able to protect herself. Tara had always thought they were excuses just to have fun with her, now she wasn't so sure.

"It is a starting point, now it's time for the real course. You are going to have to learn quickly. We've not got the time to learn everything. You are just going to have to learn to wield an essence blade and how to use it."

Tara got the impression that Samuel was all business and no play, and the next few days would confirm that for her.

****

Tara felt like she had been practising forever, by the time they had stopped for the night. Her body ached all over and she couldn't stop thinking that she would have to do it all again tomorrow.

She had taken the longest bath she had ever taken, to tried to remove the knots in her muscles. The heat helped, but sleep was what she needed.

She was led in Nick's bed looking out of the windows. She'd turned off the lights, as she'd climbed into bed, and was staring out into the night sky through the large, slightly open window, on the east side of the room.

She hoped that Nick could see the stars with her at that moment. She wished that his arms would encircle her, and he would hold her, as he told her about the stars. The moon shone brightly and illuminated the room. She wasn't even sure if she was under the same stars as him. She vowed that once she got him back - and she would - that they'd watch the stars together.

She found herself thinking about him all the time. She kept reflecting about the day he had taken her to Japan. He had shown her parts of the world that she had never seen before. He had completely expanded her world. She wanted him back safe, his family needed him. She needed him.

Tara told herself to stop thinking about it and to recap over what they had been doing in the training room. She had not yet got to the stage of wielding the essence blade. They had only been using the wooden swords. Samuel noted on her patience and control, but she needed to learn to anticipate her opponent.

They had practising for five hours, but it had felt like a lot longer. It had wiped her out completely. Samuel told her to be back in the training room by eight the next day. She would have to do another full day of training.

Stephanie had completed her training and had been practicing her sword play with Alistair. Stephanie clearly felt the need to be ready for what was to come next.

Tara was worried about how they were going to fight Jenifer. She had more power and so many more years on her, than any of them. Hopefully, it would not come down to that. *This was a rescue mission not a battle,* Tara thought to herself.

Frozen

Soon, she was asleep in Nick's bed. She had not meant to fall asleep there, but she had wanted to be close to his things. To be close to him in some way and his scent filled her with longing.

****

Eight o'clock had been and gone, then nine, then ten and then even eleven o'clock had gone. It was quarter to twelve and they'd stopped for a break to eat some food and discuss their next move.

Stephanie had run out to grab chicken from the kitchen. Apparently, Alistair was capable of eating an entire bowl on his own. Tara supposed that with the amount of training he must do and his sheer size, that he would have to consume copious quantities of food.

When she returned, they sat in the centre of the room. Tara listened to them talk of all the things that had happened during training with each other. Even Stephanie was laughing. It was something Tara thought she may never see.

"Tara, are you okay?" Stephanie asked.

"Yes, sorry I got caught up in my own thoughts," Tara replied. "However, I do have some questions."

"Go ahead," Samuel encouraged.

"I would like to know why you are all getting involved, I mean won't you get into some sort of trouble for this? For creating and pulling off your own plan?"

"Maybe," it was Alistair that spoke. "I'm sure that if we make it back with Nick, they won't even notice that we acted out on our own. Nick is our friend, our family. We will not let him suffer for one woman's path to destruction."

"We are small in number, but that will give us the advantage," Samuel remarked. "Shall we continue?"

Samuel stood up from the mat effortlessly. It made Tara feel uncomfortable. She stood up with no grace whatsoever, her aching body seizing up after being given a respite.

Tara wondered exactly how old Samuel was. He was clearly older than Stephanie or even Alistair. It brought her to also question what sort of battles and fights he had been part of.

They continued for another long half an hour. Samuel had disarmed her again and again. She grew frustrated.

"Find your own advantage, your own strength. Samuel's is grace and balance. Alistair is Strength. Mine is control. What is yours?" Stephanie said, from the corner of the room.

Tara pondered on this while Samuel disarmed her repeatedly. What advantage did she have? The question rolled and rolled around her head. She was none of the things that Stephanie had mentioned. What made her more capable at this?

My ability.

How could she not have thought of it before? She took down her block and started to hear the stream of voices in her head. She began to single out Samuel's thoughts and remove everyone else's until she had it. She locked it in place.

Left arm.

Tara moved so that he was out of reach of her left arm. She moved to strike his right side. But he dodged just in time.

Swing, twist, and strike down.

Tara did the opposite of every move he made. She ducked from the swing. Moved away from the twist and then finally struck up at his own wooden sword. The reversed movements continued until she noticed his left side was open on some of the swings he made. - something her told her to look out for that morning.

While waiting for him to make his move, she continued to block him. Keeping him from disabling her. There was nothing she couldn't block. Then with one minor opening, she stuck at his left side. Holding the wooden 'blade' just firmly enough for him to notice the contact. She had done it. Tara had disabled the training master.

"Well done," Samuel said to her. "Use your ability, but only when you can't use your sword."

"You finally worked it out then," Stephanie remarked at her. "It's easy when you know how, huh?"

"You can influence people's decisions, can't you?" It made so much sense now.

"In a way yes, I cannot make a decision for them, but I can persuade them to take a path they have already considered," Stephanie explained.

"Samuel barely touches the floor when he fights. Light footed or something else?" Tara asked wanting to understand them better.

"Samuel's ability is to master weapons and fighting techniques. Before he discovered his capabilities, he could not fight at all." Tara thought she might understand why he was so withdrawn all the time - his ability might make him more prone to violence. She voiced this and he replied with a confirmation. It was the negative side of his ability, his curse in a way. Fight first, question later.

"That leaves Alistair, who I hope that you have easily worked out?" Stephanie questioned.

"Strength," Tara replied.

"Yes, unfortunately he is incapable of hiding his ability while we lack the ability to shift. He avoids human contact. Unless it is completely necessary." Stephanie looked towards Alistair. Tara could see the pure power in his muscles as he moved. Suddenly she was very grateful for her invisible gift.

For the rest of that day, they sat with each other. Doing nothing more than discussing what they were to do next and how they were going to retrieve Nick from Jenifer's grasp. Her fighting was far from capable, but she was less defenceless.

Tomorrow they would have everything to lose or everything to gain. It would be up to Tara in the end. The thought scared her.

Frozen

Chapter 22

After Tara had finished talking through the plan with Stephanie, Alistair, and Samuel, she headed home. It had been two nights since she had seen her mother and Tara knew that there would be questions when she walked through the door. Until the moment her mother asked them, she wasn't aware of how she was going to answer them.

Tara's mother opened her arms and held her as soon as she'd walked through the door.

That was all it had taken for every emotion and everything that she had been holding back, to explode from her in violent sobs.

"It's okay, my darling girl," her mother comforted. They collapsed to the floor in the open doorway. She ran her soothing hands over her daughter's hair, just like she had done to stem every fear of the dark that she had had as a child.

"They took him mum," Tara managed between gasps. "They took him, and I don't know how to get... *gasp*... him back."

"Neither do I sweetheart, but I know my daughter," Her mother comforted. She tipped her daughters chin, locking her gaze on Tara's eyes. "You are strong, capable, loving and the best person I know."

"Thank you, mum," Tara replied.

"I think that it might be time for you and me to have a chat about what has been happening," her mother concluded. She picked up her daughter from the floor and led her to the sitting room.

"Let us start from the beginning," Tara's mother said softly. "How did you come to discover that Nick was a Shapeshifter?"

Tara told her mother everything that had happened. From the day Nick had saved her from the falling lamppost to the day the Shadows took him from her. She told her mother of the people she had met and the plan that Stephanie was working on to get him back.

It was the hardest thing of all, to admit all the feelings that she had been having over the last month. How fast and hard she had fallen.

Frozen

"You love him?" Her mother questioned.

"Yes, I love him," she admitted to her, while feathering the cushion in her lap. "It feels like home when I am with him. He makes me feel complete. I feel like I could take on the world with him by my side."

"Wow!" Her mother exclaimed. "You really do love him."

Tara didn't reply. She knew that she loved him, that she had for some time now. It seemed so surreal that she could fall that quickly. *Love at first sight indeed,* she thought to herself.

"I think that now might be the time for me to share with you something that your father left for you," her mother offered. Tara looked up at her mother as she let out a long breath.

Tara's mother took her by the hand and led her up to the library. She sat her down in her normal spot in her father's chair. Walked over to the bookshelves and pulled out a book. It was an old book, one most likely added to the collection by her father.

Tara's mother handed her the book the correct way around and Tara took it with both hands. Across the dark blue leather bounding was pressed the words, 'Great expectations, Charles Dickens'.

She had seen the book many times on the shelf and already knew that it was one of her father's favourite books that he had managed to collect. It had cost a pretty penny and for that reason Tara had never picked it up.

"What has this got to do with what is going on?" Tara asked.

"Open it," her mother instructed.

Tara opened the cover to the first page. Written in her dad's cursive handwriting - clear as day - was her name.

For my dearest daughter, Tara.

For when expectations and choices collide. I hope you find the contents of this book helpful.

Your loving Father.

Tears began to stream down Tara's cheeks. She had heard her father's voice in the words written on the paper. A voice that she hadn't heard in years.

"Your father told me to give you this when or if the Shapeshifter world came knocking," her mother said, running her fingers over the indentations on the paper. "He'd said, that if he wasn't here to tell you the things that you would need to know, then this book would hold the answers.

Tara picked up the book and flicked through the pages. She wasn't sure what she was expecting to see but she mostly certainly wasn't expecting nothing.

"I looked, at least it tried to," Tara's mum chuckled. "There has to be something in there that only

Frozen

you would be able to work out. I know what you both were like for doing puzzles together. All I could find was boring info, nothing specifically for you."

Tara began to flick through the pages slowly, trying to find a clue.

"I will leave you to work this out," she said as she placed a kiss on her daughter's head. "You know where I am if you need me."

"Thanks mum," Tara replied, still delicately flicking through every page.

Tara had no clue how much time had passed. She sat there going through the book over and over. However, when she got to the end again and found nothing, she let out an exasperated sigh. She closed the book and turned it over in her hands. There was nothing more that the title and the author. There was a pattern that scrolled across the cover in gold.

It was a beautiful book, but what the particular book had to do with Tara and the Shapeshifter world, she didn't know.

He turned over the page and looked over the inscription her father had left for her. It dawned on her that her father wouldn't have defaced such a precious book. So why had he.

Tara looked through the book again. This time paying attention to the actual book. This story was not *Great Expectations*. Young Pip was nowhere to be found within the pages.

She turned the book back to the cover and began to look around. Now it was evident that the cover could be nothing but a cover up.

She ran her hands over the front and noticed that the cover bubbled. Like there was something under there. She turned the page over to look at the inside. On the page where her father had written, the edges we not as neat as she would expect them to be.

She carried the book over to her father's desk and retrieved the letter opener from the draw. It was an old silver letter opener, and the handle were made to look like leaves on a vine trailing down to the blade.

Tara took the opener to the edge of the page going to pry up the corner to remove the paper. She had to pause. The idea of defacing this book was unbelievable. She would just have to do it carefully and hope that she was correct.

As the letter opener slid under the page easily, her heart rate calmed just a little. Her nerves were still just as bad, and she knew this from the way her hands shook slightly.

The page finally came away. Hidden underneath was what Tara assumed was the original book cover. Though the blue leather from the exterior was covering the edges of it.

Tara took the letter opener to this next, but it was harder to take off than the paper her father's scrolling script was on.

It took her several moments of being careful and prising the edges away slowly. Once she'd pulled up all

Frozen

the edges, she placed down her father's letter opener. She was hoping that she was right, but as she closed the book the doubt began to ooze out.

Tara stepped away from the desk and the book. She needed a moment to steady herself. There could be anything under the cover. What would her father have left her that he would hide it like this?

She took a large inhale and then slowly exhaled. She took the now free edges and pulled them around the edge of the hard cover and towards the spine.

It seemed too simple. Hidden behind the blue leather cover, was an envelope with nothing but her name written on the front.

Tara took the envelope out and held it at arm's length. She slowly made her way back to her father's armchair. She opened the letter with trepidation.

Then sure enough, the recognisable scrolling script of her father, caressed the pages of the beautiful paper he had written on. She held in up hoping to smell her father's scent rapped in the pages, but unfortunately it only contained the familiar smell of old musty books. A deep earthy and humbling smell.

She took another deep and reassuring breath before she could bring herself to start reading.

My clever girl you found it,

Though if your mother gave you this book and you have found this letter, then you know the truth. You carry the genes of the Shifters. The same gene, that I have carried.

I hoped that this would never happen, my girl. I hoped that you would get a carefree and normal life. That my old world would not collide with yours. I am sorry that I have brought this upon you.

If you have also had to find this letter, then my assumption and conclusion is that - I am no longer with you. Though I will always be with you in your heart, my beautiful girl. I wish that I was there to guide you and to show you the ways of the Shifters. It is as dangerous to be aware of the Shifter's world, as it is fascinating.

If you don't already know, then I need to make you aware of the fact that there are many forces that the Shifter world is fighting against. Their open and loving nature makes them easy prey and although I know that there are many within its community, I worry that it will not be enough against one of its deceitful own.

The largest and the most worrying of all, are the Shadows. There isn't much known about them, and they are a formidable foe. I urge you to genuinely think about what you are doing, my child. About where you may end up if you follow this path.

However, I know you, my girl. I know that you are more capable than anyone I know. I know that you have a heart of gold that is able to love more openly, than I have ever thought possible. I also know that you are stubborn and are so easily persuaded.

I ask only that you make the choice to enter this world, not because of the expectations that maybe on your shoulders, but for your own reasons, your own choices.

This book was more than a vessel to give you this letter. It also has information about the Shadows and their world. I

Frozen

stumbled across it years ago and knew that the knowledge on it papers needed to be shared with the Shifter world. I could not bring myself to give it to anyone, for fear it would be passed on. I knew, like many others, that there was someone on the inside that enabled the Shadow attack at the gathering.

There is so many things that I wish I could explain and tell you in these pages, but I am afraid that I am going to end up writing an entire book! Though I could never compare to the work of the greats.

Instead, I offer you help in the form of family. Your grandparents do not know that you exist. I have been hidden and removed from the Shifter world and have tried give you the same level of protection. Nevertheless, I feel like now is the time that you seek them. They are the only two Shifters I know I can place my complete trust in. Therefore, I know that I can trust them with the one thing that is most important to me – you biscuit.

Their names are Mary and Cain. They are two of the oldest Shifters alive still today and are also Elders on the Shifter Council.

Tara nearly dropped the letter. Mary and Cain were her grandparents. Her father was their son. Tara supposed that they probably had kids, but to think that they were her grandparents, and they didn't know. How was she going to process that!

Find them Tara and tell them what I have revealed to you. Show them the book, but no one else. It may help the Key when she is found.

"Oh, Daddy! I wish you were here," Tara sobbed aloud.

All that I have left to tell you, my sweetheart. Is that I love you and I am proud of you. Please, be careful. If your mother has, I fear lost me, then she will not cope with the loss of you too. Tell your mother that I love her.

Your ever-loving Father x

The tears would last no longer. They flowed down her chin and dripped on the letter now dropped in her lap. It had been hard to read. Yet, she wanted more. She wanted her father to hold her and tell her everything was going to be okay.

Tara's father and always been the one that had guided her. Even through death he was still at her side, encouraging her and lending his strength.

****

It had been hard the night before for Tara to get home and it was easier for the reverse. Stephanie had taken Tara to meet a man called Michio. He has the ability to create doorways through the fabric of space.

It was a challenging thing for him to do to a specific point. It wasn't like Nicks - he simply thought of a place and that was where he ended up. Michio had to know exactly where he was sending someone. It was

Frozen

also dependant on the ability to create an opening without exposing them to all the human world too.

It was decided that they would open a portal into Mrs Tyrell's home, and she had to trek home from there. She could have called her mother. However, it would mean revealing the location of Mrs Tyrell's and without her permission, it felt wrong.

The way back to the mansion was easier. She drove her own car to Mrs Tyrell's leaving it parked behind hers.

Luckily for her, Stephanie was from the twenty-first century and had a phone that Tara could easily dropped her a message to.

It took only a moment after that for a bright light to start in the middle of the room. It glowed the same warm glow that Tara had seen looking for energy.

The light grew bigger as it swirled faster and faster, until it left a round, open window to the other side of the portal. On the other side stood a man with a singular hand up towards the circle. His eyes closed and his face plain.

He was a short man, of no more than five-foot. He also looked like the eldest Shifter she had seen. Tara assumed him to be Japanese with the clothes that he wore. She assumed it was a simple and informal kimono of some sorts. He wore dark, loose-fitting trousers and top with a light-coloured belt around his centre. Draped over the top of this was a very loose - *dressing gown?* Tara thought - in a soft dove grey. His silvery beard sat just on his chest and his silver-streaked hair was half tied back and half down.

Michio nodded to Tara in acknowledgement for her to come through. Tara thanked him, stepping over to his side of the window. He gave a small incline of his head and left the room.

"It isn't you," Stephanie told her. "He barely says anything to anyone. I have no idea why."

"As long as I haven't offended him," Tara hoped.

"How was your mother?" Stephanie enquired.

"Worried about me, naturally," Tara went on to explain about the letter and the book. Then about Mary and Cain.

"Holy crap," Stephanie said stunned.

"Yeah, so once you are done getting your jaw back up off the floor, can we please go and find them. I have a lot I want to talk to them about," Tara pressed.

"Do you have the book with you," Stephanie enquired.

"Yes, I do," Tara acknowledged. "No, I haven't read it, to answer your next question."

"Hey, out of my head!" Stephanie shouted.

"You shouldn't think so loud then," they smiled at each other.

Stephanie took Tara down a myriad of corridors, until they arrived outside of a large oak door, with metal plates and pins. Stephanie gave it a knock and then lent against the door frame.

Frozen

After a few short moments, Mary came to the door and opened it with far less effort than Tara thought the door might have required.

"Tara," Mary greeted. "Is everything alright?"

"There is something that I wish to discuss with yourself and Cain, if I may," Tara explained.

"Of course," Mary said opening the door wider. "Please come on in."

"Come find me at the training room when you are done?" Stephanie asked Tara.

"Yeah, sure," Tara agreed.

Once Tara was inside, she could see that Cain was sat in a winged, emerald green, leather armchair. He'd had hold of a book but had since put it on the driftwood side table next to him. In truth he had added it to the top of a pile of books already there.

"Hello Tara, to what so we owe the pleasure?" Cain queried.

"I have some information to give you regarding myself and the Shadows, Tara told them.

"I am not sure of what help we can be, but if there is anything that you require, then you only need ask," Mary offered.

"It isn't about what you can give me, but more what I can give you. I have found out somethings about myself. Things that effect you," Tara started to explain. "It might be easier, if I start at the beginning."

"Very well, my dear," Mary granted.

Tara went on to tell them, about her discovery of which parent carried the Shifter genes. He had kept hidden from their world and fell in love. The way he had protected his daughter from the Shifter world and Shadow world alike.

She went on to explain that her mother knew, but extraordinarily little and it was always going to be her father's job to let her know about her heritage. She talked about how he had died in a tragic accident and had left her mother and herself, on their own.

It didn't take long before she brought up the book and the letter. It was here where it became hard for Tara to continue.

"Would it be easier for you if I read the letter aloud?" Cain asked her.

Tara nodded in agreement handing him the letter. Cain began to read it out loud. He didn't sound like her father, but there were certain similarities in the way they both talked.

Tara sat in silence fiddling with the bottom of her sleeve, waiting for him to get to the part about them. When it finally got close, she looked over to Mary. Tara guessed Mary had already worked out what was coming. Her eyes were streaming like rivers. The deep brown of her eyes never left Tara.

Cain's voice continued in the background until he paused at their names. "It cannot be!"

"Tara, what was your father's name?" Mary asked, without losing eye contact with her.

"Joseph Kingley," Tara clarified.

Frozen

Cain took the few steps toward Tara. Mary did the same, until Tara had both of their arms wrapped around her.

"Our son, our beloved son," Mary sobbed into Tara's shoulder. Tara had no idea what to say or what to do. To them, they had only just lost their son.

It was Cain that pulled away from her first and was shortly followed by Mary, who's eyes were still red and streaming.

Cains hands lifted slowly towards Tara and took a gentle hold of her cheeks. He studied her face.

"You have so much of your father's light in you. He was too pure and too good for our world. You have our protection, our sweet girl," Cain said touchingly.

"We are here for you Tara," Mary said, kissing Tara's cheek.

For the first time, in a long time, Tara felt accepted by someone new.

Chapter 23

"There's a reason it's her though," Stephanie was concluding.

"I don't think she's ready for battle," Alistair shared.

"I admit, she isn't strong enough to battle against anything major," Stephanie agreed. "But there has to be more to her, if she is the Key. Maybe the way to win this, is not with brute force."

Tara was stood outside of the room listening in on them. None of them said anything she herself wouldn't have, but to hear it from them gave her doubt.

Frozen

"She is the Key. That much everyone seems to be sure on. I vowed that no matter what or who she was, she would have my sword," Samuel declared.

"She'll have mine too," Stephanie concurred.

"Then mine she shall have too," Alistair agreed. "I do not doubt her getting us there. She has more heart and soul than all of us here combined. I just worry that her lack of experience in combat will be her downfall."

"Then it's a good thing she has us," Stephanie smirked.

"I am lucky to have you all," Tara exclaimed, as she worked her way further into the room.

"We are rather fabulous," Stephanie acknowledged.

"Have you told them about the book and about what was in the letter?" Tara changed the subject.

"Yes, we are aware," Samuel admitted.

"Mary and Cain's granddaughter?" Alistair asked - with no intention of waiting on an answer. "I mean... WOW!"

"Even I haven't wrapped my head around it yet," Tara admitted aloud.

"It might take a while for that one princess," Stephanie retorted sarcastically. Tara rolled her eyes in her direction.

"The book?" Samuel questioned.

"Mary and Cain are reading it through. If there is anything that will be of use, they are going to let us and the Council know," Tara explained.

"Do they know of our plan for Nick?" Alistair queried.

"They know nothing of our plan," Tara told them. "They know that I want to get Nick back though. They also agreed that due to me being the Key, I need to have as much information as I can. They also offered their aid."

"Then the plan continues as it did," Samuel announced. "Mary and Cain are good Shifters, but their need to protect you, won't help our plan."

"Of course, not sherlock!" Stephanie exclaimed, "but their knowledge and experience will be invaluable."

"With that, I can agree," was Samuel's simple response.

"Then what do we do next?" Tara wondered.

"I have already pulled some books from the library about dimensional travel and getting into other worlds. I will continue to read through those and try to piece together a thorough plan on how we are going to get there," Alistair explained.

"I will investigate the Shadow-world and what we might encounter when we get there. We will need kit and weapons. Samuel?" Stephanie probed.

"I will take care of the weapons and any further equipment you see fit to come with us," Samuel accepted. "Though firstly, I think it would be a good idea to further your weapons training, Tara."

"I thought I had done the basics?" Tara said. She didn't want to train anymore. There was so much to work and preparations to do.

Frozen

"I will not take you untrained, into a hostile world, which will have no greater pleasure than to destroy the Key," Samuel said firmly. "We train or I pull the plug."

"Then I suppose that I have no option!" Tara sulked.

****

Later that afternoon Tara was dripping with sweat. She was as sticky as honey but smelt a whole lot worse. She was hungry, tired, and really in need of a shower.

Samuel was working her harder than he had before. He had her correct her stance, her hold on the sword and every movement she made.

"You are off balance again," Samuel scolded as he gently nudged her shoulder, causing her to rock to the side.

Tara readjusted her feet to be shoulder width apart. Samuel nudged her again. This time there was less movement.

"Better," Samuel granted.

"I don't think I'll ever get this right," Tara sighed. Her confidence had deflated with every criticism and incorrect move she made.

"Take a break Tara," Samuel instructed.

Tara never replied. She placed her wooden sword back on the rack, grabbed her water bottle and sat herself in the corner with Alistair and Stephanie, who were scouring books and taking notes.

"Damn girl! You look wiped," Stephanie recognized. "He's working you hard."

"I understand why, but I don't think I will ever get to any real standard," Tara admitted.

"Samuel's standard? No," Stephanie said bluntly.

Tara took a deep breath and sighed. *How could Nick be so sure that I am the Key,* she thought to herself.

"But then neither can we," Stephanie finished. "He simply wants you to reach your highest potential. Not mine, not Alistair's and not his."

Tara looked up into an encouraging look from Stephanie and Alistair.

"Everyone has different strengths because we are all different. What you have learnt this week, is months of training crammed into the space of a few days. I am pushing you hard, not for myself, but for you. You are the Key, Tara. You are also a friend, a daughter, a granddaughter, and a compassionate, strong, young woman," Samuel explain from his seated position on the mats. "No one here wants to leave you vulnerable or an easy target."

Tara was on the edge of tears. She hadn't only gained her grandparents, but a whole family. The Shifters had known her for a couple of weeks and had taken her in completely. Accepting her for who she was. They would embrace her, protect her, and help her be the best version of herself. Not through punishment,

Frozen

demoralisation, or frustration, but though kindness, compassion, and love.

Tara got to her feet, retrieved her wooden sword, and took her stance on the blue training mats. "Again," she said simply.

Samuel stood up with his hands held behind his back. "Sure," he agreed. "But let's take it up a notch." He walked over to the weapons stand and took down one of the glass bladed ones.

"Am I ready?" Tara wondered aloud.

"Only one way to find out," Stephanie pointed out.

The moment Samuel fully gripped the sword, the glass like substance sparked to life. A glowing light - like the energy she had been learning to see in the world around her – emanated from it.

Samuel took a hold of the sword's blade with his left hand, realising the handle and offering it to Tara. Its light died down to a faint glow, the very second that Samuel removed his grip from the hilt.

Tara nervously took a grasp of the essence blade, expecting it to come to life. However, it remained as glass in her hands.

"You have to give your light to the blade," Samuel explained as he saw the creases that furrowed on Tara's forehead. "Relax. Take a deep breath."

Tara followed the instructions, but the blade remained as dull as before.

"Close your eyes," Samuel added. "Concentrate on your breath. In and out." Tara listened to the soothing sound of her breath as it rolled over her tongue and escaped her partially parted lips. "Now imagine your light travelling from your centre. Travelling along your arm, it gathers in the palm of your hands and then into the hilt of the blade."

Tara continued to take even breaths, allowing herself to concentrate on the lulling calm it brought her. When she was ready, Tara began to picture the light that was at her centre. A beautiful and pure light. The light that made up everything, including her. She imagined the flow of the light all over her body, making its way to her crown, her feet, and her hands.

Tara's hands seemed to warm as she concentrated the light into her right hand, which was holding the essence blade. It began to tingle and pulse, like she had her hand placed on a small electric current. It tickled more than hurt, but it was an odd sensation. One that took her thoughts from her eased breathing.

Upon opening her eyes, she had to blink to adjust to the light that was before her. Not only had she managed to fill the blade like Samuel had, but the light that came from her blade seemed to glow that much brighter.

"Damn!" Stephanie blurted.

"Is it meant to be that bright?" Tara quizzed.

"Everyone's light is a little different," Samuel revealed. "Although... I don't think that I have come across an energy this strong, since the gathering.'

"Did I do something wrong?" Tara asked.

Frozen

"Not at all. This is a perfect example of redirecting your energy into an essence blade. The purpose of this is to banish the darkness," Samuel continued with his training. "Primarily, these blades were created for the use on Shadows, but they can be used on other beings too, but that is a topic for another time. Take your stance."

Tara did as she was instructed and took her stance, just like she had done with the wooden sword. The essence blade was heavier and balanced just a little differently. She was glad when it didn't take her long to adjust.

Samuel went tougher than he had before. Tara could do nothing but remain in defence. Their swords clambered against one another, leaving a distinct ringing in the air.

Stephanie and Alistair stood at the edge of the room. The former lent against the wall playing with the knife in her hands. The latter was eating what looked to be a slice of watermelon, but Tara could only manage glimpses at the corner of her eyes.

Samuel was hounding her. The sword was striking repeatedly. She pushed back with everything she had. Hoping to put him off balance, but no matter what manoeuvre she used, he was able to counter.

Tara grew tired quicker with the essence blade. She thought it was the weight at first, but her arms had relaxed into the essence blade quickly. The only thing that she could assume was causing her to tire, was the constant ebb of her energy into the blade.

"Use your strength already," Stephanie hollered from the bench, which was now behind her.

"I am!" Tara shouted back her arms aching.

"Not the kind of strength that I am talking about!" Stephanie exasperated.

"Then what are you talking about?" Tara queried as she blocked another blow from Samuel.

Tara had expected an answer, but she didn't get one. She was sure that she could sense an eye roll from Stephanie.

Samuel continued to move, to dance around her. Though he wasn't landing a finishing blow, Tara was sure that he could if he put his mind to it. The only reason she could imagine, was because he was waiting on her.

Unable to stop him coming at her, she needed a better plan of attack. What was her strength? Her mother had always said it was her ability to love, but that was unlikely to help her in this situation.

Then she remembered back to some training they had done days ago - though it felt like weeks to her now. She had an advantage, one that she couldn't always rely on, but one that she should use if necessary.

She tapped into her ability. Casting her net over Samuel and taking in his thoughts.

One, two, three and four. One, two, three and four.

Tara looked at Samuel, who gave her a playful smile back. He was trying to make it harder.

One, two, three and four. Something wrong Tara?

Frozen

It took her by surprise. Samuel nearly managed to push past her defence with a low swing to her left. She managed to block and steady herself. No one had ever spoken to her directly through their thoughts. She would have to go deeper.

With a gentle push at first, she managed to get passed the continued counting in his head. However, she was confronted with another problem.

Cover my thoughts. Hide my thoughts.

He was good, Tara would give him that. She had never experienced levels in people thoughts before. Jumping from one thought to another was something that Tara was aware of already, just from her own head. Levels would be far more complicated. It would mean delving further in than she had ever done before.

With a deep breath she pushed down harder through the net and into Samuel's thoughts. They expanded into her own head. It was like she was no longer her - she was Samuel. Yet she was still able to move and control her body with ease.

It was like sinking into a lake. Everything that she knew of herself was above the water, clear and bright. Everything that was Samuel was in the water, murkier and dark.

Left arm. Up. Right side. Sweep up.

She had it. Tara reacted to every move that she read in Samuel's head. Until he left an opening and she attacked. It took her several more moves to take him down, but she managed it none the less.

"Well done," Samuel congratulated her.

"You were taking it easy on me," Tara announced.

"Yes, I held back," Samuel confirmed. "It would not be fair for a weapons master to pull everything in his arsenal, against a girl that has only been training for a few days now, would it?"

"I suppose you're right," Tara agreed.

"Though that was badass," Stephanie added from behind her. "I am impressed."

"Thank you," Tara said. "But is it enough to go up against Jenifer?"

"Do you want the honest answer?"

"Yes," Tara simply replied.

"Jenifer is hundreds of years old. We don't know what she is capable of. We don't know exactly what powers she has managed to keep hold of or gained," Stephanie explained. "But... we think we have found a way into the Shadow-world. The only hope that we have is to get in, get Nick and get out without confronting her."

"It will not be easy," Alistair continued. "We are few in number. Not to mention that we don't know the land or exactly where Nick is. However, you are the Key. Samuel is the greatest warrior we have. Mary and Cain are trying to help. We can do this. We can get him out."

Knock Knock.

Cain came into the room holding a book in his hand and with Mary in tow behind him.

Frozen

"We found something that you need to know," Cain began.

Chapter 24

The sun had long since gone past the horizon and the moon was glowing bright through the window of the library. The main table in the seating area was covered with books maps and food wrappers. Their whispers were trailing throughout the otherwise empty rows of books, like the scuttling of bugs. There was a sense of hurry in the way they spoke, but the hushed level insinuated secrets.

Tara gazed down on them from above, as they scoured through the mountains of books. They talked among themselves, as they tried to solve the riddle that had been given to the six of them.

Frozen

The Shadow-world was a dark one. A hostile place that would hunt them from the moment they set foot on their land. The book that Tara's father had found and left her, had given them many insights into the world they were trying to get to.

Tara had removed herself from the never-ending stream of information. It was hard to keep up with everyone's pace. They had clearly done this all before. Research, plan, and then execute, but it had given her a headache.

Her life had been turned upside down. An unsettled part of her wanted to run. However, she knew she could never bring herself to do it. Nick needed her and a large part of her needed him.

"Everything okay?" A voice came from behind her. Tara spun to see who it belonged to. Cain stood a few paces away. She hadn't realised he was no longer below with the others.

"I'm okay," Tara replied.

"Hmmm, maybe," Cain said softly. "Or maybe this is all just new and hard to process."

"Yes and no," Tara answered. "It is all new and hard to take in, but it feels right. It feels like I belong here."

"Only you can determine that. But there is always a place for you here," Cain offered.

Tara went and gave him a hug as a way of thanks. She may not have been able to see her father in Cain, but she could feel her father's tenderness in the way he held her and stroked the back of her head. Tears began to well in her eyes. She missed her father, and while she will never have her father back, she'd gained a grandfather. She hoped that they would have the chance to build their relationship properly once they'd rescued Nick.

"I think we have most of a plan together. The only thing left to work out is how to get into their dimension. It was the only thing that wasn't in your father's book," he told her.

"Is there nothing in the other books here?" Tara queried.

"If there was, there isn't now."

"Then how did Jenifer..." Tara trailed off into thinking.

"What is it?" Cain asked as he moved Tara away from him slightly to look upon her.

"Jenifer had been taking books out of the library to find a way to get everyone's powers back," Tara began to explain. "What if she wasn't looking into that at all? What if she was looking into the Shadow-world and a way to get the powers out for herself."

Tara's feet began moving before she had even acknowledged where she was going.

"Tara, what is it? Where are you going?" Cain threw questions at her, but Tara didn't answer a single one.

Jenifer's room was one of the very few doors that Nick had pointed out to her. One that wasn't a library, gallery, or kitchen door. He hadn't shown her where anyone else's rooms were, except the location of

Frozen

his own. However, on that day he had gestured to a door just off the corridor, that ran from the gallery to the library. *Conveniently placed herself,* Tara pondered.

Minutes later, Tara had her hand on the handle of Jenifer's room and was twisting the nob. Cain was stood behind her, his breathing still steady unlike hers. Regardless of the fact Tara had him practically jogging down the halls.

The room was large, neat, and awfully plain. Tara didn't know what she had been expecting to see on the other side of the door, but there was nothing here that showed who Jenifer was or what she liked.

"Tara?" Cain roused her back to the moment and away from her thoughts.

"Jenifer was taking books from the library. I saw her with her arms full of them once. They looked old. One had a pitch-black cover with a red trim. I might be wrong, but what if she was looking into..."

"Darker things," Cain finished for her.

"Exactly and what if they never left her room?" Tara thought aloud.

"I doubt that Jenifer would be as unprepared as that. To leave behind something that might led us to her," Cain added.

"Maybe. However, she left in a rush. Maybe, she didn't think about it," Tara stated as she rummaged around the room.

There were basic pieces of furniture placed around the room. Like Nick's there were several doors leading to other rooms.

In the main room there was the usual sofa, coffee table, bookcases, and side tables. From first glance Tara could see many books, but not the one that she recalled Jenifer having. She made her way around to the side table, where a stack of books was placed, and a used cup sat beside them.

The books were of no consequence. One about British history, another about map making and another that was in a language that Tara couldn't place.

Cain had gone over to the bookcases and was slowly taking in every title. Moving left to right and down each shelf meticulously. If there was anything to be found here, they were going to find it.

The first door to the left of main door was ajar and lead into a bathroom. Elegant though it was, there was nothing of use to be found in there. Tara pulled the door to and moved onto the next one.

The bedroom had given as much information as the bathroom had. Books filled the room. They sat on the bedside table, some were placed on the dresser, but none were the book that she was looking for. Tara combed under the bed and in every draw. Going through Jenifer's personal items felt wrong to Tara. Although, this woman had destroyed the Shifters world and taken Nick from her, it didn't make it right to be going through her things.

The wardrobe had been fairly empty too - besides some little girl's clothes and some hats stacked on the bottom. Knowing she needed to find Nick, Tara got over her guilt quickly.

Frozen

"Tara," Cain called from the living room.

Tara walked out closing the door to the bedroom behind her. When she looked towards Cain, she was happily surprised.

He was stood with his back to the bookcase, a singular book in his hand. It was the one that Tara had described. The pitch-black book looked darker than night. The red edging looked more horrific when the book wasn't being held between other books. It looked like blood seeping out from its dark pages.

"I assume this is the one that you were looking for?" Cain motioned to the book in his grasp.

"Yes," Tara agreed looking to Cain.

"This is an enormously powerful book, Tara. This isn't a book that will tell us anymore about the Shadows or even how to get there. This book will take you there," Cain told her.

"I don't understand," Tara responded.

"I have heard of this book. It is an ancient and powerful book. A book I had long thought had been destroyed," Cain explained. "Many, many centuries ago, I met a young Shifter by the name of Thema in Ghana. She had the ability to access another world by simply writing the true name of each dimension."

"Is she still alive?" Tara asked. "Could she help us?"

"I cannot tell you what happened to Thema. She disappeared years after I had met her. Many believe she died using her ability. Others believe she got stuck in another dimension. Either way, there's not enough time to find her.

"This book has her abilities in it. This was a book that she wrote. A book that she would use to jump in-between and through. The binding is made from materials of another plain. It was made to hold her power and very few ever knew it existed.

"I cannot tell you, if this book contains a page that can get us to the Shadowlands and I cannot tell you, if we can get back using it. I can tell you, that this is powerful and complicated magic. We need to be careful how we use it. Jenifer hid this and for good reason."

Cain nudged his head in the direction of the floor. Tara moved around the sofa to see what he was hinting at. At the foot of the bookcases, a plain piece of wood was covering the bottom. The panel that Cain must have gotten the book from behind, was open. The piece of wood was hinged on the left side. It would have been completely invisible.

"How did you know something was under there?" Tara wondered.

"The edge of wood is slightly worn. She's been using this to hide things for a while," Cain explained, pointing to the worn edge of the wood. He was right it was obvious now, but you would have to be diligently looking to spot it.

"What do we do with it?" Tara asked.

"We take it to the others. Mary knows more about this book than I. It was Mary who was charged with destroying it," Cain admitted.

Frozen

****

Everyone was still sat around the same table they had occupied all evening. Tara would guess it was past midnight by now. They'd been at this for many hours, and they must all be exhausted.

"Mary?" Cain called to his wife.

"Yes, my love?" Mary replied, slowly looking up from the book she had her head in. "What is..."

Mary never finished her sentence. The book that was in her hands dropped heavily on to the table, catching everyone's attention. Mary slowly moved towards Cain. All eyes were on her.

"How?" Cain asked her.

"It was hidden," Mary managed to choke out. "I couldn't destroy it. I tried everything. Hiding it was the only option left. It took three of us to place enough wards on it. I don't understand. Where?"

Cain explained how they had found the book. Mary wasn't the only one that listened. It took far more explaining for everyone to understand exactly what had been found.

"Why didn't you tell me?' Cain asked his wife.

"The fewer that knew its location, the safer it was. I wanted to tell you, but I was bound to a promise not to reveal it," Mary explained. Cain simply nodded - a clear indication that the conversation would be finished in private later.

"Can this help us?" Tara eventually asked her grandmother.

"Yes, it can."

Frozen

Chapter 25

It was late the next morning, when Tara was awoken by the rays of sun shining through Nick's window. It had become a routine during the preceding days, she would seek solace in his space, but end up falling asleep in his bed.

The plan for the day had been unclear when they scattered the night before. Mary had been muttering something inaudibly to Cain, presumably about the book. They headed towards their room, which were in the opposite direction to where Tara went.

Stephanie, Alistair, and Samuel had said a brief, exhausted goodnight. It wasn't a warming good night from Stephanie, but Tara had the feeling that she was growing on her – albeit slowly.

Tara hoped there wouldn't be any training today and they would finally nail down a plan to save Nick. Everything seemed to be taking so long to progress. She hoped they would depart soon. She didn't know if Nick was okay or if he could wait another day.

The thought of losing him sent her down into despair. She sobbed into the covers of the bed and let herself really feel it. She had been holding it in for days now. Moving from one activity to the next, but with nothing to occupy her and no concrete plan in front of her, it had begun to spill.

Twenty minutes later with her throat burning, her face wet and her chest screaming she got up, went to the bathroom, and showered.

The feel of the water beating down on to her, soothed her aching heart. The warmth took away the coldness that had spread across her body. Determination sunk into her once more.

She would visit Mrs Tyrell. She should have done it earlier, but she had got so wrapped up in saving Nick and everything that went with it, that she hadn't thought to go a visit her teacher.

****

Mrs Tyrell's condition had not changed. She was still unconscious, but otherwise well. Whatever Jenifer had done to her, she had done it well. Sandra's investigation had been fruitless, she hadn't found a way to bring her around.

Frozen

Tara knew the doctor had been up many hours of the night, pouring over books. Stacks of them lay in her office and the evidence they'd been read, could be seen in the dark circles under Sandra's eyes.

Sandra would probably have gotten rid of her bagged eyes if she still had her shapeshifting abilities. One thing more for Tara to give back to her people – assuming she succeeded, and fate unclasped its grip to let her.

Catherine looked almost peaceful, tucked underneath the hospital sheets as Tara read *Charlotte Bronte's Jane Eyre* to her.

****

Tara read to Mrs Tyrell for the next few hours. It had given her something to concentrate on and something to escape, too.

Mrs Tyrell hadn't stirred within that time. She was still, like one of the photos that lined her walls. The gentle rise and fall of Catherine's chest, were the only tell-tale signs that she was alive.

Tara glanced up at the clock, the hands depicting one o'clock. She was due to meet with Stephanie to go over what they may have discovered about the ancient book and the possible reasons Jenifer needed it.

Firstly, she would have to grab some food. She'd have to head to the kitchens on her way to the training room. Tara closed *Jane Eyre* and placed it down on the bedside table.

A hand grabbed around her wrist loosely enough that Tara didn't feel threatened, but surprised. She looked around to find out where the phantom hand had come from. Catherine's open eyes blinked at her.

"Jenifer," she hoarsely whispered.

"Gone," it was all Tara knew to say. How was she going to tell this wonderful woman, that the man she had raised as her own child had been taken.

"She is the one...," Catherine cleared her parched throat. "... that is," she coughed again.

"... the one that has been working with the Shadows," Tara finished for her, tipping water from the glass jug into a clean glass and handing it to Catherine.

Catherine weakly sat herself up in the hospital bed and drank its full contents.

"Sandra?" Tara called through to the doctor.

"Yes?" An exhausted reply came.

"Catherine is awake." It only took those simple words and Sandra was next to her bed, checking her pulse and asking her basic questions. The weariness that Tara had seen on doctor's face earlier, had been replaced with hope.

"Sandra, please stop fussing," Catherine pleaded with her friend after she had begun her examinations. "Honestly, I feel fine. Hungry and sluggish, but otherwise fine. There are more important things to deal with," Catherine asserted and looked to Tara.

"Sandra, I need you to get some of the Elders here, please," Catherine requested. "Don't look at me like that. You can do all the tests and checks you want

Frozen

to do... After I have communicated everything that I need to."

"Fine! But to be clear - I am not happy. Your well-being should come first. You are my patient!" Sandra exasperated.

"Yes, but what I need to say is for everyone's well-being," Catherine explained. She didn't have to say anything more to the doctor. Sandra was out through the door, looking like a woman on a mission.

"Tara, there is somethings that I need to explain to you. They may ask for you to leave when the Elders get here and I am not sure if I will get the opportunity after that," Catherine rushed.

"There is something that I need to tell you first," Tara spoke down to her clenched hands.

"What is it child?"

"Shadows took Nick. Jenifer was behind it," Tara said quietly. As if they were spoken in whispers then perhaps, they might not be true.

Catherine went pale instantly.

"He will be okay," Catherine said softly, comforting herself and Tara. "It wasn't your fault. He is strong and we will get him back.

"Now I need you to listen Tara," her eyes pleaded. "As I am sure you may have worked out or guessed by now. I became aware of Jenifer's intentions. She had been so careful to only plan and choose each move as it happened. She knew that there were holes in my power, and she utilised them. She plans on releasing and harnessing the power she contained in that orb all those years ago.

"She has been trying and failing repeatedly. She remained with us so she could find a way to harness that power. She has found her answer. There is a substance found in another dimension. If crafted correctly it can contain small parts of the light. The wielder or bearer would have the ability to siphon small bits at a time. It's possible for it to then replenish itself, just as we replenish each other.

"She has been trying to get into this other dimension. I stumbled upon her while she was planning her moves once she got through a dimensional gate. It's possible that she has already been to retrieve this material.

"You are the Key Tara. I am not sure how much the Elders will be willing to share with you. I believe that you need every piece of information that you can possibly get.

"It is with a heavy heart that I tell you this," Catherine looked on the verge of tears. "The container that she originally used is far more volatile. If you overload that container, it will burst. Jenifer will not be able to use our light, for whatever horrors she has in store. This will come at a great cost. Once the container is destroyed, our powers will go with it.

"This decision will have to rest on your shoulders. If there is no other way to retrieve the orb or stop her, you may have to destroy it."

Frozen

"I can't make that kind of choice," Tara started hyperventilating.

"For the good of our people, for the good of this world and potentially others, you may NEED to make that choice," Catherine instructed. "All I ask is that you consider it if the time comes. I will stand with you."

"O… okay," Tara said calming slightly. "I have to get Nick back."

"We will. I will do what I can with the Elders. They may see Nick as expendable now that he has delivered you to us, but come find me again in a while?" Catherine asked.

"Of course," Tara replied as Mary, Cain, Adam, and another woman – recognisable from the Council room - that she couldn't put a name to.

She was tall and slender with black hair that was sleeked back into a tight bun. She looked incredibly severe, until she smiled at Tara. She wore a black high-necked dress and black boots. Tara supposed that if she'd lived as long as some of the Elders and had seen the things that they'd seen, she might seem severe too.

"Good afternoon, Tara." Adam said inclining his head towards her. Tara reciprocated with a slight bow of her head. He moved around his daughters' sick bed to plant a kiss upon her forehead.

"I don't believe we have been formally introduced," the severe woman addressed Tara with a strong American Accent.

"I'm Dorothea."

"It's a pleasure to meet you properly," Tara politely responded.

"The pleasure is mine. You are the Key." Dorothea smiled broadly at her. Tara was stuck between thinking this pale, slender woman was either kind and sweet, or potentially a vampire. *If they even exist*, Tara chuckled to herself.

"I will see you soon Mrs Tyrell," Tara told her.

"You can call me Catherine, Tara," she smiled at her. Tara headed out giving her grandparents a slight nod and a brief smile.

Chapter 26

This would paint a very odd picture, Tara thought to herself. She wasn't wrong.

Imagine six people - or in this case Shifters - stood in a circle. They are all wearing battle gear, dressed head to toe in black. All carrying different weapons except one, they all had an essence blade hanging in a sleek black sheath.

Furthermore, they were all surrounding a black and red book that lay closed on the floor. A very strange picture indeed and not where Tara had imagined herself ending up.

Mary had told them little about the book. Whatever she knew about it, she didn't want to share.

To Tara it felt like her grandmother was reluctant to use it.

The things Cain had told her about Thema and her abilities, were confirmed by Mary. The book had been put under various protections after the continual failed attempts of destroying it. Mary only added that she knew how to use it and could.

The story that went with the book was obviously a deep secret Mary was unwilling to share. Tara – for maybe the first time in her life – didn't question it. Mary was willing to use it to access the Shadow-world and save Nick. That was enough for Tara.

"Everyone ready?" Mary checked, gently pressing her hands on the edges of the black binding.

Tara wasn't sure she was ready, but like, she agreed.

Mary took a deep breath and turned the cover of the book over. She ran her finger down the list of things written upon the page. *What language is that?* Tara could only guess at Arabic.

Tara's grandmothers' young hand, stopped at a line about two thirds of the way down the page. She flicked towards the end of the book and opened it to reveal a double page covered with a pattern of black ink. It had a geometric design that focused around a large, black square in between each page.

"Whatever you do, do not fight it," Mary told them. "These pages are thin, and the struggle will only change the destination, like changing the page."

Frozen

Wind started to circle around them, like it was pulling them into the book. The dark space in the middle grew larger and larger. Absorbing and morphing into the shapes around it.

Tara's heart began to race faster and faster, keeping in time with the speed of the wind. Tara took one last look at the circle of people around her. She took one deep breath to steady herself and thought of Nick. *I can do this for him,* she thought.

A dark mist then began to unfurl from the book, wrapping itself around them. It pulled them towards the book. The last thing that Tara saw was Mary's concerned eyes.

****

A darkness - unlike anything that Tara had seen before - surrounded her. Not a single drop of light. Not a streetlight to be seen. No sunlight or moonlight graced the sky. The only dim light was that of the stars that sparkled so distantly, that their light barely penetrated the dark.

Tara got up off the cold, wet floor she had inelegantly fallen onto. She attempted to dust herself off, but the mud had been damp. It clung to her gear in clumps, Tara was sure it was the least of her worries.

It was quiet - too quiet. She wasn't certain what to expect from this world or what the vegetation and wildlife would be like. She did know that she should be hearing the hustle and bustle of another five people around her.

Panic began to creep in. Realisation that she was alone sunk in. With no idea where she was or how to locate them or even Nick.

Calm down Tara. She thought to herself. She closed her eyes and took a few steadying breathes.

She couldn't afford to panic and loose the precious time that she had. The plan was to get to Nick swiftly, get him out, and if possible get the orb too.

Mary said that they would land south of the place they believed Jenifer may have taken Nick and kept the orb. North she would travel.

She thanked whatever deity she could think of, that she had a compass in her small backpack. She retrieved it from the inner most pocket and was glad to find that it worked in this world. It might be completely different than earth, but at least there appeared to be the fundamentals of earth - water, gravity, stars, oxygen, and a similar magnetic field.

Tara had to focus and squint to see which direction the little red needle was facing. There just wasn't enough light on this dark shadowy world. She knew she could pour her light - her energy - into her blade, but she deemed it imprudent. She might need it later.

While she walked further and further north, she began to acclimatise to the dark. She began to see the shape of the land and make out where the vegetation around her was.

Frozen

The density of the foliage became less and less. At first, she was having to brush things out of her path and bend spiked ferns. Now she was able to walk more hastily.

There had been no sign of her companions. There hadn't been any sound or movement, other than the slight rustle of the leaves around her. There were no footprints that Tara could see or broken branches that would suggest someone had been this way.

Tara continued her trudging. Her feet ached in her boots. She hadn't had the time to really break them in. She was chilled to her bones. The steady breeze and unending darkness sapped at her strength.

My strength, Tara thought to herself.

She cast her mind out as far as she could. Trying to pick up on anything. Casting that net further than she had before. Until she could see the pulse of blue light edging through that net in her direction. She held onto that connection and followed it.

It was too far away for her untrained skill, to make out any words or coherent thoughts. Tara had no way of knowing how far away this person was or whether it was one of her group.

However, she knew staying stationary was not going to help her. She had to get moving. She would have to swallow the pain from her feet, and she would need to forget the bitter icy cold.

At that moment, a growl emitted from the trees behind her. She had disturbed something.

Tara turned facing the darkness that held this unknown creature, slowly stepping backwards. Another growl came from the darkness.

Tara couldn't see anything. Not a single thing. Although she knew it was there. She asked herself, if it was worth the risk, to pull her essence blade.

The light might attract something bigger, or more of them. Yet, if this creature attacked her or was able to move faster than she could run with her blistered feet, she would be dead anyways.

Despite this realisation, she ran in the direction of that faint blue current in the net. She would have to take that leap of faith and hope that someone would be there to help her. The chance of attracting more beasts was not an option if she was to save Nick.

The beast was hot on her trail. Following her with every turn she took. She was not losing it and she was not out running it. She had a blood hound on her scent and no way to shake it.

Tara ran desperately like the wind, regardless of her pain. The tether that she had held onto became brighter and brighter. Though the beast got closer and closer.

Tara took a sharp left - turning past the tree in front of her - but the damp ground claimed her as a victim once more. It felt like her left hip crunched as she hit the ground, sending a flare of pain down her leg.

She scrambled to get to her feet as the beast rounded the corner. It was closer now and her adjusted eyesight could make out its shape.

Frozen

It looked like the silhouette of huge dog, if not a wolf. However, this creature had no fur and no skin - that Tara could see. It was like a pulsing black shadow. Its four limbs rippled and ebbed like smoke. Its body was the same wisping smog and was completely black, except for the blood red, glowing eyes.

It lunged with no warning, barring its onyx black teeth, in its gaping, crimson red mouth. It was on her in the blink of an eye.

Tara instinctively raised her arms to protect herself, unsure if she would be able to stop the smoke demon. Her hand touched something beneath the black swirling mist, though she did not know what. Then she screamed as teeth sunk into the flesh on her left arm.

The demon snarled and snapped at her arm, over and over. It's teeth drawing more blood and ripping tissue into ribbons.

Then it stopped.

"There you are," Stephanie simply stated.

Chapter 27

Tara would never have believed she would be this relieved to see Stephanie standing over her, while wielding a sword. Yet here she was, covered in her own blood, a granite black demon dead on top of her, as Stephanie smugly looked down upon her.

Stephanie enjoyed the hunt and the kill, Tara realised. This is what she was trained to do, what came naturally to her. It should unsettle her, but it didn't. Stephanie was a lot of things, but she would never kill an innocent.

Stephanie's hard exterior portrayed a cold personality at first, but Tara saw nothing except kindness now. In the last few days, Tara had learnt to see past that toughened barrier.

"Next time you decide to disappear, try not to pick a fight with a Shadow Hound." Stephanie grinned at her.

"I will bear that in mind!" Tara replied shortly. The hound may have appeared as light as gas, but in actuality it was heavy enough to crush Tara into the damp ground beneath her. Her unhealed back burned anew. Tara hoped she hadn't pulled any stitches. She didn't dare glance at her arm, the pain was excruciating, and she knew it was bad.

"Alistair, over here. I need your help!" Stephanie shouted.

Alistair approached from around a large tree, sword held out in front of him, ready to use. The essence blade wasn't glowing like it normally did, there was no light coming from it at all. Tara turned her head to look at Stephanie, who's sword also wasn't glowing.

"Your blades?" Tara managed to wheeze out.

"We can't let them light up the place now can we. It would let every creature in this god forsaken land know where we are," Stephanie explained as her and Alistair prepared to lift the Shadow Hound off her.

"How?" Tara questioned.

"We just..." Stephanie paused as her and Alistair heaved the animal from her. "... don't send our energy into them. Well, we actively stop it from trying to enter the blade. We didn't have enough time to teach you."

"More training when this is all over, I'm afraid," Alistair smiled at her. He knelt beside her and took a gentle grip on her elbow, being careful not to touch the horrific wound.

"Great!" Tara winced.

"We need to get this wrapped. Did you bring medical supplies?" Alistair turned to ask Stephanie, who is checking the parameter of the clearing they occupied.

"No, I think Samuel is carrying them," Stephanie explained.

"Then we need to find them and quick, or Tara is going to bleed out," Alistair concluded as he gave Tara a winced smile. He took the strap - that held his sword sheath like a belt - from around his waist and made a tourniquet on Tara's upper am.

Alistair laid Tara's arm across her chest, which almost had her crying out in pain, but she bit her lip as tears threatened to spill out from her eye lids.

"Then let's get back to the rendezvous point," Stephanie agreed, while she continued to pace around the clearing.

"I am going to carry you," Alistair told Tara.

"My legs work fine, thank you," Tara retorted back.

"I am aware," Alistair chuckled. "But you have lost a lot of blood and you are going to struggle to keep up. We need to travel fast."

Tara wasn't happy about it, but she nodded her agreement. How could she ever save Nick if she didn't survive?

Frozen

****

"What happened?" Mary practically yelled, as she spied their approach.

"Shadow Hound," Stephanie explained simply.

"Samuel, the medical supplies?" Mary asked frantically and Alistair laid Tara on the ground in front of her.

Samuel slung his backpack off his shoulders, rummaging through the bag before it hit the floor. He handed over the medical supplies and waited to help wherever he was needed.

"How bad is it?" Tara asked, though she wasn't sure she really wanted the answer. She could smell a metallic tang in the air.

"I have seen worse," Cain answered, trying to soothe. He took the space on the other side of her. Tara couldn't see where everyone else was, but she assumed that they were circling the area, in case of an attack.

"We need to take her back," Mary explained.

"No, we need to save Nick!" Tara pleaded.

"We will, but you are our priority right now," Cain stated.

"NO! Patch me up and we carry on! Please!" Tara nearly screamed.

"Okay, stay calm," Mary took a hold of Tara's arm. "The last thing we need is you getting worked up. I'll patch this up for now, but really you need a doctor."

Tara glanced down at her arm and instantly regretted it. She felt queasy immediately. The first thing she saw was blood, the second was ripped flesh and the third was white, the white of the bones in her arm.

"Don't look," Cain pleaded as he took his granddaughters face with both hands and turned her head gently to the side.

"This is going to hurt," Mary said before the all-encompassing burning sensation took over all of Tara's thoughts. It felt like liquid fire was poured over her arm.

Darkness crept into her vision, until everything went black.

****

"Tara? Tara?" A familiar voice beckoned her.

"Yes?" Tara answered, as she opened her eyes and took in the scene that was around her.

She knew that she was being carried instantly. She could feel the pounding of feet on the floor, her body bouncing slightly away from the body that held her with each step that they took.

Once her eyes had adjusted to the darkness and her mind lost some of the fogginess of sleep, she looked up to view Alistair's big eyes staring down at her.

"Finally!" He exclaimed to her. "You have been out for about an hour now. Mary managed to patch your arm up."

Tara lifted her arm to take a look. The pain threatened to overpower her again. Her arm was

Frozen

covered in an expertly wrapped bandage. A slight red tint showing through in patches.

"It will scar, I am afraid," Mary chirped in from behind her. Tara swung her head to the side and back and could see Mary keeping pace alongside Alistair.

"But I will be okay, I will still be able to use my arm?" Tara worried.

"I cannot tell you right now. When we return, we shall take you straight to Sandra and see what can be done," Mary looked at her with sympathetic smile.

"Thank you," Tara said sincerely, hoping that it would ease some of Mary's pain. Tara could visibly see Mary was on edge. She could feel it too. It couldn't be easy to discover you have a granddaughter, then have to patch up her arm and ignore your maternal instincts.

"We have been on the move for some time now," Samuel piped up. "If the shape of the land is anything to go by, we are coming upon the destination that we set."

"I think Samuel is right," Tara heard Stephanie agree from somewhere in front of her. Stephanie was pointing to something in the distance, and everyone came to a stop.

They were situated on a hill or ledge - Tara couldn't say which. In the distance, where Stephanie had pointed, Tara could see the faintest of blue light. It was hard to make out any details. The darkness that perpetuated this world didn't allow anyone to see much further than a few meters in front of them. The light was at a lower point than them, nestled into rock. It was possibly a cave, but Tara couldn't make out enough to guarantee it was.

"Now, what use would this world have for a source of light like that?" Stephanie questioned. "Unless of course, it was for something or someone that didn't belong here."

"You think Nick is there?" Tara asked pushing out of Alistair's arms and stumbling on the floor. Despite her clumsiness, she managed to keep upright.

"I don't know about Nick," Stephanie stated honestly. "I suspect that Jenifer is there though."

"Then we head for the light," Cain concluded.

"We will need to be more cautious from now on," Alistair warned.

"Alistair is right. The more light there is, the more Shadows there are," Mary expanded.

"Then what do we do?" Tara asked anxiously.

"We split into two groups," Samuel declared. "The Shadows will likely be in front of that area, where it is lighter. I suggest that we circle around this area and approach from the sides where we will be less visible."

"I agree," Stephanie established. "But why would we split up?"

"Terrain," Samuel simply stated and received an understanding nod from Stephanie.

"I still don't get it," Tara quizzingly looked at Samuel.

"We do not know for certain what lays on either side of where we are. It might not be possible to get around," Samuel explained. "If we split into groups, we then don't have to double back on ourselves. We'd have more of a chance of reaching Jenifer or Nick."

"I get it, but won't that make it more dangerous?" Tara questioned.

"There is a strength in numbers, yes," Samuel agreed. "But I believe that time is our enemy right now."

"We split into groups based on our strengths then," Stephanie answered.

"How do we decide teams?" Tara queried, not convinced with the idea. She could acknowledge that they were the experts though.

Chapter 28

It was decided one group would be - Samuel, Cain, and Tara. Leaving Mary, Alistair, and Stephanie in the second group. Tara was the weakest, not only because of her severe lack of training, but also due to her injury. Therefore, they'd placed her with the strongest warrior amongst them - Samuel.

It had taken the group sometime to decide who else to add to her group. The first thought was for Mary to join her granddaughter, especially as she had more knowledge on their current situation. However, Samuel knew enough about how to read the land for Tara's group to continue, without Mary's knowledge.

Frozen

They stayed at the ledge for some time, and they answered their grumbling stomachs. They knew there would be little time for such luxuries once they got moving again. In between bites, they discussed and determined the last member that would go with Tara.

"Maybe, it should be me that goes with Tara," Stephanie had said.

"I disagree, I think that each group needs to contain someone that knows Nick well enough. This is a mission to save him," Alistair had stated.

"Then it's between Cain and Alistair," Tara concluded.

"Both of which have very similar skill sets and both can be utilised by either team," Mary put plainly. "I would prefer Cain to go with our granddaughter."

"Cain goes with me and Tara," Samuel said. "Unless anyone has anything else to add?"

That was exactly how it ended up. They split the supplies of food, water, weapons, and medical supplies between them. Then everyone said their quick goodbyes. No one wanted to dwell on the fact, that they didn't know when or if they would next see each other.

Hours later, it left Tara trying to keep pace with Samuel, who led the way. They were to approach the cave from the east, doing a large enough arc to avoid the light.

It was hard for Tara to keep up, the wound from the Shadow Hound had left her drained of energy. Her head felt fuzzy and cloudy.

"Keep drinking the water. Fluids will help with the blood loss," Cain explained, caringly.

He'd been behind her the entire trek. Placing his hand on her shoulder encouragingly or giving her a hand when she needed to climb.

Samuel had taken on the role of leader and protector. Tara could see the concentration on his face. He was listening to every sound, watching every movement, and planning several steps ahead of where they were. Tara began to realise that he was much more than just a weapons master.

"How much further?" Tara asked.

"A bit," Samuel replied. Tara deciphered his true meaning - there was more than enough walking left in front of her. She fought down a moan. It wasn't about her. It was about saving Nick. She would walk greater distances, just to know that he was safe.

"How does Samuel know how to navigate somewhere he has never been?" Tara curiously asked Cain.

"I am not sure," Cain shrugged. "Ordinarily, I would have suggested that he has a good sense of direction and uses the stars to navigate."

"Except, that there are barely any stars to follow," she concluded.

"Precisely. It leaves me with the impression that he simply has a sense of where we need to go. He is probably using every tool and skill in his arsenal to head in the correct direction. Plus, Mary would have given

Frozen

him at least some idea on where we are heading and how to proceed."

Tara spent a brief moment admiring Samuel's abilities. Meanwhile with no skill, she put her every effort into taking one step after another, in what felt like an endless pursuit.

The blackness around them seemed to lighten as they trekked through the strange wilderness. Tara supposed that her eyes were adjusting to the continued night that enveloped them. Although, there seemed to be a constant appearance of fog.

She began to make out some of the plants and creatures they passed. They felt foreign and strange. Tara observed the changing wilderness, and it was like something described on a documentary about the Mariana Trench. Evolved to sustain themselves on the tiniest amounts of light, it gave them a peculiar look.

Though the more she thought about it, they hadn't adapted to live without light. They had in fact been made for the endless dark.

Plants had little to no leaves, but had large, thick, long roots. Roots that Cain had been helping her to climb over, for at least an hour. Tara supposed that all the nutrients the plants needed to grow, must come from the depths of the soil.

Insect looking creatures skurried and jumped around the roots, clearly at home in the tangle. They looked heavily armoured, dark in colour, and they were lighting fast. They were able to move at a such considerable pace, that Tara was only able to glance them as they escaped her trudging feet.

The strangeness didn't end there either. On earth, plants gave out so much energy that you could bask in it. Even taking a walk in the woods could elevate your mood, make you feel positive, and humble you.

Here, she could feel the plants trying to reach out and take her energy. If it hadn't of been for the lessons she had received back at the manor to guard and ground herself, she wouldn't be able to continue this already exhausting walk.

"The cave is over this ridge," Samuel finally declared. "We shall rest here for a short while."

Tara didn't respond. She sat down on the closest root that made a good perch. She was tired, sore, and frantic about getting Nick home.

"I am going to scout the edge of the cave," Samuel declared.

"If you haven't returned within ten minutes, then I shall come looking for you, Samuel," Cain told him.

Samuel nodded his head to Cain, dropped his bag next to Tara and disappeared into the starless night.

"He is braver than anyone I have ever met," Tara explained.

"Indeed," Cain let out a chuckle. "I think we would be hard pressed to find much that could scare Samuel. When you have faced as many adversaries as he, then you may appear braver than you are."

Frozen

"He seems to have no fears," Tara replied lowering her chin to her chest. "I am jealous of it."

"Bravery, my child, is not the absence of fear, but the ability to acknowledge that fear and continue regardless. It is to put aside your fears, in order to accomplish what needs to be done."

Tara had no immediate reply to Cain's profound point. She thought of all the bravery that she had seen. Nick's sacrifice, her mother sharing what scared her the most and every single Shifter who'd journeyed with her. She was surrounded by it.

"I will be brave for Nick," Tara said. It was aimed more to herself, but Cain replied, nonetheless.

"You are already brave, Tara. Not many would enter a world void of light to save someone. There are even fewer that would continue their mission after receiving such a wound," Cain bolstered and nodded towards her arm.

"You make me sound like the heroine of a novel," Tara laughed awkwardly.

"You are the heroine of your own story Tara. You always were," Cain smiled at her, and she smiled back.

"Coast is clear," Samuel stated moments later as he appeared from the gloom.

Chapter 29

The initial few meters of the cave were narrow like a corridor. Everyone had to duck, so that their heads wouldn't hit the ceiling but there was enough space width wise to fit the three of them next to each other. They chose however, to remain cautious and stayed in the formation they had used in the wilderness outside – Samuel front, Tara middle, Cain at the rear. Using tentatively light steps, the group progressed in a near silent manner. It would do no good to be found now.

After a few minutes of walking, it began to open into a large, spacious cavern. Tara was glad to stand upright again and began to scan the cave. Stalagmites and stalactites dominated the edges of the circular cave like fingers grabbing for the dark. An eerie turquoise

Frozen

light shone onto every damp surface - illuminating everything, except the outer reaches.

While pressed to the outside wall - just beyond the passage - Tara noticed the form of a crystal that appeared to be the source of the glow hanging from the domed ceiling above. One large, upside-down, tear drop shaped crystal was surrounded by varying sizes of smaller ones. It would have been beautiful, was it not for the situation they were in.

It was too quiet, far too quiet. No drops of water echoed. No animals scurried about their business. It was still, too still. Tara felt like they lurked into a predator's den.

Emanating from the crystal, was a perfect conical beam of light, which created a large ring on the floor below. Within the ring stood a large wooden frame. Lashed to it like an animal for slaughter - was Nick.

His head was lolloped forward. His hair crumpled. His wrists red raw from the rope bindings. His skin and clothes as dirty as the floor on which Tara stood. He looked completely beaten.

Tara barely recognised him. Her limbs started to move before she had time to register. A hand held her back. She looked over her shoulder. Samuel stood directly behind her with a finger to his lips. The statement was clear, they had entered the lion's den with no idea where the lioness was. They would approach with caution.

Tara itched with anticipation and worry. He was so close now and yet still, Nick was out of her reach. Her heart ached to go to him.

They made their way around the outside of the cave, using the larger stalagmites for cover. Their steps were soft and their breaths low. Stealth was the only thing that mattered in this moment. They followed the curved wall and therefore, they also circled Nick. He didn't move or stir once, almost like he was utilising the absence of Jenifer and the Shadows, to get a few moments peace.

They were parallel to Nick, when a section of the north wall, began to slide and grind. A pitch-black doorway was formed in the stone. There she was - Jenifer - strolling out like a queen of darkness, with a mass Shadows on her heels.

It was near impossible to make out how many followed her. They seemed to huddle together, morphing, and stretching into one larger Shadow.

While remaining behind the safety of a stalagmite, Tara watched them follow Jenifer like she was their pied piper. Well, until they got to the circle of light that the crystals beamed to the floor. It was like a charged force field to them and held them a short distance away.

Jenifer however, continued right up to Nick. Tara held her breath and tried to remain still as anger rushed over her like a wave on rock.

"She's still not here to rescue you?" Jenifer laughed. "Pity, I thought the fun might have begun."

Jenifer lifted Nick's head up by his chin, so that he looked directly at her, "I can see that your hope of rescue is gone. Given up already? I thought you were stronger than this."

Frozen

"I never wanted rescuing," Nick growled, not from anger Tara noticed, but presumably from thirst. Tara danced from foot to foot, itching to run to him.

"Ever the sacrificial lamb, I see," Jenifer said snidely. "Well, it matters not. Tara and her band of misfits will be on their way, I am sure. You may be willing to sacrifice yourself, but something makes me think that they won't allow it. They still believe that 'good trumps evil.' What a notion!"

Nick didn't reply or acknowledge Jenifer's ramblings. Jenifer didn't seem to mind, and she continued rambling.

"It's an exciting time Nick. Once we have opened the potential of the orb, me and my friends will be able to do unspeakable things. I have spent too long in the shadows. Ha! Excuse the bad pun," Jenifer smirked. "I have had enough of sharing my abilities for 'the collective good'.

"Why limit people to the average when we could be something extraordinary! I was not born into this immortal life to be nothing but average. I was meant to be something bigger."

"Like leader of the Shadows?" Nick snorted.

"They are a means to an end Nick, and watch your tongue! I am still your elder," Jenifer jabbed sternly.

"You gave up that right over 100 years ago, when you plotted against your own kind and stole from them," Nick retorted.

"Shut your mouth!" Jenifer shouted as she slapped him. The sound vibrating off the curved cave walls. "You know nothing of what I have endured. The sacrifices I have made to better our people."

Tara's need to run to Nick flared. She didn't know how much longer she could hold herself back. She needed to get him out of this forsaken place.

"To better yourself you mean," Nick concluded, then spat - what could only be blood - on to the floor.

"Oh, you clever boy!" Jenifer cackled. "You attempt to let my anger get the best of me. You think that if I kill you now, then it will all be done with. Fear not Nicolas. I have better control than that."

Jenifer took something from the table that was located at the edge of the light. She spun around, her gaze landing upon him. "Rest now sweet Nick. Our girl will be here soon enough."

Jenifer left the ring of light. As she did the Shadows were on her within seconds. Following her heels like obedient hounds.

"Now?" Tara asked Samuel.

"Slowly," he mouthed back to her.

Tara took her first apprehensive step towards him. When nothing happened and Samuel did not recall her, she took another. Soon she was side stepping stalagmites with speed, more anxious than ever to get to Nick. Her breathing had quickened, and heart thundered in her rib cage, like the pounding of hooves.

It wasn't until she got to the edge of the light, that Tara slowed down. She cautiously placed her foot inside the beam of light and waited. She wasn't sure what she had expected, but she hadn't come this far, just to set off some form of other-worldly alarm. One that might notify Jenifer of their arrival.

Frozen

When nothing happened, she fully stepped into the bright beam. Her shadow disappeared completely underneath her, only viewable as she removed her feet from the ground below her.

"Nick?" Tara whispered when she reached him. She wanted to touch him, to make sure that he was there, but it was clear that placing her hands on him would do nothing but cause him pain. He was in a worse shape that she had thought.

"Nick, it's me," she announced quietly. He did nothing to acknowledge her. While she gave him a brief pause to respond, she took the chance to check him over. His face was badly bruised. Different varying colours covered him. It was like a patch work of purple, green and yellow. All at various levels of healing.

His wrists were so raw, that it almost looked like his body couldn't heal them anymore. The gashes looked angry, and the rope was scabbed with old blood. Tara couldn't help but feel guilty, they should have got here sooner.

"Nick, please?" Tara pleaded for a response. She reached out to place a very gentle hand on his hollow cheeks. He looked so withdrawn. The clothes that had fit him well, now hung from him. Had he had any food in the time it had taken them to get here?

"I wish I got to see you one last time," Nick whispered hoarsely. Tara broke at his statement and tears began to flow like waterfalls down her cheeks. He didn't believe that she was there.

Samuel and Cain had since caught up to her. Samuel stood on the inside of the light but faced outwardly. Guarding the doorway that Jenifer had used before.

Cain quickly observed the table that Jenifer had taken papers from. He pocketed some of them and came over to Nick.

"He doesn't think we are here. Help him, please," Tara begged. Tara went for the ropes around Nick's wrists.

"No Tara," Cain said, placing his hand on hers. "His cuts are raw. If we remove them, it will cause him great pain to separate the ropes from his skin. The scabs have bonded him to the rope."

Tara's next question was answered by Cain removing a knife from his belt and passing it to Tara. "You will have to cut them carefully, above his wrists. I will take his weight."

Tara waited for Cain to lift him onto his back slightly and then began to saw at the rope, ignoring the pain that shot through her arm. It was thick braided rope, but the knife was sharp. She made quick work of it and before she had time to register, Nick's arm dropped to Cain's side.

Nick winced. He slowly became aware of what was happening. "No!" He tried to shout.

"Shhh! It's going to be okay," Tara tried to soothe him and then moved around him to start work on the next binding.

"You have to leave! Now! You can't be here!" Nick was distraught, but had no energy to shout or to move.

"Quickly, Tara, there isn't much time!" Samuel hastened.

Frozen

Tara took hold of Nick's arm, as she cut through the last of the rope and placed it gently over Cain's shoulder.

"TARA! RUN!" Samuel shouted as the sound of an essence blade scrapped against a sheath. Its light scattered over the surfaces around him. Apparently, now was the kind of time to fill the blades with light.

"Well, well, well... exactly as I planned Nick. I told you she was predictable," Jenifer's voice came from the darkness.

Chapter 30

Chaos.

That was all it could be described as. Complete chaos. Jenifer stepped into the cave from another hidden door. It was located a few meters across from where Samuel had been guarding. Her minions were again on her heels. She was carrying a small wooden box in her arms.

The Shadows expanded and grew, until every edge of the light was surrounded by their riving darkness. Leaving them with nowhere to escape.

Throughout the commotion, Samuel had strategically placed himself between Jenifer and their group. His intentions were clear – Jenifer was to go through him first.

Frozen

"Well, I would have expected Samuel to be here. The rebel that he is, but you Cain?" Jenifer tried to question him, ignoring Samuel. "This is a development."

Cain gave no answer and Jenifer began to prowl the darkened edge, then finally took a step into the light. Her smile was cruel and expectant. Jenifer was enjoying this, Tara realised. The toying and the game.

"I see that you aren't going to explain how you ended up being here then, Cain," she sardonically aimed at Cain. He gave her no explanation but scowled at her. "Nothing to say at all? How very boring of you - as always.

"You were fun once Cain. Many a moon ago, you, me, and Mary were the pinnacle of the Shifters. We used our powers to take down those that would harm us and protect those that were defenceless. We worked year after year, lost friend after friend and still our foes kept coming.

"Do you know what I came to realise?" Jenifer paused, waiting for a response that would never come. "Where was the gratitude? Where was the prize? Where was the reward?

"Well, I will tell you... there never was one!" Jenifer nearly shouted. Her anger was getting the better of her and she set to pacing back and forth.

Tara looked away from her and tried to find a way for them to get out. Everywhere that she looked there were Shadows. How were they to get past so many?

"I have taken my own reward. The reward that I have earned. The reward that is my right to have. I just need to unlock it," Jenifer smiled crookedly at Tara.

"I won't help you," Tara retorted.

"You will, whether you want to or not," Jenifer said confidently. "I may only have access to a fraction of the Shifter's powers – Thanks to the crystal above you – but do not be mistaken, Tara Kingley. I have the power to make you comply."

Tara took notice of the crystal necklace that clearly hung around Jenifer's neck. It had the same eerie, turquoise glow that the crystal above them had. It was a roughly cut, wand shaped crystal that was attached to a simple chain around her neck. It lay just below her collar bone and cast a mysterious light up under her chin.

"A hundred years I have been waiting for this," Jenifer explained opening the box in her arms. Immediately, a second light source bounced off the objects around her. It was a warmer and softer glow. Jenifer placed her hand inside the box and pulled out a spherical object - which Tara could only describe as an orb.

"This is the Shifters power," she announced. "Contained in another, exceedingly rare crystal. It was the only way I could collect it. It took me centuries to find the right material. Not that it is important right now. I was under the impression that once it was collected, I would be able to access what was inside. Thus, I was fooled and those that fooled me, paid a heavy price."

The implications were obvious enough to Tara – she had killed them, mercilessly. Just how she would with Tara, Nick, Samuel, and Cain. She wished for the other group to reach them and yet hoped they didn't.

Frozen

Tara dropped her mental wall and reached as far as she could, seeing if she could hear them. All she heard was white noise. Something was wrong, very wrong and they needed to get out of here.

"Somehow, Tara Kingley, you are to unlock this. This is what you were born to do," Jenifer smirked at her.

Click

Suddenly, Tara was pulled forward from the rest of the group. She tried to scamper back, but she couldn't move her limbs. She could hear Nick shouting her name, the sound echoing off the cave walls.

Samuel moved – his light filled blade drawn in front of him - ready to protect her. Then he just came to a stop and lowered the sword.

"Ah, yes. Did I forget to explain. You see the crystal above you?" Jenifer asked rhetorically. "The crystals light will dampen your powers. Basically, while you are inside its light you can't use your abilities.

"Hence, why your good little soldier, now doesn't know what to do. Oh, how pathetic you look now, Sam," Jenifer teased, glancing at him, and heading to Tara.

What Jenifer hadn't noticed, was that Samuel was now inching to the edge of the light. He may not be able to fight as well within the light, but he was more than capable outside of it. Tara was unsure what he was waiting for, as he paused at the edge and never left the circle.

"Now Tara darling, I am sure that you are questioning why I can use my powers," Jenifer smiled up at her. It was still hard to look into the eyes of this young girl and see an enemy in the form of a child.

"Come now, I am sure that you have guessed," Jenifer almost laughed at her.

Still unable to move Tara simply glanced to the crystal that was around Jenifer's neck. When she looked back into Jenifer's eyes, she could she the twisted fun that she was having by toying with them. Maybe there was more to her being a youngster than just her appearance.

"Finally!" Jenifer exasperated dramatically. "One of you actually has some sense and cleverness. She is younger than all of you and has double the wit.

"You are right of course. The crystal around my neck allows me to use my abilities. More accurately it channels it through the light around us. You see, your powers are still there, it just can't travel through the crystal's own capabilities. When I wear this, it believes my own powers are its own. It is why I chose this location."

Click

Jenifer flounced toward her as Tara's body was forced to kneel. She took no care with her, and Tara winced as she hit the floor. Her knees stung. Her skin splitting on the rough unhewn stones.

"Now, unlock it," Jenifer instructed.

The orb was held directly in front of her, and she could see more of it now. It was covered in frost like it was frozen - like the Shifters powers, she supposed. The icy forms danced in the light that emanated from the glass-like sphere. Inside it swirled and eddied like a liquid gold. It shone and sparkled with

Frozen

a milky, white pearlescence on its surface. The liquid didn't move based on Jenifer's movements, but on its own accord. It was like it was trying to find its own way out.

"No," Tara finally responded.

"You will open this girl or your boyfriend's life will be forfeit," Jenifer scowled. She took Tara's hand and placed it on top of the orb.

It was not cold to the touch, like Tara had expected. The fractured veins of frost gave it a texture she could feel underneath her fingertips.

"OPEN IT!" Jenifer demanded.

"I don't know how," Tara explained.

"Then what use are you as a Key!" Jenifer shouted and then slapped Tara with a force that sent her falling to the floor. How this tiny girl had that kind of strength Tara couldn't explain.

Click

Nick moved from Cain's back and was thrown to the floor beside her. He weakly held himself up on his elbow and stretched his hand out to her. Suddenly he stopped. His face scrunched with comprehension - he couldn't send her away this time.

Tara reached out to him and placed her hand upon his. She looked into those beautiful eyes and wished things had been different. That she had been able to save them all. Maybe she wasn't the Key after all.

"Unlock it!" Jenifer shrieked. She clicked again and Nick helplessly threw his bound hands to his own throat - powerless to resist her unspoken instruction.

"STOP IT! PLEASE! I don't know how to unlock it," Tara pleaded, tears streamed her face once more.

Nick scratched at his own throat, trying to remove a threat that he couldn't see. Tara reached out to him. She couldn't help. She couldn't stop her. She couldn't save him. What use was she?

"Just stop! I will do it!" Tara bluffed and hoped Jenifer didn't see it.

"That's more like it," Jenifer smiled and released Nick.

Tara stood and walked the few steps to Jenifer. She glanced at each of her companions as she did. Her long-lost grandfather looked pained and motionless. She realised that Jenifer had pinned him still. Samuel still stood toeing the line near the edge of the light. Nick was the one she looked at last, and her eyes lingered upon. He looked so broken and beaten, she knew that she never wanted him to know pain like this ever again.

"Last chance Tara," Jenifer warned.

Tara placed her right hand upon the orb in Jenifer's outstretched hand. She felt for the energy inside. It called to her. Inviting her into it, but she couldn't access it through the casing.

With her other hand, she swiftly grabbed Jenifer's Crystal and ripped it from her throat. She threw it to the floor and brought her foot down on it as hard as she could. It shattered as easily as glass.

Jenifer screamed her outrage.

Tara heard other sounds filling the cave. The sounds of fighting distantly behind her. She saw Samuel moving around the edge of the circle behind Jenifer,

Frozen

sword illuminated. Shadows writhed against the wall of light.

Then she felt nothing but pain.

Chapter 31

Tara instantly felt cold. Her vision began to blur at the edges.

"NOOO!" Nick screamed and ran to her.

"NOW LOOK WHAT YOU MADE ME DO!" Jenifer hurled at Tara.

Tara's hand went instinctively to her stomach — to the place where the pain was growing. Her hands touched upon Jenifer's clasped hands. Tara looked down.

A metal handle was protruding from the end of Jenifer's fist. The handle of a dagger. The blade hidden within Tara's own flesh. She could make out a faint light coming from her wound, Jenifer had used an essence dagger.

The pain took over. Her body collapsed to the floor once more. The second shock to her knees went unnoticed, as the blade was pulled from her body, slick with her own blood.

Jenifer rounded on Nick as he approached. His weary body finally taking flight.

Tara took in his beautiful face. The fullness of his lips, his hazel eyes, and the warming glow that encompassed it. She was glad that he would be the last thing she saw before death claimed her as his own.

A tear rolled down her face, she blinked it away. Another came, but she didn't blink again.

Death had come.

****

Nick hurled himself at Jenifer. Tara had removed her power when she destroyed Jenifer's crystal. Leaving her nothing but a helpless child.

She was, however, still armed and had hundreds of years' worth of fighting knowledge over Nick. This made him cautious but didn't stop him from attacking.

"NICK!" Cain shouted finally having the ability to move. He threw his second sword to Nick. He jumped slightly to catch it with his left hand. The blade lighting up again on contact. Uncomfortable as it was in the wrong hand, a blade was a blade.

Jenifer saw the oncoming attack. She dropped her dagger and slipped the orb inside the box in her left hand. She removed her essence blade from its sheath with her right hand. The blade was much smaller than Nick's but glowed just as brightly.

Jenifer countered Nick's approaching attack with a sidestep, trying to take his unprotected side. Noticing her gentle and precise movements, Nick aimed to land his blow wide, hitting the floor while spinning on his feet to come face to face with Jenifer, giving him the chance to change the essence blade to his most dominant hand. His body was screaming at him, it was weak and injured, but he could not give up, not while Tara lay helpless.

"Are you sure you want to do this, Nick?" Jenifer smirked, but her words were not filled with the confidence she had earlier. She was on the defence now and Nick had seen it.

He lunged. He may have been bigger and stronger than Jenifer, but every move he made she met or counteracted. Knowing her own weaknesses and how to defend them. Neither was getting the upper hand as sword clashed against swords – the cave ringing like bells.

Cain joined Samuel at the edge of the light. Taking down as many of the Shadows as possible. They were getting over run, but it was the only way that any of them would be able to leave this pit of hell.

Samuel moved with such swiftness that it was like watching a dancer perform in a national ballet. His

Frozen

feet were so light you could barely hear them move. His posture shaped with strong determination. He was as swift and as agile as a hummingbird. He struck down his foe's again and again with a precision that Cain would never have.

Cain fought and fought with everything that he had in him, but was distracted by the safety of his granddaughter. He couldn't see her face, but he knew that her time would be running out. This battle needed to end fast.

Cain swung at a Shadow, but his blade passed through the creature and bounced off a longer stalactite. The rock vibrated and must have loosened some of the crystal above. A reasonably large chunk fell to the floor and shattered – sending shards in all directions. Cain noticed that the circle of light shrunk slightly. He made note not to hit any structures. Nick needed that light to take down Jenifer, while she had no back up.

Cain took a glance towards Nick and Jenifer. Nick was holding his own. Although, he wasn't getting anywhere near bringing her down. He needed Cain's help. He would have to leave Samuel to take the Shadows on his own.

Where are you, Mary?

Nick took another swing at Jenifer. She parried the blow. Nick took a step back. The length of Jenifer's essence blade meant she had to move in closer. He kept as much distance as he could between each attack. Her small child-like body would never have been able to manage a lengthy sword. Her unnatural abilities may have given her the strength to wield a larger sword, but her height hindered her ability to keep a sword of such length at her waist.

"This is fruitless, Nick," Jenifer admitted, still tightly grasping the box. "I have all the skill where you have all the muscle. My skill will find your weakness eventually. Concede now before you end up like your beloved."

It was an attempt to distract him and to give him doubt. Nick, however, was wiser than to take her poisoned speech. Tara needed him and the only way that he would be able to help her was to go through Jenifer first.

Hold on Tara. He directed his thoughts loudly toward her. He knew it was a fruitless endeavour for the crystal above would silence him, but it didn't stop him from hoping.

Nick went in for the attack again when he paused. The sound of more swing swords echoed through the narrow entrance to the cave. Jenifer's fear-stricken face said it all.

The cavalry had arrived.

****

Cain knew as soon as the sounds echoed off the curved walls, that his wife had arrived. He also knew that nothing would stop her from fighting her way to her granddaughter.

Frozen

Knowing that Stephanie, Alistair, and Samuel could hold off the Shadows on their own – Cain brought down his glowing blade on his current advisory.

He jumped into the light of the crystal and aimed for Jenifer. Never had he been so fuelled by hatred.

The stalemate was over.

The Jenifer's advantage had now become her downfall. Once the necklace was removed, she lost her power over them, but she had forsaken more than that.

The very space she used to remove the Shifters powers, was also her own isolated island. Where Nick had support from his fellow party, Jenifer had secluded herself from her dark vile servants. Simply, she had no back up.

Jenifer stared down her opponents, worry creasing her young forehead. While her eyes darted between her two foes, she took every opportunity available to search the situation for a viable exit.

She found one.

While she was stranded in the middle of the light she was irrevocably cornered. However, if she left the light she would be in a sea of her followers.

"You cannot escape this fate, Jenifer," Nick hissed at her. She took a step backwards. "You have doomed yourself with your greed for power."

"Oh, sweet Nick," Jenifer leered. "You think that you will win this because you are on the "good" side! You are naiver than I gave you credit for."

"It is you that is naive," Nick retorted. "You think that you can take our power, that you can take a loved one from us, and think that we will simply give up? No Jenifer. All you have accomplished is to unite us more. To drive us to protect the ones we love."

"Love?" Jenifer laughed taking another step, her foot reaching the edge of the ring of light. "Love will give you nothing!"

"Love gives us everything. Love gives us something to fight for together!" Nick cried.

"Where has that love got you N..." Jenifer stumbled.

"Love gives us hope," Mary whispered into Jenifer's ear.

Jenifer's gazed with horror at her chest. She glanced up to stare death in the face, Nick's face as he swung his blade cleanly. Blood sprayed anything nearby.

Jenifer's head rolled and lodged itself between two stalagmites. Her body fell with a thud to the floor. Her blood drenching her dress and then the floor beneath her.

The orbs box fell from her grasp and hit the floor. The boxes clasp failed with the impact. The lid opened exposing the orb, as it bounced back into the air.

Nick lunged to reach it. He barely made it. His hand touched on the top of the orb, but its gravitational fall was not stopped entirely.

The orb cracked as it hit the floor.

Frozen

Nick, Cain, and Mary gasped with horror. Mary noticed a small wisp of light escaped through the fissure. It curled its way up Nick's exposed arm. As it did, it sunk beneath his skin.

Nick hadn't seen the wisp. It would have been the least of his concerns. It didn't seem to of affected him. He stood and placed the orb into Mary's blood drenched hands.

He turned towards Tara's body.

Chapter 32

Nick darted to where Tara lay crumpled on the floor. He dropped his sword to the ground, the light instantly dying, and a clattering echo was sent thundering through the cave. Nick threw himself onto the gritty floor, skin ripping from his legs. He numbly grasps for her cold hands, silently screaming her name – his thoughts trying to call her back to him. His hands find their way to her already paling face.

Nick could barely stand to look and yet he couldn't bring himself to look away from her ashen skin. He already knew what her vacant expression meant. His emotions crashed over him like a violent stormy sea. He screamed.

Frozen

She couldn't be gone, not after all this time he'd had without her. How cruel fate was to give him this sweet, delicate girl for only a passing moment of his life and then to strip him of her presence.

Nick lent over her huddled body to bring his arms around her lifeless form and caringly lift her to his chest, wishing that the warmth of his body would warm hers. He wanted to pour his entire life force into her. He would give everything just to bring her back. He lowered his face into the gap between her neck and shoulder, as tears ran down his face and streamed onto her torn and dirty top.

Nick held her even closer. He loved her. Truly loved her, but it hadn't been enough. He spilt all the love he had within him into her lifeless form. It had always belonged to her, he had no need of it without her, she could take it with her.

He wished that he could join her, to be with her in whatever came next. He was hers, just and she had been his.

He softened his grip upon her to look into her eyes. Eyes that he would never forget.

"I love you," he whispered to her softly. He placed his right hand over her heart, closed his eyes and repeated his words.

"I love you," it came from deep within his being.

"I love you," he whispered again as his hand warmed, and he felt a stir, a fluttering under his palm.

The fluttering came again. He dismissed the sensation and the hope he felt with it.

But then it came again.

Thud... Thud... Thud.

It grew faster and began a rhythm that was familiar to him.

It can't be, he thought to himself.

Tara's heart thundered and then her lungs filled with air as she gasped.

"Nick?" She wheezed. Her brilliant blue eyes stared up at him. Her cheeks beginning to turn from storm grey to a rose blush. He had never seen anything so beautiful.

"Tara!" Nick exclaimed and pulled her close again.

"I love you, Nick." she ardently replied. His heart skipped a beat.

****

After Jenifer's fall, the Shadows didn't stick around. Stephanie, Alistair, and Samuel had fought off any of the remaining beasts. They hadn't been privy to everything that had happened with Tara, but it hadn't been long until Cain had explained what had happened – or at least everything he had understood.

Tara's sudden and unnatural return made no sense to any of them. One doesn't simply come back from the dead because their loved one wills it. Do they?

Cain approached Mary who was very quietly sorting through things that Jenifer had left on the table.

Frozen

Many things were left unanswered and some of these documents may give them more insight.

"Are you alright?" Cain asked his wife and he put his arms around her from behind. Embracing her middle.

"We lost our granddaughter today," Mary stated as an explanation.

"Then by some miracle we got her back."

"It wasn't a miracle, Cain. I saw what happened," Mary confessed.

"What do you mean?" Tara questioned. She'd moved closer to them with the aid of Nick.

Mary spun around quickly, not having expected Tara to be there. Mary's face warmed as she beheld her granddaughter. She reached her hand out and took Tara's in hers.

"While you were..." Mary paused trying to find the right word, "...out, Nick and I took down Jenifer."

Tara looked over to where Jenifer's head was suspended between two stalagmites. It was clear the first time she spotted the dead eyes staring from the perched head, that she was never coming back.

"The orb box, that she was still holding fell from her hands. The box took most of the impact, but the orb came free," Mary explained.

"But I caught it," Nick told Tara.

"Yes, but some damage was done to the orb," Mary announced as she turned to the table behind her and removed the orb from its box.

She turned the orb over to reveal a small crack. It was less than an inch across, but it was there.

"Nick did manage to catch it and if he hadn't, I believe that we would have lost the Shifters abilities along with it," Mary concluded.

"I don't understand. What has this got to do with Tara coming back?" Cain queried.

"When the orb hit the floor and the crack appeared. Something came through. I believe there was a temporary moment where the crystal separated slightly to allow something through. It then must have forced itself back together somehow, as nothing is now coming out," Mary continued.

"What came out?" Tara quizzed. Stephanie, Alistair, and Samuel had now come closer, having overheard the conversation.

"I cannot answer that," Mary sighed. "There is a lot about all this that we are unable to answer right now. We are still unaware of what this orb is made off and how taking our light in the first place took our abilities. Once we are back at the mansion, I will begin research. Starting with everything that Jenifer has left behind."

"You have a theory though?" Cain presumed.

Marry nodded. "Whatever came from inside this orb headed straight for Nick. It could have gone anywhere, but it chose to go to you."

"What?" Nick said shocked.

"When you had hold of the orb a tendril of the light within, went up your arm and then beneath your skin," Mary described what she'd witnessed.

Frozen

"What will it do to him?" Tara asked anxiously.

"I believe, nothing harmful." Mary stated. "We know that this orb contains the Shifters powers. Like calls to like. I believe that as soon as it was free it went home. It took the fast route available."

"Because Nick was the closest Shifter," Stephanie concluded.

"Precisely Stephanie. I think that some of the Shifter's power entered your body and then you used that power with love to restore one of our own. I cannot explain to you how it worked, just that it did."

"Then why don't we break the orb and let the power free?" Stephanie asked.

"There are thousands of Shapeshifters powers within this orb. If we were to break it - and it takes the path to the closest source of Shifter – we would be exposed to more power than a body could manage. That is why Jenifer never did it."

"Then we call a gathering and expose many of us at the same time," Alistair suggested.

"Same problem," Samuel concluded.

"Exactly, Sam. We do not know if it would head for one source or spread out evenly amongst us. It could be a slaughter," Mary sighed.

"Then what do we do?" Tara asked.

"We take all this back to the mansion. We research and find a way. We have our power back and the Key. All we need to do now is discover how to unlock it," Mary assumed.

"Then let's head home," Tara announced.

S. M. Clair

Frozen

Chapter 33

Mary had done the best that she could, while they were still in the Shadow-world, with the gaping wound Jenifer had inflicted on Tara. She had washed it with some of their drinking water and bound it with the meagre medical supplies they took with them. It had been nearly as painful – if not more painful- than receiving the wound in the first place. Tara had screamed and potentially caused Cain's comforting hand irreparable damage. Mary had given her some painkillers, but whatever she had given her was not strong enough by far.

Whatever Nick had done with the sliver of light from the orb, had saved her internal organs and saved her life. However, the wound was open and required stitches. Mary had explained to Tara that she might require internal ones and decided that it would be best not to seal the wound up until Sandra could see to it.

Tara hadn't fared well for her first battle. She had taken a Shadow Hound to her arm and a revenge-filled Shifter had taken a dagger to her torso. Still, she was glad to have Nick back safe and sound.

Sandra was, however, more than horrified when she saw the damage after their return.

"You should be dead!" Sandra yelled, as she undid the bandages from around Tara's midriff.

"This arm is a terrible mess, but this..." Sandra paused to wave her hand above Tara. Tara wasn't sure if she was referring to her wound or Tara in general, but Tara didn't want to know how badly she looked right now. "...It should have killed you."

Tara had given Sandra no explanation. She was too weary, wearier than she had ever felt. Sandra didn't probe her for answers and Tara supposed that she would get her answers once the Elders had told everyone of the events in the Shadow-world.

Tara was taken in front of the Elders immediately after they had come back to their world. Nick had tried to convince her that she needed to be treated first, but Tara wanted it over and done with.

****

Frozen

"You mean to tell me that you brought her back from death with power from in this orb?" Adam asked for clarification. "Our power?"

"Yes," Nick replied simply.

"How?" He questioned, shock emanating from him.

It was Mary that answered, "We are not entirely sure. This is all going to take time to dissect."

She was stood next to Tara in front of the other remaining Elders. They had been questioned about everything that happened in the Shadow-world and the events leading up to it. Tara had a suspicion that Mary and Cain may be in trouble for going against the Council's wishes. Even though it had meant retrieving Nick and the orb.

"We have the orb, Jenifer's research, and we have the Key," Cain interjected. "It will take time but there is every hope that we can understand this, that we can still release our powers from it."

"Tara," Dorothea addressed her, the cracked orb sat in front of her on a scrap of fabric. "You have retrieved the orb, but I fear that is just the beginning. The Prophecy states that you will restore our power, not just bring it back. I hate to ask this of you, nonetheless, are you willing to continue to work with the Shifters to find a way to undo what Jenifer did? To join us?"

Tara paused. It was a simple question to answer, and she already knew what her response would be, but she took a moment.

The pain in her stomach was slowly taking her entire attention. She has already lost Nick, travelled to an alternate dimension, been bitten by a savage beast, stabbed, and learned to fight – with a sword!

She took in all the faces around the room. Not the Elders sat on their cold stone chairs, but to the people that stood with her, the people united with her.

She looked to Stephanie with her aloofness. She was stood toward the exit lent against a wall twirling her daggers. Stephanie simply shrugged at Tara. Tara wondered if that hard shell ever cracked, and she wanted to be there to see it. The thought made Tara smile.

She looked to Samuel with his ever-calm demeanour. Stood erect as ever, next to Stephanie and Alistair. She wondered if anything could ever phase this mighty warrior.

She looked to Alistair with his ever-smiling face. That smile alone let her know that she would always have a friendship with her very own gentle giant.

She looked to Catherine who was sat feebly in a chair. They still didn't know what Jenifer had given her, but Tara was glad that her teacher and friend was on the mend. Her ever bright inner light shined with so much compassion and hope.

She looked to her Grandparents. Cain waiting ever patiently while Mary itched to know if her Granddaughter would be staying. Tara at least knew where she got her impatience from and hoped that one day, she would learn to have Cain's patience.

Then finally she looked to Nick, her Nick.

Frozen

No matter what you chose, I will support your decision.

Tara turned to Dorothea. With a steadying breath she announced, "There is nowhere I would rather be."

Tara had found a home here with her friends. *No,* Tara corrected, with her family. She had found somewhere she fitted in and felt a sense of belonging. Somewhere that she could make a difference. If this wasn't where she was meant to be, she had no idea where was.

"Thank you, Tara," Dorothea replied gratefully. The entire room seemed to take a moment. *Were all of them that scared she would have chosen to leave?*

"Now, if it is okay with the rest of the Council, I am taking my granddaughter to Sandra," Mary stated, but she didn't wait for a response before guiding Tara to the door.

I'm so proud of you, Mary shared as she took some of Tara's weight. Tara hadn't realised she had felt so tired.

****

Nick had come with her to the hospital wing. He had perched himself on the bed next to Tara's, worry etched into his features for her entire examination. He looked exhausted.

"We are safe now Nick. Why don't you get some rest?" Tara suggested.

"I will need privacy Nick," Sandra added. "She needs stitches."

"Can I have a moment with her please?" Nick asked solemnly.

"I will fetch what I need," Sandra gave as an explanation as she covered Tara's wound. "I will put Cain and Mary's minds at rest while I'm gone too."

Nick gave Sandra a warm smile in response, but when he turned to Tara there was so much pain in his eyes.

"What's wrong Nick?" Tara enquired.

"There was something that I kept from you," he began the moment Sandra had left the room. "Something that I couldn't explain before now."

Nick didn't continue his explanation. He just sat there quietly for what felt like hours to Tara.

"What is it?" Tara eventually prompted.

"The Prophecy it states…" Nick hesitated.

"It this about how you knew I was the Key?" Tara guessed. Nick only nodded.

"Surely, its not that bad?" Tara asked, although she had to admit that she was worried. He had never seemed so anxious to talk to her. Hesitant, that he had been, but this was different. She could see it on his face even though he wasn't looking at her. She recognised his fear of voicing his next words, and their potential consequences.

"It states…" Nick began after another pause. "…that the person who delivers the Prophecy would find the Key."

Frozen

"You already told me this." Tara said nervously.

"I know," Nick took a steadying breath and then everything he wanted to say tumbled out. "What I didn't tell you was how I would know. I knew straight away. I knew the moment that I saw you and that's when the deceptions started.

"I only went to your school because I knew you were there. Catherine only knew that you needed to be saved because I asked her to keep an eye on you. I knew where you would be and how to bump into you when you weren't at school, because I had watched you for months. I had to be sure. I could not bring the horrors of my world into yours without good reason. You seemed so happy, and I didn't want to ruin that."

"You stalked me?" Tara snapped.

"Yes, if you want to label it," Nick sighed and finally looked at her. "Tara, please understand that I did none of this without thinking of what it would mean for you. You have been my priority from the moment I knew. I needed to be sure. Surer than I have been about anything."

Nick stood up from the bed. Tara saw him wince, but barely. She wanted to take his pain away, no matter his past actions. Maybe what he had done was not right, but he had to have done them for good reasons.

He moved to sit on the edge of her bed but slowly enough that she could refuse. Did he really think so little of himself to believe that she wouldn't want him near her?

"What did the prophecy say Nick?" Tara questioned.

"It states that I would find the Key. That I would know because they would be the first person that I would love, truly love."

"Oh Nick," Tara breathed, some tension leaving her. She had expected something worse. Then it began to dawn on her. The implications of what he was tell her.

"Oh," Tara let out.

"Please say something more than 'oh'," Nick pleaded.

"You have been in love with me this entire time? You have been trying to see if I could love you? Have you been trying to seduce me into loving you? How far does this go Nick? Do I even know the real you? Is this why you haven't had a relationship before?" Tara began to spiral, began to question everything. She shifted in the bed, the need to move stopped by the sharp pain in her gut.

"Tara. Breathe." Nick took a deep breath, encouraging her to replicate. She took one, but only as deeply as her wound would let her.

"Yes, I have been in love with you from the start. I selfishly wanted your love in return, but I did not press you to, I only hoped. I have told you nothing but the truth. I hid my feelings from you and that is all. This is why I have stayed away from relationships, I could not risk hurting anyone. I had to be certain before I brought anyone into this world. Into this mess. If I had brought someone into this and I was wrong, that could never be taken back."

Tara was dumb founded. *He had been in love with me from the start?*

"But you explained to me that you had to be sure I was the Key?" Tara quizzed.

"I already knew. I just didn't want to subject the one that I love to the darkness of my world. I did not think that I was worthy of you," Nick admitted. "The more that I got to know you, the less that I wanted you to be the one that I loved. This isn't what I wanted for you."

"Nick, do you not see?" Tara asked rhetorically. "You sacrificed your own happiness to protect me. You continually try to protect me. Do you not see that your actions only proved that I am the Key? That you truly love me, that you are worthy of me."

"But look where me loving you has brought you Tara?" Nick said, as a tear rolled down his cheek. "You died. I lost you completely. The moment you died was my breaking. If you had not come back to me, I do not know what I would have done."

"I did come back Nick. I am right here," Tara tried reaching for his hand to comfort him. Her tears began to fall. "You cannot force love. My love for you is of my own creation. I made my choices, and you cannot protect me from them."

"No, I can't, but can you forgive me for my deceptions?" Nick asked, as he took her outstretched hand.

"There is nothing to forgive you for. You have been battling between your love for me and the love of your people. How can I be angry with someone so selfless?" Tara explained.

"I love you, Tara. I have loved you from the first moment I saw you," Nick declared.

"I love you too." Tara returned as Nick lent over and placed a gentle kiss on to her lips.

Life might be hard, painful, and unkind, Tara thought to herself, *but being with Nick makes all the pain worth it.*

Love will always be worth it.

Frozen

Epilogue

The cavern was nearly empty of all light. Like everything else in the world of Shadows, it was deep in eternal darkness. There was no bright glowing light from the crystal that once hung from the ceiling. All that remained was the broken shards that made speckled patterns on dark floor.

The Shifters had taken much of the crystal with them. Clever Shifters, so very clever.

Her body laid in its own pool. The dark crimson liquid dried and crusted on the ground. The tiny body almost lost in the darkness of the cave. Her once pristine dress now resembled a dirty rag.

She had been a fool. Such an old fool, to think that she was able to finish what they had started so long ago, by simply torturing one Shifter. Baiting the Key into her den. Stupid careless woman.

Now the orb was lost. Taken by the very people she thought she could control. It reeked of Shifter arrogance. It made his nose rib in disgust.

There was one bonus to this outcome he supposed. He would not have to listen to her moan at him again. Her incessant talking had nearly been enough for him to end her himself. She had been a means to an end, but this was not the end that Jenifer had promised him. How dare she defy him.

He had told her that it was folly to think that she would be able to persuade the Key, force the Key into doing her bidding. Did she know nothing of human determination? Or was she just that desperate after so long of trying to release the power from that blasted orb?

Another thing she had not thought through. Shifter arrogance indeed.

He stretched out his clawed hand, reaching between two pillars of stone. Lifting a severed head out from between them.

It was in no better condition than the body. Red liquid clung around the wound. What strange creatures to bleed this deep red viscous material. It stuck to her and crunched in his palm as he grasped her head. Hair was twining the tips of his claws.

Her eyes stared back at him. Open and glassy.

Even in death she looked outraged.

He tossed her head towards her body with no delicacy. She had been nothing but a tool for him. A tool that had become defective.

Frozen

He left her body there. It would rot in the dark and no one would come to mourn her. She had chosen this path of destruction.

He was on the same path, but it would not end in his ruin. Emotion could not bring him down.

This was not over.

This wasn't even close to over.

The Shifters weren't ready for what he would unleash on them.

They were not ready for the destruction he would bring upon them.

Their ending had begun.

Printed in Great Britain
by Amazon